The ghost of the spell flew on and faded.

Having cheered and applauded with crowds in the past when someone used flair to end a spell not of their casting, Ben spun to take in the crowd with hungry eyes and ears.

"Tradition's blight."

Instead of appreciation, insults where thrown as the crowds—which had formed a communal protective magic circle around him—began to move away. Tinted the same colors as their various robes, their translucent mystic barriers popped like a rainbow bubble and sparkled away.

ADVENTURES OF BENJAMIN BAXTER: YULETIDE YIELD

Book Three of The Darkness Within Trilogy

EZEKIEL JAMES BOSTON

ELSEWHERE
E
P
PUBLISHING

Adventures of Benjamin Baxter:
Yuletide Yield

Published 2016 by Elsewhere Publishing
www.ElsewherePublishing.com

Cover art copyright © 2016 Lim Chuan Shin

Book and cover design copyright © 2016 Elsewhere Publishing

ISBN-13: 978-1-62538-054-8

Elsewhere Publishing
www.ElsewherePublishing.com

Dedicated to:

Family & Friends
Mentors & Minions
Kay McGarvey

Ezekiel James Boston

The Adventures of
BENJAMIN
BAXTER
YULETIDE YILED

Book Three of The Darkness Within trilogy

Chapter One

YULETIDE'S YIELD

HAVING five seconds before the next attack, Benjamin Baxter scanned the throng of starwise patrons around him at Bauman's Bazaar. *Five.* The sea of brightly colored robes, cloaks, and wraps of the shoppers receded, clearing a forty-foot radius around him.

Four. A handful of shoppers and hawkers—who had stopped lending their voices to the constant chorus of sale barking—watched his plight.

Three. None had the intense gaze it took to control the ongoing spell and none were willing to help—and, worse, he didn't see a hint of tan trench coats anywhere. *Where are the guys?*

Two. Ben spun.

The bright metal of the whirling scimitar—a blade he had only seen in use by bodyguards from the middle east—reflected the corridor of lights vendors had set up to highlight their tents, tables, and wares in the largest outdoor night market in Las Vegas.

One.

Centered on him, for some reason, the tumbling blade stopped as the pommel seemed to press against its range thirty-feet away near an abandoned pewter mug at an abandoned table. The steel morphed into a rapier—*or is that a cutlass? Which one is it that pirates use again?*—pointed at his chest.

Now.

It shot at him.

Ben twisted sideways and bent.

The blade swooshed by. In its wake, the scent of delicious spiced cider.

Keeping his gaze on the blade, Ben jammed his hands into his coat and came out with his Anvilsmith tablet and mouthpiece.

Five. Though he didn't need it anymore, Ben jammed the mouth guard in as, by muscle memory, his fingers worked his tablet to press *Spells*, *Enchantments*, *Achilleus*, and *Cast*. The welcomed scent of fresh-cut pineapples pillowed in his nose as the spell flowed into him, winding his fast-twitch muscle up for action.

Four. To keep up appearances of what people were used to seeing technocaster do, Ben quivered his arms and worked his chin as though the magic had to be forced into his body.

Three.

"Daddy!" A small girl in a long, absurdly pink, full-length fur coat screamed and pointed at him.

The man in red furs next to her grabbed the child's upper arm, scooped her into a defensive hug, and bellowed, "Ape casting!"

Two.

A fierce-faced woman—*the mother*—leapt in front of

the man and began to work the air to build a mystic barrier. She wasn't alone. Eyes wide in surprise, fear, or wonder, over a hundred casters' hands worked the air to throw up protective power to shield themselves, and loved ones, against his magic. More people had been keeping an eye on him than he had thought.

One. Ben hadn't seen this many spells thrown at once since the Arcane Alehouse wizards had stacked dozens of Hold spells on him. *They have no idea what spell I cast.* This knowledge made him smile around his mouthpiece. He sucked at the pineapple that had worked into his saliva, and turned back to the sword. It had already switched back to a scimitar. Ben stood sideways to present a smaller target. *Now.*

It whirled at him.

He waited.

It closed.

Leaning, Ben slid back.

The sword whooshed pass his chest.

He snatched at the hilt as it rotated—*got it!*—and found something small in his hand as the bright blade dispersed into red whirling mist.

The ghost of the spell flew on and faded.

Having cheered and applauded with crowds in the past when someone used flair to end a spell not of their casting, Ben spun to take in the crowd with hungry eyes and ears.

"Tradition's blight."

Instead of appreciation, insults where thrown as the crowds—which had formed a communal protective magic circle around him—began to move away. Tinted the same colors as their various robes, their translucent mystic barriers popped like a rainbow bubble and sparkled away.

"Lack wit."

The circle around him stretched into an oval as other bazaar buyers began to move through.

His eyes found the face of the little girl in the pink fur coat scrunched up in a tiny scowl as she stared at him over her father's shoulder. "Nobody likes you." Innocent disdain clung to her words. "Go home, ape."

That slur! Reflexively, Ben's fist balled.

The Nilosian font, the energy Ben regarded as belonging to Bastion—the monster in his head—flashed hot. Boiling, his vision dimmed momentarily as The Beast raised its head.

Ben tensed at Bastion waking and tried to relax. *I can't blame her for her parent's bias.*

Committing her face to their memory, Bastion sneered at the girl.

Ben's brow furrowed and he sneered.

No! Having expressed Bastion's reciprocal disdain, Ben covered his face. *Diffuse your emotions, Ben. Cool down.* He closed his eyes and lowered his head. *There's no way to change their prejudice. To them, their casting method will forever be pure and superior while 'techno-wizardry' will forever be an affront to 'true magic-users' everywhere.* His jaw and fist began to loosen.

Recalling the hard lesson he had learned from the Arcane Alehouse, Ben wanted to yell, *None of us are real wizards.* Instead, he took a deep, calming breath. *She's not a threat, Bastion.* He took another breath and insisted. *She's not.*

Unconvinced, Bastion snorted. Wary, it went back to rest.

That was close. Focused on his shoes—month old Tore Vex boots he got through Meadows Towing—the seams remained slack. His feet weren't growing to bastion-size. He exhaled his relief.

Adept Love had, in his nasal whine, warned against coming to Bauman's Bazaar which had set up in Vegas for a week before moving to Los Angeles next month. "It's a den of derision," he'd said. Love had been filling in for Senior Adept Collins, who went absent after the Samhain Festival. "You may be attacked, openly, and no one will come to your aid." The small man's face took on a shrewd smile. Everyone knew Bauman's Bazaar was the only place where an Archon Private Academy student could get the spells the Academy wouldn't—or couldn't—teach. "Which is why I'm breaking you all into groups of four. You will be responsible for each other."

Ben's throat rocked at the memory. "Hmph." *Responsible for each other, ri-i-ight.* Having been attacked, he temporarily forgot that he, Neil, Kevin, and LeRoy had agreed to split up to find vendors who sold technomancy spells. Remembering, Ben shrugged. *Guess Love knew what he was talking about.*

Curious about what he held, Ben opened his hand to see a miniature duplicate of the scimitar in his palm.

"Hey, showman," a high-pitched feminine voice called before he could really analyze what he had in his hand. "Give you a gold for that."

Chapter Two

RISKY BUSINESS

BEN SUCKED one last time at the pineapple flavor in his mouthguard before he pulled it out. The effect of his Achilleus spell persisted and he found it hard to keep his amped-up, thrumming body still. He closed his hand and looked to where the voice had risen above the clamor of vendors selling and shoppers haggling. He picked up on something he hadn't noticed earlier. *Everyone's dealing in one ounce units of precious metals...*

No vendor offered or accepted local, regional or global currency. Currency was backed by an institute or agency which would go after a seller if you got a really bum deal. No one backed ordinary gold or platinum. *Wow, guess all sells are final.*

"Right here." A tall, bald, slender woman—*that's a really long neck*—raised a hand. She stood in a light green sleeveless dress before a ten-foot wide emerald canvas tent. One of the flaps had been pinned inward showing a bare hint of what lay within the tightly packed rows. Something about her—*the large eyes?*—

made her quite comely. Her neck scarcely bent, giving him the slightest degree of a courtly greeting.

Ben made sure to return the gesture. *That probably looked fast-forwarded.* He focused and gave a proper—*so slow*—bend of his neck.

She nodded in return. "You did well in defending yourself, trencher, so why not profit from the momentary inconvenience?"

Trencher. Elder Komir had call him that, too. Hearing it again made Ben smile. *Heck, why not?*

"I'll give you two gold." Another woman, almost alike in every way except her dress had full sleeves and she stood in front of a red silk gazebo. "One and a half for the spell focus and the extra for the wonderful show."

"Two and two silver." The lady in green counter-offered. "My first offer was low just to get your attention."

"Two and five." Confidence accompanied the second's bid as she motioned to the opening to her gazebo. "That's the highest price it will fetch."

Ben gently squeezed the small blade in hand. *If that's the most it'll fetch here, what's it really worth? Better yet, do I even want to sell it?* While he wouldn't dare take the tiny thing home where his family could find it, it would look rather nice in his basement lab at Meadows Towing. *I'll hang it next to the soldering iron.*

The first woman, who Ben—lost in thought—had turned to face extended her hand to the red tent as well. "She is correct."

"Lies!" A squat rotund man called from across the way. He stood before a crimson-and-violet stripped pavilion made of hard, opaque plastic. His dense, parted mustachio wound two wide loops on each cheek. "I have a cousin who collects such items. If you look closely, ape, you'll see two tiny gemstones on the pommel. It points to its origin and true value." The man hooked his thumbs on his thick black belt. "The info is free and I'll give you the truest offer. Three gold." He raised his chin. "Neither gazelle will top it."

Though Ben had made his mind up on keeping it, the man calling him ape made him want to prove a point. He looked back to the women. *Long necks. Large eyes. I can see why he called them that.*

The woman in green bent her neck slightly, again, but both signaled open palms to the man, conceding to his bid.

Though the passing crowd, Ben examined the man. *There's something about him… besides him calling me ape…* Ben couldn't figure out what about the man bother him, but there was something there.

The mustachioed man raised his head a bit higher and a slight smile spread his face open in pride of winning Ben's business. Figuring Ben would follow, the man turned and walked to the door of his store. "This agreement is beyond far, but the focus will thrill my collector cousin to no end."

Ben turned and bowed to the woman in front of the green canvas tent before approaching her. *She was the only one who extended any courtesy.* He made a point of speaking loudly, hoping the man would hear him. "Though your offer was the lowest, I would like to see what you can offer in trade."

Her neck bent again and, this time, her body folded slightly, too. "I will be honored."

"Three and two!" The man called. "A full ounce of gold more."

Ben did not look back as he moved to her tent.

"Three and five! No, four full!"

Ben crossed the threshold. The din of the bazaar faded, then fell silent. Soft music, like a string quartet playing from beyond the door behind him, took the place of the hustle and bustle of the marketplace. Sandalwood incense filled his nose as he took in the twenty-foot depth of tightly packed rows of similar cherry wood shelves covered with various traditional knickknacks, brick-a-brac, foci, totems, and spell components. Dangling from the center of the tent, a brass brazier caught his eyes.

"*Rawk.* Right this way." A green parrot with a hooked yellow and red beak whistled, and repeated, "Right this way." Its perch appeared to be the handle of a strong box in the far left corner.

Guess she's not worried about being robbed.

Next to the bird, the woman pushed on the canvas back wall. With a pop, it parted to reveal to a secret room.

Okay, that's cool. Making sure to go to the opposite skirt, along the edge of the tent opposite the parrot with the wicked beak, Ben carefully hustled along the narrow walkway to get into the back room. *She's got spells!* He spied the SD cards on a shelf in a glass display. Of his schoolmates, he'd been the first to find one of the rare merchants who had items to sell to technomancers. A bit less carefully, Ben picked up his pace and pressed the Anvilsmith's volume button down twice to signal the rest of his group.

The fact that he might be walking right into a trap didn't occur to him... until *after* he crossed the threshold.

Chapter Three

RELAX... RELAX

A SOFT LAVENDER SCENT—*ALMOST the exact scent mom keeps at home*—filled the seven-foot by seven-foot room. To the immediate left, a small round folding table with a pale green checked table cloth. Floating inches above the table, a manila ceramic teapot with cherry blossom trees—*they're moving*—painted on the side. *The falling petals look so graceful.* As the tiny pink flowers rocked to the base, a sense of serenity eased into him.

While he'd thought about raising his guard as he stepped in, as soon as he entered the room, all semblance of worry slipped from him.

Cool. A cherry blossom had spiraled away from the teapot to land on the side of one of the two thin-lipped manila tea cups set upon similar ceramic saucers. More drifted from the pot to the cup, which filled from the bottom up releasing a fragrant—*oolong?*—brew.

Voice softer in the quiet room, she said, "Feel free to take your coat off."

Ben didn't much feel like taking off his trench coat.

Due to the magical enchantments placed upon it, he never felt discomforted from it and it regulated extreme temperatures to nothing more than either a slight chill or a subtle warmth. *Still, it sounds like a good idea.*

Checking to see if Bastion, who had a supernatural sense of when things were about to go wrong, had cause to be wary, Ben found the beast soundly asleep.

Well, why am I not surprised? A faint, pleasantly warm fog filled his mind. *With how peaceful this place is...* He slipped off his coat and looked for a place to hang it.

"There." She extended her long arm to point a long finger at a single-peg coat rack in the opposite corner. It stood at the foot of a long, narrow emerald green canvas camping cot—*heh, it and the blankets match the walls*—which, coat-rack notwithstanding, ran the full length of the right wall.

Something about the bed—*no, it's a cot, cots aren't comfortable*—felt inviting. His nerves jumped.

"Don't think about the bed." She gave his shoulders a slight rub before giving a mild directing push. "Just hang your coat on the peg."

Ben did. A price tag—*two hundred and fifty... 'Two hundred and fifty' what? Is that the number of days that I've worn it?*—flipped from the tip.

"Don't forget your tie."

"Oh yeah." *Did I want to take off my tie?* With the wonderful warm fog filling his head, Ben found it hard to tell. *Why'd I come back here in the first place?* In answer to this thought, his shoulders gave a lop-sided, drugged shrug. *Well, I took off my coat.* He slipped the red silk tie off and looped it over his coat collar. The rack sucked the tag back in and flipped another from the tip. *Two hundred and seventy-five. Weird. What does that mean?*

"If it chafes..." She began.

Ben faced her.

Nothing remained of what he thought the woman out front looked like. Instead—*the dress is the same*—a young lady, very similar to both Penelope and Alice—*if the medusa didn't have scales*—stood. The two semblances seemed to struggle against one another as though uncertain which visage it should take.

She took a step toward him. A soft lilac smell—*Alice's scent*—washed over him and all traces of Penelope faded. Voice tentative and hopeful, a human version of Alice suggested, "You can hang your tablet harnessss too."

What's with the hiss on harness? Ben recalled Alice ticking off common misconceptions of her cursed race. *She isn't sibilant.* The warmth in his head cooled a bit. He patted the holster that kept his Anvilsmith at easy reach over his leg. "No, I'm good."

"Sure, understandable." She said. All hint of hisses vanished. She lifted the two ceramic cups with cherry blossoms settled on the base, sat on the edge of the bed —*it's a cot*—and extended a cup to him. "How about we sit and have some tea?"

Without thought, his arm extended to accept. Ben pulled back just short of taking the cup. *Wait, Alice can't stand me!* The fog vanished.

Kevin, who always talked as though he were in a competition to get the most words out in a minute, chattered. "Come out from wherever you are, Ben. We got your location ping."

Tone confident and sharp, LeRoy called. "You know you're not going to scare us."

Ben glanced to the canvas wall separating him from the main store. A light from the other side projected Kevin and LeRoy's shadows on it. When he shifted his gaze back to where Alice had sat on the bed—*cot*—the tall, bald, lanky woman from early sat there, sipping tea... And had been there the entire time. *Well, I think she's been there...*

"Oh good. More customers." From her expression, the tea—*or something*—put a bad taste in her mouth and made her words sound bitter. "Perfect timing."

Something weird was going on. Ben tried to recall exactly what, but could only recall cherry blossom, oolong tea, and the smell of Alice's skin. *Why am I thinking of Alice? Better yet, why'd I take off my coat and tie?* He snatched both from the peg, gave the woman a dirty look. *Trickstress.*

She shot him a tight smile.

The glass rack of spellcards, which has been there all the time, seemed to sneak up on him.

Ben jumped away. *Whoa, that's right. Spellcards.* He called out, "In here, guys. Check this out."

Chapter Four

SOMETHING LIKE FRIENDS

THOUGH LEROY, Kevin, and Neil had done a great deal of haggling and some buying in the green canvas tent, Ben had remained a few steps behind. First, mentally, as his schoolmates worked hard for the best deal, then, physically, as the three of them left the tent and had to come back for him to pull him along.

In fact, the four of them had walked well out into the expansive dirt parking lot and located their cars amidst the thousands—*if not tens of thousands*—of hastily parked vehicles before, still smelling lavender, Ben finally started to come back into his own frame of mind—*they're like scattered cherry blossoms*—puzzling out the, mostly horrid parking situations much further away from the bazaar.

If the Bauman people laid down chalk parking lines, everyone would follow suit.

Late-comers were often the third, or fourth car blocking in people who had come early. Others parked to the side of a horizontal row meant for two cars to pass, narrowing the lane to one, in which—if two cars came toward each other with too many cars behind them—the lane would become yet another row of parking, locking in even more cars.

And thus his earlier plan to have at least have one direction to get out by parking side-by-side—Kevin's luminescent orange flame-tipped next to Ben's matte black—backed-in behind Neil, and LeRoy's A.P.A. approved, stock, bright reds had been foiled.

Both sides—*as far as the eye can see*—had been blocked in. *If this were my event, I'd have lines drawn and offer valet.* Ben found his head shaking. "This is atrocious."

"Oh, he's back." Kevin rattled, "Welcome back, Ben." He raised a powder blue spellcard with a large white energy bolt painted on the flat which branched out to seven strikes high near his crazy brown swath of windblown hair. "Check it. Chain Lightning."

Trying to focus on the spellcard, the mental image of raining cherry blossoms and phantom smells of the woman's back room finally faded to the buzzy ozone smell of too many arcane-powered vehicles in close proximity. Each of schoolmates, in their school uniform of white dress shirts, red ties, brown slacks, and tan trench coats, leaned on the corner of their cars facing the space between them.

Not remember anything after having parked, Ben tried to quickly piece the night back together. *We came right after Spell Programming, split up. Someone attacked me with a sword. No...* He opened his hand and rediscovered the small masterfully crafted light, high-quality silver, three-inch sword whose hilt alternated between strips of cooper and steel. *The ruby chips... The husky vendor had the highest bid, but I... I went to the lady in green...*

"Hey, wizzes." A guy in a dark trench coat and long oily hair called to them from the end of the row." For five hundred Strong or seven hundred M.U.s, I can get your car out. Then a second ride for half as much."

Wizzes. Ben used to toss the friendly, casual slang for unknown casters quite a bit. Now—*we're all sort of delusional*—now it just felt false. *No, it's pretentious.*

"Nah, wiz." LeRoy called back. "We're good for now. Please hit us up later though."

"You got it." The guy waved and walked on.

Ben asked, "How can he get our cars out."

Offhandedly, LeRoy answered, "He's a porter specialist." As though that explained everything, he turned his attention back to Kevin. "Nice buy." LeRoy shuffled several cards and presented a silver one at his hip near his red leather belt held closed by his Top Junior Caster belt buckle. The low angle helped the lighting from the Koffman floating lights to highlight an embossed sword. "But not nearly as hot as my sweet Mage Sword."

Ben wanted to pry into porters, but his thoughts were still preoccupied. *She— She bewitched me and tried to rob me.* He balled his fist on the blade. It bit into his palm. *Ow.* He relaxed his hand and kept his fist closed so the cut could heal before being noticed by the others.

Kevin laughed a challenge. "You can't cast seven stones."

LeRoy shrugged. "You cannot cast Chain Lighting."

Kevin and LeRoy are jaw-jacking again, and Neil's off—as usual—in his own little world. None of them probably wouldn't have noticed if he held his hand opened and showed how the small cut on his bloody palm was healing shut.

LeRoy flipped the SD card over his knuckles, making it dance on top of his hand. "Perhaps you should master Lighting Bolt first?"

Ben winced. *Low blow!* While, between the four of them, he could out program and engineer the others put together, Ben wouldn't have dared to brag about it. LeRoy, on the other hand, had made direct reference to the spell he used to finish Kevin, twice back-to-back, to become the school's Top Junior Caster for last school eighth.

Kevin stopped laughing.

LeRoy drove the point. "I mean, it should come naturally, now, since you know what it tastes like."

"Want to go right here?" Kevin pointed to the ultra-narrow, walk-side-ways-only lane between the cars that had them blocked in. "Go ahead. Step out."

This spiraled fast.

Nonplussed, LeRoy rocked his head on his shoulders. "The duel was supposed to be a best of three match... You didn't even take one."

Oh, no! Ben extended his arm to stop Kevin from moving to the row to call LeRoy out to duel.

"Move, Ben." With contact being frowned upon, Kevin stopped short of Ben's arm. "All I need is one."

LeRoy flipped the card over his knuckles again before putting it into his pocket. "Easy, Kevin. Do you think the Magistrates want to be pulled from the Bazaar?" He crossed his arms and pressed more of his weight on his car. "This is like their vacation time."

Kevin's spoke slow dread through clenched teeth. "It would only take a minute."

Strength left Ben's arm. *The hawkish nose, flat cheeks, pronounced brow. Kevin looks just like Collins when the jerk threatens us...*

"Less, actually." LeRoy slid his hands into his pocket. "What's up with you, Ben?"

Ben studied Kevin's face a bit longer. *Could the number-two caster and the Senior Adept be related?*

Kevin stole a glance at Ben.

"Uh." Ben shifted his eyes to LeRoy, and lied, "Nothing."

Finally moving, Neil pushed a few strands of his white hair behind a pigmentless ear, and held up two of his four cards. One had a clear case to show off the circuitry within while the other was black with a faint gray line. Voice soft and steady, he said, "I don't know which I am more proud of..." He presented the clear one. "Wind Wall." Then the black one. "Or Enervation."

Ben eyed the black card. *What's Enervation?*

"Neil the Techno-Necro-mancer, you gotta know it's the Enervation," LeRoy answered with a sneer as though the question lay leagues beyond stupid.

Kevin's chin relaxed a bit as he raised a leg to his car and, in his normal fast patter, agreed, "Hands down."

Clever. A slight admiration kindled in Ben for Neil; the smallest, and softest spoken of the them. *He changed the topic and neither of them seem the wiser.*

"Yes, it is necromancy, which I adore." Neil slid the black card into the pocket of his heavily starched shirt, presenting the clear one. "And yes, it is more useful in combat, but this one completes my collection of standard three-stone spells."

What? Ben's ears rose, and his focus shot to Neil who still eyed the card. *I know he comes from a wealthy family, but if he has all three-stones...* Not sure if his question strayed into an area considered too personal, Ben asked, "So, you have all single and double stones too?"

Neil nodded absently as he bent over the card, putting his pigmentless face closer to it for inspection instead of raising the card before his powder pink eyes. "Interesting. There's a faint brick wall in fine white paint."

"Wait." Kevin stood again. "You mean to tell me you wasted coin on Erase?"

Neil bobbed his head again. He ran a finger on the flat. "Talk about craftsmanship. The paint is in miniscule grooves."

Kevin waved a hand. "Man, that's the most useless spell in the world."

Having programmed it for extra credit, and used it to keep Collins from seeing a letter of complaint he had composed against the Senior Adept during Spell Programming III, Ben ventured to disagree, "It has its uses."

"How?" LeRoy shook his head. "Okay Ben, there you are, standing across from me at dueling length. How would you use it?"

Ben opened his mouth to try and back out of LeRoy's hypothetical before it could accidently spiral into a real challenge. Another flash from earlier in the night came to him. *Crap. I had a vision of dueling him, but we were between tents. Man, I really don't want to—*

Neil interjected, "Ben doesn't duel."

"In this example, he does." LeRoy looked from Neil, who hadn't stopped marveling at the card, to Ben. "So, there we are, hooks in and ready to throw." He stood and, in an instant, drew his hand from his pocket as though he held his tablet. "Somehow, in this fictional world, you gain the dominant caster's advantage." Staring into Ben's eyes, LeRoy took an aggressive step forward into Ben's personal space.

What are you doing LeRoy? The manner of approach meant 'go time.' *What's this about? You don't like someone disagreeing with you?*

Bastion—the Nilosian monster that could steal control of Ben's body—remained fast asleep. In its slumber, the beast uttered an annoyed grumble at the challenge.

LeRoy stared intensely.

Tension seized Ben's shoulders, back, and brought his brow into a tight knot. *Man, I really don't want to duel you LeRoy...* Ben stood up straight. *I really don't.*

Chapter Five

QUIET CONFIDENCE

LeRoy's breath smelled of bacon.

You want to start something from nothing? Ben took a small step forward, tightening the narrow space between them and a faint, invisible static, as though they were Tesla rods attracting dimensional energy, built between them. *I may not win, but I'm not going to slink away.*

"Shit." Kevin leapt forward to get his arm between them before they bumped chests.

Counter to the seriousness of the moment, a group of people—*they're enjoying themselves, why can't we be like them*—laughed. Staring into LeRoy's African brown eyes, Ben found an intense pinprick of cobalt blue at the center of the black pupils.

"You have first bang, Ben." LeRoy gave a dangerous grin. He lowered his voice to a threat. "I dare you, piss it away on Erase."

"First, I don't start fights." As he said the words, Ben tamped down the desire to cast Erase on LeRoy just to see if the Top Junior Caster would have attacked him. "More importantly, tactically, it'd be a waste again you."

LeRoy nodded a, *I didn't think you would* nod. "Exactly."

Ben added, "However—"

Breath hitched, Kevin bristled.

LeRoy's eyes narrowed.

Neil looked up to them.

Ben continued, "—since we're talking fictional events." He gave a dismissing wave to negate LeRoy's scenario and took half a step back. "Say you and a traditional caster are battling for real. Life or death. No minimum distance. You both have just enough juice for a single low-level spell." He slipped his hands into his coat pockets and dropped the miniature sword as he turned a small circle.

Paying them no mind, Koffman Lanterns floated above patrons moving to and from the bazaar.

Ben stepped back, bumping into Kevin's arm which bumped into LeRoy. "So, there you two are. Eye to eye. Nose to nose." He yanked his hand from his pocket. "He pulls a scroll!"

Expertly, LeRoy said, "I blast him."

"Yeah," Kevin agreed.

"Really?" Ben's brow eased. *He didn't even think to try and rip the scroll away.* His eyebrows raised. "It's not enough to take him down. He's mystically shielded."

LeRoy blurted, "I punch him!"

"Ah." Ben stepped backward and raised a finger. "Your spell hits, but he's made of sterner stuff. The strike lands, a solid shot, but we're not martial masters so it doesn't knock him out." Ben took another step back and leaned on his car.

LeRoy's eyes bounced around his sockets as he searched for another answer.

Ben added, "In fact, this trad-caster is well practiced at concentrating through such damage and activates the scroll."

Rapt in the scenario, knowing that LeRoy would have to eat whatever came, Kevin found the breath to ask, "What spell is it?"

LeRoy raised his chin and tightened as though he were preparing to take a punch. "Yeah, what spell?"

Ben hadn't thought the scenario that far. *Not important really. You're already cooked.* He shrugged at the two constant contenders for Top Junior Caster. "It could be anything, but to be sure, it's offensive and, remember, traditional mages can fit up to four spells on one of those scrolls. So, after the first, another would come, and another, and—most likely—another. Then, he still has juice for a personal spell."

Stunned by the reality of being totally screwed by his choices in the scenario, LeRoy stepped back from Kevin's arm.

Dumbfounded, Kevin still stood there with his arm out like a crossing guard at an empty street.

"Tactics, LeRoy." Ben peeked in his Transcend to check on Tex. The other guys' knee-high Golemcasts where there, but not his. *Darn it, Tex.* If the others check their robots, they'd see his missing, and then the awkward questions would come. Hoping none of the guys would, Ben returned his focus to LeRoy. "The main difference between you and me—in this scenario

—is that I would make a play at grabbing the scroll and using my last arcane watt to erase the magic."

LeRoy frowned slightly. "But you'd still be at an impasse and he'd have a tick up on you."

"Yeah." Kevin lowered his arm and moved back to let his car support his weight. "What then?"

Ben gave another shrug and chastised himself. *I'm starting to act like Jek.* He looked away to the Bazaar, taking in the glorious spectacle of so many Koffman Lanterns hovering—*they're like stalking butlers*—to light people's way out into the parking lot. "Well, being civilized, we could call it a day and go our separate ways."

Kevin shook his head hard. "No. You said it was life or death."

"So, I did." Ben lifted his gaze to the night sky. He found the North Star. *Just one arcane watt...*

The horrified expressions on the Old Henderson orcs' faces when blasted their life from them came to his mind's eye and took roost. Expression left his face. The justifications—*they had Clarissa. They would have killed me*—still didn't ease the guilt.

Tonelessly, Ben said, "Then it's 'may the most determined man win.'"

"You mean the best man." LeRoy correct.

In an internal quagmire, Ben shook his head. "Winning doesn't make you the best."

"Wow." LeRoy cast his gaze to the sky as he fell back on his car. "That's deep."

"Yeah." Kevin nodded and did as LeRoy had. The two of them had a long time rivalry. While one might be the best for several school eighths, the other could pull out a win to take the Top Junior Castor belt buckle. No matter which one held the title, they tended to mirror each other.

Since looking up, Ben had felt Neil keeping a steady eye on him. Scrutinizing.

"Why are going this deep anyway." Ben tried to shake off his sense of woe. *Plenty of time for that later.* He cleared his throat. "Bauman's Bazaar is right there guys. There's bound to be more sellers. Plus, I haven't had one mug of spiced cider yet."

"Me too." Kevin sat up. "And I still got money."

LeRoy echoed, "Me, too."

"Then back into the den of derision we go." Neil tucked his clear spellcard away and stood. "Until cider come from your noses and moths from my pockets."

Ben laughed and clapped with LeRoy and Kevin, but wondered. *What does he mean by that?*

Chapter Six

NEIL

SEARCHING for other vendors with technomancy wares, the four of them crossed back into the heart of the bazaar and split up again... Or at least they were supposed to. Ben kept catching glimpses of Academy-trench coat tan when he least expected it. *One of them is following me.* Still, Ben wondered aimlessly through the bazaar, rarely pausing.

Ben came to a full stop. In the valleys of the hawkers calling out, he heard and—*mmm*—smelled bacon frying. He was standing at the corner of a pale orange and blue striped pavilion. He feigned interested by passing a curious glance over the wares in the rows and rows of glass cases with tiny glass boxes of powders, herbs, and fluids of various transparency before fixing his gaze on the deep fried bacon balls on sticks, freshly rolled in maple.

The vendor, an elderly Asian with a huge, mean-looking, twelve-legged spider tattooed on his face, eyed Ben and muttered in a Far-Eastern language.

That doesn't sound pleasant or welcoming. Hopeful, Ben approached the man.

"For paying customers only." The man waved him away. "Go feast your eyes somewhere else."

At least he didn't call me ape. Ben turned away. When he did, he got his best look at the flash of tan following him at it ducked behind two large whiskey barrels stacked atop each other. *Must be Neil. Too short to be either LeRoy or Kev.* He had a clear view of both sides of the barrels. Whoever it was, couldn't slip away around a corner like before. Ben headed back to the hiding spot. *I have to know why.*

He had made it most of the way there when a large, burley man in a long-sleeved golden shirt and red overalls stepped from a crimson dome tent with yellow and orange paisleys. The man seized something near the barrels, lifted it, and flung Neil like a sack of potatoes into the main thoroughfare.

The crowd of colored robes scattered away from Neil like frightened cats.

Can't believe how quiet everything got. Nearby hawkers fell silent. The immediate din quelled. Sales from rows over spilled in. Having just been on the inside of such a circle for the first time a short while ago, Ben scanned the crowd to note what kind of view the others had.

"We don't serve your kind!" The man barked and pulled a narrow—*is that bone?*—wand as he closed to only ten feet from Neil.

The shoppers formed a moving circle a few steps further out.

"My kind?" Neil stayed down on the packed earth

and locked eyes with the man. He motioned to his pigment-free cheek and then to his trench coat, and asked, "Do you mean *albinos* or *apes*?"

The man didn't answer.

Not at the center of attention—*they want blood*—Ben could feel the unhealthy lust from the crowd like a coming storm. They pretended to mill about when they were entirely focused on what was about to happen in the dirty duel circle.

Blending into their movements, Ben angled and joined the second rank of people moving in slow circles. Like them, he tried to give off the appearance of minding his own business.

Still on the ground, Neil had one hand tucked inside his coat—the side where he kept his tablet—as he extended his other hand toward the man. "I did not mean to offend, good sir." The pigment-free hand motioned to the stand. "I could not help but notice your small, yet impressive, dragon fruit tree."

The merchant pointed the wand at Neil and laughed heartily. "I'm not looking away, ape." He shook his head and pointed a gaudy pinky ring of his other hand at Neil. A tangerine line of energy—*I haven't seen an orange tether before*—shot out and struck Neil's leg. The line slid to the center of each of their chests, binding them for the duel. "But, if you stand, and perform a proper folding bow in apology, I'll keep the charge in my pointer."

Moving behind the man, Ben couldn't see Neil when he spoke. "In fairness, good sir, I must let you know…"

Ben passed directly behind the merchant's broad

back, he almost felt tethered himself as ambient dimensional energy flowed into the bond. A wealth of scents, chief being spiced cider and honey-mead—both staples at Bauman's—came to him and his hearing perked to hear bets—all favoring the merchant—being softly whispered.

Then he passed from behind the man and could see Neil's powder pink eyes fixed on the man. The feeling faded. No one's mouths moved. *How are they whispering?*

Neil had pulled his Triforce. "When I stand—and I will stand—I will not bend."

"Then die on the ground!" The merchant flicked his wrist. A cackling pale blue skull formed at the tip and shot at Neil.

Neil lifted his tablet.

The skull rebounded from Neil's device and zipped back at the man, striking him square in the chest. The skull squealed joyously as it disintegrated. The man crumpled.

Neil got to his feet and dusted himself off. The tan coat didn't appear dirty, but each strike knocked away small puffs. He stopped, gripped his device with both hands and jutted it out.

Dressed similarly to the fallen merchant, three guards, all more muscle-bound than their employer —*more muscle-bound than orcs*—leapt into the circle with their hands on their hilts over their shoulders. Strapped across their backs were wide, four-foot long, scabbards

Ben reached into his trench, put one hand flat on his tablet, and fingered his Shield and Orion spellcards with his other hand.

The mirror on the back of Neil's protective cover shone green as arcane watts slowly empowered the redirection enchantment. *It'll be ready to reflect again in a minute, but won't do a spit of good against those swords if they pull them.*

In unison, the guards called, "Life for life!"

Chapter Seven

RESPONSIBLE FOR EACH OTHER

Trying to ignore the strong eucalyptus smell coming from a string of six young casters in ankle-length, greyish-purple robes and their similarly dressed chaperone who wore a flat, wide-brimmed hat like only old priests used to wear, Ben eyed a narrow gap between them and their escort. None of the six were older than twelve—*they don't want to miss a thing*—and they moved a bit slower than the rest of the inner circle.

About to perform a major breach of courtmanship by making contact with a caster he was neither familiar with or indebted to, Ben reflexively scanned around for Adept Matton, and then for anyone in a tan trench coat.

The kid in the lead, a boy by the voice, leaned back and whispered to the one behind him, "I hope the ape's head comes clean off."

"Me too," the second, a girl, replied.

They've more bloodlust in them than the adults. Ben lowered his shoulder and shoved his way into the circle, which instantly adjusted to form two feet behind him.

"It touched me!" The boy.

"Another ape!" The girl.

I'm a little too close to the guards. Ben began to walk just inside the circle toward Neil.

On the opposite side, some of the those in the second rank of the shoppers rotating around them as though they hadn't noticed a fight happening, squeezed in closer. *With all these colors moving around so slowly, it almost feels like the start of a Screaming Meemie ride.*

"Friar Zane." The boy Ben had bumped pawed at the chaperone. "That ape touched me!"

Ben ignored the true accusation, kept his hands in his coat and focused on the three guards. "If things get ugly…" Halfway to Neil, Ben backed slowly toward the toward the bloodthirsty watchers, forcing them to make the circle wider and wider. He kept going until he, the guards, and Neil formed an equilateral triangle. "They're going to get real ugly."

Mimicking expression Bastion made him make at the girl in pink, Ben furrowed his brow, sneered, and boasted, "We've already got you in a pinch and you have no idea how powerful A'Neilios, the White Dragon, Understudy of Master Reynolds who, as The Shroud, held the World Dueling Federation title for eight years, truly is."

Seemingly undaunted, the guards nocked elbows amongst themselves to indicate which one of them—Ben or Neil—they were going to attack. One began to eye him while the other two focused on Neil.

They're not buying my bluff. Ben's heart began to

thump in his chest. As though concerned for those around them, Ben tried to keep his voice calm and spoke from the side of his mouth, "A'Neilios, please, I beseech you. Hook these three. You needn't close down Bauman's Bazaar as you closed the Samhain Festival."

Neil remained quiet.

The circle behind the guards began to break apart. *Some of them are buying it, but they're not the customers that I want.* Virtually everyone in the Vegas Valley, even if they weren't actually there, had claimed to be present when the pyrotechnic dragons shook free of their control and battled of their own accord. Nearly fifty people had died that night. Though all the deaths were from having been trampled, every death had been blamed on the dragons and the pyrotechnic company was still paying blood money to make amends. No one, not even Ben, knew the cause, but he did his best to make Neil seem responsible.

Regretful the guards hadn't cowered, Ben gripped his Anvilsmith and opened his mouth to call 'go time.'

"He fell from his own spell." A man in layered rubicund robes stepped from the front rank into the circle. He pulled his hood to show butchered short, brown hair.

The broken circle which had turned into a rocking horseshoe thickest behind Neil, grew accordingly.

The man started to close his hand on air. A Primary Baton appeared in his palm shining bright with Argosian red energy.

Relieved, Ben exhaled. *Thank goodness. A Magistrate.*

Neil cut his eyes to Ben.

What? Ben shrugged. *What?*

Neil turned his attention to the Magistrate. Ben did the same.

"As a Lesser Judge of Chief Magistrate Lars Lightningpalm, acting on the best interest of this event, I declare your claim of life for life to be invalid." He waved his baton at two of the guards and pointed at the merchant. "Collect your benefactor."

The lead guard kept his hand on his hilt, but the two did as they were directed.

"Hold," the Magistrate commanded, and the muscle-bound men heeded. He still had the tip of his baton aimed at the merchant. "He draws shallow breath. Stand him tall."

The guards hefted the unconscious man to their standing height.

The Lesser Judge pointed his rod at Neil. "Pick your prize, A'Neilios."

A weak orange flash shone and faded around both Neil and the merchant.

What the heck was that? Ben rubbed his eyes in disbelief. *I didn't imagine it.*

The Lesser Judge raised his rod to the crowd. "Now, go."

Instead of the circle going oblong and compacting in, everyone walked as directly away from the Primary as possible. Hawkers tried to call their attention with, supposedly, unbeatable deals, but the would-be buyers moved past the vendors and through open-sided shops.

Neil bowed formally to the out-of-uniform Magistrate. "Thank you, Lesser Judge."

The man opened his hand and the symbol of his office flashed away. No longer in his official capacity, he sneered contempt at Neil. "It was not for you, ape. It was for the good of all near." He pulled his hood to obscure his face. "One point your school, and Master, seem to constantly miss is this—" he walked after the north-moving crowd, and called back, "Tradition is Tradition!"

Most of the crowd around echoed, "Tradition is Tradition!" It came a second time with more people joining in. "Tradition is Tradition!" The pulse grew exponentially in strength and it felt like the entire bazaar boomed it on the third iteration. "Tradition is Tradition!"

Something about the calls 'life for life' and 'tradition is tradition' sounded quite familiar. Ben snapped his fingers. *Those are calls from the Kings, Clergy, and Coffers game?* Unable to afford the ante, Ben had never played. He made a mental note to verify with Dominic, a KCC junkie, and hurried to Neil to ask the question burning in his mind. Ben lowered his voice to a soft whisper, and asked, "Hey, what was that orange flash?"

Chapter Eight

PARTNERS

CALM, as though he hadn't had three large guards about to cut him down, Neil put a hushing finger to his lips. "If you want to trade questions, we should not do so aloud."

Appreciating the local silence—even with hawkers calling from a few rows over—Ben focused on bringing his heartbeat back down normal. *Is he talking about telepathy?* Considering letting a secret slip, he narrowed his eyes. *Should I let on that I know how to mindspeak?*

Neil projected his thoughts at Ben, *While telepathy would be quicker, I meant texting.*

Ben thumped his own forehead and smiled. The scent of the kid's eucalyptus clung to his arm. He frowned and put his arm down. "That's how you knew when I was going to look your way and bust you following me."

Neil's expression didn't change, but he nodded and projected, *Precisely.*

More as an afterthought, Ben shielded himself from other mind readers.

A small, brief smile flickered and died on Neil's lips. *Better. However, it still is not safe since others can pick up on waves between you and me.* Neil began to type on his device.

That green lady really did a number on me to slice through my defenses like that. Ben checked his sleeve. *How long is that eucalyptus going to cling to me?* He sniffed it and shook his head against the strength. *Lesson learned, never rub up against—* He paused. While he knew the school uniforms of the Las Vegas Valley and neighboring prefectures, the cut and length of their robes proved a conundrum.

Movement caught his attention. A young girl—*she can't be older than ten and she's shivering*—in jeans and a heavy, cream-colored winter coat came from between shops toward where the confrontation had been. *She must be freezing.* For the first time in a long while, Ben sent a thankful thought out to the universe for the comfort enchantment on his school coat. *Guess she didn't hear the Primary tell everyone to go.* Something about the fact that she didn't have her elbows tucked tight to her sides, or the way her eyes shifted side to side to take in the area, put Ben on guard. *What does this kid want?*

One of the large guards came from the shop. Anger —*perhaps disgust*—dug deep lines across his forehead and knotted his brow. Staring blades at Neil—who had his attention firmly fixed on his tablet—the man squatted near the fallen spellcaster's wand.

The preteen sprang around the guard, scooped up

the white wand, and dashed between the shops on the opposite side.

The guard cried, "Stop! Thief!"

Vendors and their guards reached out for the girl.

She proved too nimble and, grabbing one of the maple bacon balls Ben had eyed earlier, disappeared into the crowd the next lane over.

Not looking up from his device, Neil said to the guard, "If you were not trying to intimidate me, you would have possession of your master's wand."

Ready for an attack, Ben turned to the guard.

His furrowed brow, cheeks, and neck had flushed with blood. Instead of coming at them, or going on a fruitless hunt for the girl, he stomped back into the merchant's shop.

I would've never pegged Neil as one to salt another's wounds. Ben's tablet chimed as a deep grey text made to look like fine calligraphy in a white bubble appeared holding Neil's message. "Was what you said about Master Reynolds being The Shroud true?"

Ben hadn't gotten around to formatting what his text balloons would look like on others' tablets, so his words appeared in the Anvilsmith's stock emerald green stencil on steel. "Yes. What about the orange flash?"

Neil texted, "I'll prepare a document for you." He then motioned down the lane. "Come on. Let us continue our search for Technomancy vendors."

Ben said, "Okay. Follow me."

Neil followed Ben as he took the path the girl had taken. He kept from whimpering as they passed the maple bacon balls on a stick. Stepping through to the next lane, he walked side-by-side with his schoolmate.

Surprisingly, the various starwise patrons moved away to let them into the flow.

The parting wasn't only to let them in. The mostly bright robes around them—age, gender, and affiliation notwithstanding—afforded them an additional five feet of space... Even if they walked down the center of the lane. *So, when I walk alone, I'm—more or less—accepted by the crowd, but walk next to another Academy student and they give us air.* Though he thought it wrong to enjoy the feeling of power, Ben couldn't readily find shame in it.

From the general din of the bazaar, his ears began to pick up on a constant murmur of "Apes" which both preceded and followed them. While being called one grated his nerves, the word proved a small price to pay for commanding an area. Soon, the slur lost its impact and began to feel like a warning to everyone else to get out of their path. Though Ben knew the space granted them came from a place of fear seated in the souls of those around him, this proved to be the first time he had been afforded something that might be mistaken as respect. *And, most amazingly, it's actually for attending the Academy.*

His device chimed. Neil's text bubble had two document plus signs along the top. "I have sent you my notes from Dueling I and II. This should settle both your stepping in to back me and the information deficit created by your sharing the information about The Shroud."

"Thanks!" *Wow, notes from Dueling! Fantastic.* Ben's thoughts shifted. *Can't believe he didn't know about*

Reynolds being The Shroud. Though he recalled getting the information from his mom, he figured if she—as a pacifist plant-based caster—knew, then everyone must've known.

Information deficit. Ben rolled the words around in his head as he spied an eight-foot tall man in a black shroud step from one tent to duck into another. *Given Neil's lineage, he must know lots of stuff I don't. Wonder if he'll be open to exchanging more.* Not wanting to share anything too heavy—*like Node Keys, what I know of the Mystique or the existence of the pocket realm where the Komirs reside*—Ben scanned the around for any sign of tan coats. Not seen Kevin, LeRoy, or any other A.P.A. folks, Ben whispered about technomancy. "Did you know that you can copy spells from one spellcard to another?"

Neil cleared his throat to warm up his voice again. "Of course you can move from one to another."

"I didn't say move." Ben corrected. "I said copy."

Neil stopped cold.

When Ben turned, the albino's index finger slid in mad dashes along his screen. *Wow, never seen him this passionate before.* Ben smiled inwardly. *Guess he didn't know that.* He looked to his device for Neil's message.

Neil presented his screen. Unlike his message, everything on Neil's Triforce was white with faint silver highlights which made anything but his message a strain to read. Ben read, *Copy, as in, not losing the original SD card?*

Ben nodded.

Neil double tapped the text and hit delete.

Ben frowned a bit. *Wonder why he doesn't want record of the message?*

Calmer, Neil's finger started a graceful slide over the keyboard.

Ben leaned in to read.

Each time Neil's finger stopped or turned on a letter, it appeared in the box. As the fingertip moved to the next letter, the tablet guessed—rather accurately—what the next letter would be. At times, full words would spring up in Neil's fancy text script after only a couple of letters. When correct, Neil lifted his finger and the word appeared in the text box.

More interesting than his classmate's typing was the symbol above the shift key where the caps lock should have been. *It's the same eye-shaped mark that accompanies stock Scry sigils. Wonder if the Triforce can be used as a divination focus?*

Neil tapped his unsent bubble. "How many copies can you make from one SD card, and is there a maximum spell level you can do?"

Ben checked over his shoulders again. *No one.* He mused, *feels like we're forming a cabal.* More in respect for how Neil acted than any real feeling that he should show discretion, Ben lowered his voice and whispered, "I've copied from my original Blast eight times." Ben cleared his throat. While him being the most disadvantaged student at the A.P.A. wasn't a secret, due to the subtle classism obvious in his non-school issued possessions and him being admitted under the Matton Grant funded by the one Adept whose classes Ben could never pass on the first attempt, having to admit it proved to be another matter altogether. Still, he had made enough room to swallow his pride. "I don't know about max level; I've never been able to buy spells."

Neil's finger went back to its keyboard ballet.

Nearby, a vendor tossed a freshly-turned-over-to-her coin purse to a guard.

The thump and jingle reminded Ben of the reward bag he'd been given for his lost spells. Ben typed a message to Tex. "Remind me to count the Komir coins when we return to the scrapyard."

Tex's reply was instant. "Remind me to never let you leave me in the car."

Guiltily, Ben sighed. *Tex would love this place. The tents. The wares. The various people and their diverse manner of dress…* "Sorry, buddy. They made a good point for leaving you guys behind."

"Look at these bots idle." The text popped up a split second before a snapshot of the other three Golemcasts in the backseat, their eyes dark and wound close. "They're Olympic class idlers, Ben." Another three full rows of text popped up. "This wouldn't be as bad if these guys played games like poker. Heck, I'd kill for Memory, Go Fish, or even Eye Spy right now. Ah! I've been slain. My assassin's name… Boredom."

Ben chuckled.

Neil looked up, finger still moving. "What?"

Ben angled his screen away. "Funny picture."

Neil frowned at the turned-away device, but returned his focus to his Triforce.

Ben typed, "Tell you what, Tex. Climb through the backseat to the trunk and pull the spare Anvilsmith. You have my permission to download any free play game."

Tex replied, "Bless you, Ben."

Ben imagined his companion army-crawling his metal body across the desert when an oil oasis appeared. Ben rolled his eyes and smiled at his imaginary Tex pinching his fixed nose while he cannonballed into the center. He added. "Nothing with a cost." Then clarified. "I mean no spending."

"Got'cha."

Almost fittingly, Ben had to take a turn at being idle as Neil worked his device. Though he liked tablets, Neil was mainly typing and pulling different documents together. *Non-cool, mundane, things any tablet could do.*

A whiff of sizzling bratwurst came to him. Casting his eyes around the nearby tents to find the food vender, Ben spied another solid green—*is that burlap?*—tent. Recalling the woman from earlier, he groaned. *Even if I see a green tent next year, it would be too soon.*

In front of the building, atop a huge, eight-foot tall, dark oak barrel set on end and tapped midway with a spigot, a little person with dense red mutton chops and wearing a seaweed-green monk habit considered them.

Accidently, Ben made eye contact. *Crap!*

Before he could bounce his eyes away, the merchant raised his squat, round mug to him with a true respectful bend of the neck.

Huh. Don't normally get both courtly, and courteous in the same gesture. Begrudgingly, Ben gave a short, almost dismissive bow in return. *Adept Matton would cut my tie and give me eternal detention if he caught wind of this.* He chided himself. *Do the right thing, Ben.* When he would've normally straightened, Ben involved his back and stopped deeper to give the man twice as much respect as was given to him.

The man struggled to mirror Ben's bow, but managed. Better still, he tilted at the waist to extend the cup in his hand in hospitable good will.

Free cider? Too good to be true! His earlier adventure into the green tent not forgotten, Ben fixed his attention on the merchant and tried to remain cool as anticipation to take the offer for a free spiced cider overcame his staunch reluctance to ever approach another vender in green. *This time, I have back-up.* He took a couple of steps toward the vendor and urged Neil, "Come on."

"Almost done." Neil replied.

I'm not going to wait. Ben moved toward the shop and spoke to his device, "Wake. Ping Neil. I'll be at the green tent five down on the left." A soft *ting—Neil's text tone sounds dull*—came from behind him.

Neil gave a dark mumble.

"Welcome." The man called in a tinny voice as he labored down a set of stairs built on the side of the barrel. "Welcome to both of you." Midway, he paused, took a gulp from the cup, and continued down. "Come in, my friends. Please, come in."

Chapter Nine

CIDER'S SIREN SONG

THOUGH THE SCENT of spiced cider and honey-mead intensified as Ben drew closer, he tried to keep his field of vision broad as paused at the wide, rolled-up entrance. *The dispensers smell like they're just inside, to the right.* His stomach rolled and gave an anxious groan. *Scope the place out first, then draw a drink.*

The little monk's habit rocked as he hobbled toward the back. Many of the tables within were the standard six-foot long folding kind. *The same style used at the Magic Faire to display projects.* To the left, past a large stuffed animal, were some lowered and narrowed tables for people of the owner's stature. A silver bell with gold leafed letters—*ring for service*—floated over each table just above eye level. *Smart. Don't distract from the wares.* To the right—*ah, glorious*—tapped, and raised up on their sides, were three quarter-kegs made of the same dark oak as the large one out front. *Whew, I can feel their heat.* Like birds on a wire, they sat next to each other, waiting and whistling softly.

The merchant, in his tiny voice, offered, "Something for that watering mouth of yours before I truly amaze you?"

Ben had to peel his eyes away from the barrel that read Goodspice's Old Fashioned Spiced Cider to look the shopkeeper in his eyes, bow respectfully, and respond to the gracious offer. An anticipatory grin spread his lips. "Only by your urging, of course."

"Of course! Of course." The monk laughed and waved Ben on to the kegs. He raised a warning finger. "But only spiced for you, my young friend."

"Wouldn't want otherwise." Ben crossed the threshold. Littered with wooden drinking cups of various widths and depths, a folding table appeared in front of the kegs. One last fleeting defensive thought seated by his experience in the tall, bald woman's shop flickered through his mind—*I can still hear what's going on outside which means they can hear what's going on inside*—before he relaxed.

The smallest goblets were nothing more than hollowed-out barrel plugs while the larger cups were like lidless, thirty-ounce timber steins. *I am feeling a powerful thirst.* Ben smiled at the greedy thought. Something about the merchant's mannerisms encouraged excess. He took the second-largest mug.

A light snort came from behind him.

Ben turned.

What he had dismissed as a stuffed animal on the inside left proved to be a living, breathing, minotaur. His—*wait, there're udders*—her thick, wooly brown coat made Ben want to reach out and stroke her. However, the array of hilts on her waist and over her back and shoulders kept his curiosity in check.

He gave her a tentative nod.

She nodded back.

If she wanted to cut me down, she would have. Ben faced the quarter kegs and—*it's so nice that Bastion's out for the count*—smiled. The beast probably would've been pounding at his temples for turning his back to a being as armed as she. He held the cup beneath the rightmost spigot. Aromatic, deep brown cider sloshed in, building a mountain of tan bubbles. Ben licked his lips, relished the mug warming in his hands, and kept it under the spout until it petered out. The fully-developed head threatening to spill over the lip.

Wish I could dive in! Ben dipped his nose into the fragrant foam and stole a slow sip of the hot beverage. The mixture of cinnamon and nutmeg—*so good!*—complemented the robust apple flavor as the intense beverage washed his mouth. Through tight lips, he mumbled, "Quite good!" He then swallowed and paused. A subtle flavor—*walnut?*—washed his palate and poofed away. He smiled fondly at the disarming aftertaste. "Neil, you gotta try this!"

"No, thank you." Neil replied. "I am not thirsty."

Ben turned.

Still engrossed in his tablet, his finger still doing its mad ballet, his schoolmate had stepped just inside the entrance and propped himself, leaning against the minotaur. Not really out of his own thoughts, Neil nodded. "It does smell delicious, though."

"Old family recipe." The merchant gave his paunch

a proud pat. "And now, without dinner..." He hobbled to the olive green back wall. "...time for dessert."

Ben followed.

A section as wide as the front opening rolled up and hung there. The merchant lowered his hand. To the left, at a table set for four, a dice game was in progress—*wow, they're playing KKC with real dice*—three guards in brown studded leather, each with a set of wooden and live-steel short swords on their hips, settled into their seats. The little man swept his lowered hand in a gameshow assistant's arc around the room.

Ben's hungry gaze skipped past the gaming table and bopped across multiple oak bookshelves stacked deep with display cases chockfull of spellcards. To the right, seven tablets were presented face-out. His jaw unhinged. He snapped his mouth shut and it eased open again. Ben blurted, "Paydirt!"

In his amazement, Ben had let his drink tip. Searing liquid spilled onto his fingers. *Ah! No!* More splattered and spilt with each rapidly worsening corrective tilt that he made. *No, no, no! Please don't let me drop it!*

The mug lifted from his hand and steadied, hovering in mid-air.

Thank goodness.

Holding it by the handle, a fourth guard—previously invisible—appeared. "Thanks." He winked, took a sip, then sat at the formerly vacant fourth spot at the gaming table, and set the cup next to his dice.

Beyond caring about his lost drink, Ben turned back to Neil, windmilling his hand in small, excited circles. "Neil. Neil!"

"What?" His schoolmate didn't even look up.

All right. Guess I'll shock you into moving. "Get off that minotaur and come in here."

Neil frowned at Ben, and stumbled away from the door guard when he realized he had been resting against a living being.

The minotaur's mouth moved, speaking in the Servant-Giant tongue. "Now I wonder not why the small, oblivious caster could resist the power-aroma of master-class cider, mead, and spirits."

Working his device in spell-prepping taps, Neil took a few worried steps, inching toward Ben.

Seeing where Neil's pale fingers moved, the upper right of his tablet—*he's readying a spell*—Ben decided to offer, "That wasn't a threat."

Neil's power pink eyes flitted to Ben's empty hands before returning to the minotaur. "You speak its language?" Coming next to him, Neil whispered, "What did it say?"

Ben hooked an arm around Neil's shoulder, guiding his schoolmate to the back room. "*She* said, 'nice tablet. Want some cider?'"

Neil continued to whisper. "Tell her, 'thank you, but no thank you.'"

Continuing to direct Neil, Ben glanced back at the door guard and, not thinking about how hard he hit the consonants, replied in the dialect of Giant reserved for leaders and rulers. "He said, 'you're huge and guard well.'"

The minotaur gave her chest a proud thump and snorted.

"By Smitton's Forge," Neil breathed, speaking under his breath signaling his equal astonishment with what the merchant had for sale. "Paydirt, indeed."

Ben removed his arm. He pressed his volume down twice to call Kevin and LeRoy. "Just pinged the guys."

Neil turned to face him. His free hand raised as though to grab Ben's lapel and lowered. He showed Ben his screen. "Is a contract." Neil hit send. "Until you read it, can I get a tentative, verbal response, battle-buddy?"

Battle-buddy. I hadn't even thought of that when I stepped up. "Sure." Ben said, "Pending a thorough read, you have a yes."

"Great." Neil slung his Triforce into its holster. He clapped his hands, hard, once, and turned to the merchant. "Impressive selection of spellcards you have, my good man. How much for one of each?"

Chapter Ten

CONTRACTUAL OBLIGATIONS

WITHOUT BUYING POWER, Ben began to feel sorely out of place. Deciding to put his time to use, he pulled a more manageable cup, filled it with the hot, fragrant cider, and—figuring the minotaur to be the best indicator if trouble broke out—moved a chair to sit on her left.

Not only had Kevin and LeRoy joined Neil in buying stuff, Neil told him later, but nearly every Junior Apprentice, Apprentice, and Senior Apprentice who attended the A.P.A. had come through in an unbelievable precession, haggled, bought, and left before he finished his own in-depth deal.

Engrossed with the contract, Ben hadn't noticed.

Twice he filled up his cup and saw different schoolmates. Each time, the clamor of the bazaar had dropped until by the time Neil had finished and they left the tent only a handful of vendors still called in casual volumes to the meandering patrons which had thinned to the point that the full lengths of several of shopping rows were visible under the soon-to-be dawning sun.

Ben had paused his reading while they returned to their cars in the mostly empty lot. He bid Neil a good night, directed Tex to plot a path to Meadows Towing, and read as his companion directed the car. He didn't notice when they stopped, or even when the sun rose just enough to affect the brightness of his screen.

A freezing chill rushing across the scrapyard got his attention. "Whoa!" Ben sat up straight and scanned the area. A four-foot tall, high-speed frost wave flashed away toward the city. From the wide arc trailing into the distance, the spell must've originated miles further out in the Might-Lands. Still, Ben gave a casual search for incoming casters. None.

The windows on the first floor of Meadows Towing were iced-over. Rows and rows of wrecked cars—*wow, it started off ten feet high*—sported frost, and he could see the power of the spell diminish toward the front gate in the receding level of frost on the row ends. *Well, it's not an attack.* He rubbed his face and tried to stretch away the weariness that had settled into his bones. "Tex, someone's casting *big* magic out there."

Holding the spare Anvilsmith tablet with an iced-over screen, his companioned faced him with an equal film of ice over his lenses. "You don't say."

Ben chucked and pulled the thin sheets away from the round sockets. He didn't know the name of that spell, but had seen the effect before. That wave of frost would continue until it coated enough obstacles to absorb the frost. "We call him Neil the Necromancer, but we should call him Neil the Negotiator."

"Huh?" Tex had remained still like a trained dog being groomed. "I don't think I was a part of whatever conversation you're continuing."

"You should have seen him haggle, Tex." Ben slid his tablet away, lifted his companion—which clung to the extra Anvilsmith—and stood. "Before I went to read, he had already talked the guy down twenty percent; and, from what I'm reading on the forum thread about the bazaar, he got everyone an amazing deal."

Ben stepped over his car door. The top layer of desert hardpan crunched under his boots as he stretch-strolled to the front door. "And then, from what he laid out in this contract... not only could we make some serious coin, we could make almost every spell available for every technomancer to buy."

"Ben," Tex motioned Meadows Towing sign. "The scrapyard makes coin."

"Yeah." Ben gave a non-committal shrug as he entered the spotless kitchen. He set Tex down and went to the refrigerator that had once had been the nastiest appliance he had had ever laid eyes upon. The handle had been so caked-over with crud that only the dull tips of chrome were visible. Now, two months later, he could clearly see his reflection in the handle he would've once only touched with a gloved hand. *The goblins really whipped the place into shape.* "But whatever this place makes belongs those who operate it on a day-to-day basis."

"I don't know..." Tex trailed off. It seemed that he had more to say on the matter, but switched topics. "Mind if I take a look at the contract?"

"Please do. Go ahead and pull it." Ben took an icy cold water bottle. *This should wake me up.* The heater kicked on. *Man, the place sure is quiet...* At home, his family always kept two mundane televisions going, each tuned to a different news channel. He often went to the roof so he could study in relative peace. *...And boy is it nice.*

His device dinged at Tex pulling the document.

Ben cracked the seal, popped open the sports top, and took a swig. *Ah, refreshing.* His eyes went wide. *Ah crap!* He set the bottle down and sent a text to his parents. "Going to be out of the house this weekend. Please reach out if I'm needed for anything."

Apparently waiting for communication, his mother texted back. "Okay."

Ben nodded at the reply. Ever since the Samhain festival, they've been giving him an unbelievable amount of latitude. He stifled a yawn. They no longer batted an eye when he went out or said he was staying out. *Also nice.* His mind switched back to the offer from Neil to go into business together. *Can't believe I have a chance to make real money and help others get spells.*

He scooped his bottle, made his way into the dining room and—might as well get working now—made a left to go down into his basement laboratory.

No sooner had he made it down the last carpeted step, though, then his eyes landed on the spare twin bed he kept near his desk. *Didn't realize how tired I am.* Soft breathing came from the hammock the goblins had fashioned by stitching together scraps of leather upholstery and hung by car door springs. Next to each other, Nuk and Uk'so's combined weight barely weighed the sling down. *Oh yeah, nearly forgot that they're communal sleepers. I better get to my bed upstairs or I'll wake and find them crowding me again.*

I'll just set my coat on the chair... He took off his coat, and did. *Kick my shoes off...* Ben tried, but unlike his school loafers, the mid-calf boots refused to be discarded so easily. *Man...* He sat down on the bed. Under the mounting weight of sleep, unlacing his boots became an arduous task. *I need magic laces or something...* When he finally got one undone, he laid back to kick it off. *Time to struggle with the other...*

BEN REGAINED consciousness hearing soft tapping sounds. *Must be sprinkling.* Diagonally across him, a small warm body weighted on his torso. *Jake must've had nightmares.* He put an arm over his youngest brother and, expecting the soft somewhat wooly feel of the various Disney themed onesies Jake slept in, frowned. *Rawhide?* Almost negligible at first, the tangy smell of —ug, *what is that?*—antiseptic registered when he yawned. *Oh, no. Not again.*

Ben opened his eyes.

Instead of Jake's mess of black hair under his arm, he found the bald brown, tan, and black calico head of Nuk, the bossy goblin. *The warmth against my side, just below Nuk's head must be Uk'so.* Though the second goblin had finally become the solid deep forest green that the orcs often admired in their own kind, Ben's mind conjured the mottled whitish-yellow-green skin that had covered Uk'so's body for the first few weeks.

He fought the desperate urge to shove the quiet goblin away. *Easy, Ben. Whatever that was has been remedied.* With how hard Uk'so worked, and how often the others ignored him, Ben felt a bit of kinship with the scrapyard's least valued member.

The soft tapping sounds continued.

Feeling at ease with the goblins, Ben scanned for a window to watch the rain. All around, except for the cement-slabbed ceiling supported by wide square cement columns on cement flooring, the twelve-foot tall walls of the fifty-foot by fifty-foot space were bare, dull gray cinder block. *Wait, I'm in the basement. I shouldn't be able to hear rain.* His gaze went to where his ears estimated the source of the tapping.

Reclining against the springs, Tex sat on the top edge of the hammock, where the Frankensteined leather had been stitched around metal. The robot's lenses held a faint blue light, making its orbital sockets look like dull flashlights, about to wink out.

Ben eyed the one long pointed calico goblin ear he could see. *This'll probably wake them.* He whispered, "How long have I been asleep?"

The goblin's ear twitched.

Tex's lenses rotated to him. Matching the volume perfectly, the robot's synthesized voice answered, "Only two hours. You were up for over thirty so you've got at least six more coming. Go back to sleep."

"No." Practiced at moving Jake without waking him, Ben tried to apply the same gentle tactic to Nuk. "I got work to do."

His gruff, high-pitched voice at the ready, Nuk rolled away from Ben's grasp and elbowed the other goblin. "Up, Uk'so Tuk." Dressed in a Meadows Towing t-shirt and red jeans, Nuk shook his body in two sharp twist. Cracks and pops, clacked. "We got the work to do, too."

So glad I made them start wearing real clothes.

Groggy, the deep green goblin muttered and rolled out of the bed, clad only in blue jeans. His two twists were slow and labored.

Man, now I feel guilty. Ben offered, "Uk'so, if you want to sleep longer, you can."

The hunter green ears, a bit more pointy than that calico's perked up. Uk'so stroked his lengthy, angled chin with his three-fingered hands as though he actually considered taking Ben up on an offer—*that's a first.*

Ben had finally gotten Nuk to keep from dragging Uk'so around. This moment built hope in Ben's chest. *Do it. Just jump back on the bed and I'll back your play.*

Nuk rasped something that sounded like a heavily accented, "Saturday."

Uk'so nodded, scooped up his Meadows Towing tee, and headed toward the stairs.

Nuk followed.

Ben listened as they padded up the carpeted stairs. Nuk had a habit of smacking Uk'so when things weren't done to his exacting standard, and the slow rouse probably qualified. *You better not slap him, Nuk.* Though he gave orders, Ben figured the calico would find a way to circumvent them. A few second passed. He didn't hear a slap. Instead, a vacuum whirled to life.

Keeping an ear out for Nuk's petty physical dominance, Ben sat on the metal folding chair and made a dissatisfied face as he scooted into the shallow hollow under the four-legged wooden desk. *I need to get a real chair and a real desk. In fact, that's the first thing I'll do with my proceeds.*

Ben reached into his pocket, pulled one of the spellcards—*hmm, burnt orange case with royal blue spirals. Wonder what spell is in this inside*—and opened the shallow drawer. He took out a thin flat-head screwdriver, and pried at the fine line on the edge of the casing holding the two halves shut. *Only one way to find out.*

Chapter Eleven

PLAYING WITH POWER

THE SPELLCARD OPENED WITH A SNAP. *Crap, did I break it?* Ben checked the thin slats on the top card. All four were fine. *No matter how many times I do this, I always feel like I've broken it.* He sniffed at the rubber cement that had kept the two halves bound together, trying to get a hint at the card's origin. *Kiwi? Hmph, none of the major distributors use Kwik's kiwi scented sealant*—he paused feeling a bit honored—*maybe this card is from Australia.* He smiled at the possibility of working on a card that had traveled around the world.

Ben, set both halves on the desk, and pulled out his headband with a magnifying glass attached to it from the drawer. *Crap, the Liquid Forge Neil bought is still in the car.* Ben slipped the headband on and glanced back at Tex.

Tapping on the tablet, his companion still sat poised on the top hammock springs with one leg crossed over the other.

Ben folded a cuff back and continued to roll his sleeve up to his forearm. "Hey, Tex. What'cha up to?"

Tex didn't look up. "Playing Dragon, Deities, and Divinity."

Ben chuckled, shook his head, and worked on his other sleeve. "Hate to tell you this, but that's just a re-wrap of Kings, Clergy, and Coffers."

"Well…" Tex rocked his head to the side. "Yes and no. There are different calls to learn and more dice to unlock. In fact, I've collected all of the sets in K.C.C., including Ob, and the forums say TripD unlocks gems with an ultra-rare Ast set."

Jeeze, he sounds just like the addicts at school. All I really heard was him justifying the amount of time he's pouring into it. "Well, could you take a quick break and do me a favor?"

"Sure." Tex dropped the tablet into the hammock and started down. "What is it?"

"Please retrieve the small brown paper bag Neil left in the backseat." Ben turned back to the desk. "There should be a four ounce squeeze bottle in it."

Tex's metal feet *tinked* on the cement floor as he hustled to the stairs. "Will do."

"Thanks, buddy." Ben flipped his magnifying glass down and focused on the bottom half of the card. *Now, what do we have here?* He pointed with the flattop screwdriver as he gave the card's innards a thorough once over. *Standard Anvilsmith circuit board layout. They've got the obdurium strip at the back...* He rolled his eyes and sighed. *It's like since they found what works, no one tries to innovate any more. Wait, hold on a second, why'd they use a three on two diode config instead of three on one?*

He followed the tiny wires to the memory core interface and found two single thin obdurium steel strips fused together to accept power and trigger the memory. "Ohhhh." He grabbed his forehead. "That's why! My cards need another strip to provide enough power to trigger second tier spells."

"Ohhhh." Mocking him, Tex's voice preceded him coming down the stairs. "You do know you're speaking gobbly-gook."

Ben flipped up his magnifying glass and smirked. "Listen here, Mr. Ob, Trip D, and Ast. I don't want to hear anything about not making sense from you." Holding the chair to his bottom, Ben hiked up, turned to face the stairs, and set himself and the chair back down with a clunk. *I really need to get a swivel chair.* "By the way, just figured out why I could transfer my mid-tier spells to the SD cards, but they wouldn't fire."

Water sports bottle strapped to its chest with a thick rubber band, Tex came down without the bag. In one hand he held a glass saucer and in the other, the clear plastic bottle with four ounces of pearly white. On the front, in large, molten-steel orange text, it read *Liquid Forge.* "Ben." His companion's synthesized voice hit a rare serious tone. "This stuff is dangerous. Especially when applied to obdurium."

Ben took the saucer and the Liquid Forge. He scanned the back and found the warning. *Use extreme caution when working with precious metals. Only to be used with obdurium by licensed, bonded, and insured professional smelters.* The last line gave him a moment's pause. "Just how dangerous is it?"

Tex flipped his puncture point forward and cut the rubber band. "Oh, how about Pepcon dangerous?"

Pepcon. Ben rolled the word around in his head as he took the cold bottle of water. *It's not just a word. It's a name...* He couldn't remember. "Pepcon? Why is that name both familiar and forgettable?"

Tex asked, "How about putting it in conjunction with May fourth, 1988?"

"Nope." Ben popped the water bottle top and took a sip. *Mmm.* He read the label. *Lemon infused.* "If I have to guess, I'm going to need another clue."

Tex stroked his chin. "Old Henderson?"

"Well, besides that being from before I was born..." Ben tried to place the name again. It solidified for a split-second before fading. *Nope. Still don't know.* He shook his head.

"Wow." Tex whistled. "Before you open the Liquid Forge, let me show you something on your tablet."

Ben flipped up the cover from the holster and watched Tex's tiny fingers navigate to the HistTube video archives. *History Tube? It's not fair to have school flashbacks while on Yuletide break.* Ben's eyelids already started to feel heavy. "Not this site, Tex. Anywhere but this site."

"Sorry, they have the best info." Tex made his way back to the hammock and pulled himself in.

Ben marveled at the goblins' ingenuity. *Wow, the springs didn't make a sound.*

"Besides." Text continued, "That's just a short, two-minute clip. There's a butt-load more information there if you want it."

"Nah, two minutes should do." Ben lifted his tablet,

leaned back in his seat, and hit play. The video opened with a view from a hill showing the expansive desert brown earth around two manufacturing plants in the valley below. *Hard to believe the sprawling industrial city of Old Hendo had once been nothing, but a bunch of sagebrush. No one at school would believe it.* The video fast-forwarded to show a fire at one of the plants with white smoke pluming up to the sky.

The spare Anvilsmith strapped to his back, Tex lifted the two prize bags full of spellcards Ben had won at the Conjurers Course during the Samhain festival.

"Hey." Ben asked, "Where are you going with those?"

Tex continued toward the stairs. "Just keep watching."

Ben turned his attention back to the screen. The small fire ballooned into a massive explosion. Dirt shot up into the sky obliterating the early white plumes. A dust-filled shockwave rolled across the desert hardpan. The sight made his guts quiver. About to speak to Tex, his Anvilsmith speakers blew air into his hands when the thunderous boom of the rolling repercussion hit.

Holy! He dropped his device and scooped it out of the air before it completed a swing in his holster.

Before his eyes, a second blast—*that's more powerful than the first one*—blew black smoke up through the massive dirt cloud still in the air. He thumbed down his volume before the blast hit and it still rocked his speakers.

Stunned, Ben watched as the camera zoomed out to take in the massive black and brown smoke-haze clouds which also underscored just how powerful the explosions had been and just how unpopulated Henderson had been.

Tex came back down the stairs with Uk'so who now wore the long black apron and thick yellow kitchen gloves, which—before Ben laid down rules—had been the only items close to clothing that the goblins wore. Presenting two of the prize cards, Tex asked, "So, you see?"

"Yeah. Oh, yeah." Ben unstrapped his spellcard holder, holster—device and all—to hand them to Tex. He folded his trench coat, laid it over Uk'so's arms, and pulled his school tie off to go with the coat. Ben grabbed the Komir necklace and considered the gold castle inlayed in ruby surrounded by gold. He rubbed the small etched disc behind the highest tower. *Even the sun's not too high for them.* About to take it off, he triggered the protective charm and tethered its power need to his Argosian font. "Just in case."

Tex nodded. "Well, it couldn't hurt."

Ben patted himself down and felt a small prick. *Right, the little sword.* He took the token snatched from the magic weapon that had attacked him and handed it over. "Oh." Ben snapped the open card on this desk shut, and handed it off. "That's everything."

"Except for the Liquid Forge." Tex reminded. "I brought the saucer so you could dole some out for use."

"Yup." Following the instructions, Ben held the bottle upside down by its base and tapped the tip directly on the glass. The tip starred open and two droplets escaped before he could right-side the bottle which closed itself. He handed it off. "Here you go."

"Be careful." Tex took it and motioned for Uk'so to go with him. The goblin followed.

Ben rubbed his hands together and turned to the desk. He cracked open both SD cards, checked the slats —*both still good*—and, quite practiced at the process from changing spellcard casings, made short work of removing the obdurium strips with the flathead screwdriver and a pair of tweezers.

Okay. He removed the headband, put it away and reached for a toothpick. His mouth went dry. *Time to start making money.* He laid one of the thin obdurium ribbons on the saucer. Dipped the toothpick on the Liquid Forge and—*easy, easy does it*—applied it to most of the strip, leaving the tip dry so the excess had a place to go. *Alright, step one down. We got the bread, the spread.* He wiped his lips with the back of his hand and picked up the other obdurium strip with the tweezers. *One more slice and this sandwich is done.*

As he moved the tweezed ribbon toward the first, the one on the plate slid away slightly.

Huh? "Okay..." *Must be a matter of angle of approach.* He twisted his wrist and came at the Liquid Forge slick strip from the side. *It jumped again.*

Ben sighed. He pulled double-sided tape from the drawer that he typically used to affix his own custom labels to his spellcards. He put a piece on the saucer. *Then tap you into position with the screwdriver and press you down so you don't go nowhere this time...* Again, he picked up the dry obdurium ribbon with the tweezers and moved it toward the stuck strip.

As he moved them closer, the sheen on the stuck strip dried up. *Huh. Did it evaporate?* He bent to judge the reaction when the obdurium slivers were an inch from each other and felt slight resistance.

The ribbon he controlled curved away from the desk. A fine lather began to bubble on the stuck strip giving off tiny white flashes. *Crap!* He yanked his arm away. The flashes intensified to strobe light his action. *Horribly concerting!* A white arc spanned from the obdurium on the saucer to the strip in his hand, and he stumbled back out of his chair to get away from the one on the table.

A scorching flashed washed over him.

Then another.

"Holy shi—

One more.

BOOM!

Chapter Twelve

AGONY

*...Darkness...every bit of me...hurts...bad...*Cool water sprinkled on the back of Ben's neck and trickled down to his lower back before is spread outwards from whatever he sat against. *...Is it raining? ... Where... Where am I?...*The front of his body, his arms, his face, his ears, his head, his lower legs. All of it pounded with each pulse of blood through his system. A relentless two-tone warbled ringing filled his head. *...What's that...that noise?* He tried to lift his head to see. Searing pain washed the world white. Then unconsciousness... And again...

A faint stream of hot, thick air worked through a nostril...*Am I no longer in my lab? What...what's that horrible stench?...Maybe if I—* Ben tried to open his eyes and it felt like someone shoved coals against them. He tried to jerk away. Agony flooded his system. He went out...

...If I could look up... Out again.

Next time he came to, the steady patter of rain

around him, running cool down his back relaxed his mind for a moment. The rain also landed on his upper legs. *...Why's it raining on my back and legs...I'm—I'm sitting up—propped up. Can't open my eyes. Can't... Can't move at all. Stuck. How...how damaged am I?* Each beat of his heart pumped blood. Everywhere the blood went reported pain. *My stomach hurts the most... The ringing.*

He listened.

The horrible high-pitch whines inside his head had ceased and a horrible—*at least it's external*—alarm rung rapid—*ear piercing, skull-splitting*—bells. The rings would break for a gruff voice yelling in a harsh language full of hard consonants. Then the alarm would continue.

Slowly, open your eyes. Ben tried. *They feel fused shut, but the rest of the pain.* He considered his overall condition like a burning wood smell piggybacked on the faint air already pregnant with other horrible smells. *It's not so bad, except—* His throat tightened. He swallowed. The air passageway through his sinuses nose grew a bit wider. *Why does my stomach still blaze?* The yelling between bells repeated. *It's the same message, and in Giant. Is that Ur-Krurk?* Ben tensed. The world behind his eyes flashed white. He desperately clung to consciousness. *Impossible. He's imprisoned.*

"Put out the fire or I'll roast all of you alive!"

It is Ur-Krurk. It must be a recording the ogre made, which means that I am still at Meadow's Towing; but, then, why is it raining? A bit of sound reasoning began to return. *Try something else.*

Ben tried to move his arm. *Arm feels fine. Is something holding me down?* He forced his arm to bend and something on top of his skin cracked sending light, stinging sensations into the crook so his elbow and shoulder. *Good. I can move. Now, what's over my face?* The pressure from his hand registered on his rigidly stiff fingers and forehead, but—*something's between them*—dulled his ability to feel.

Focusing, Ben forced his fingers to bend a segment at a time. Light stings registered there, too, before feeling returned and he had a handful of the nullifier. *What is this bumpy stuff? Sort of feels like—uh!—they feel like scabs.*

His thoughts went back to the obdurium and the bubbling Liquid Forge. The Pepcon explosion—*that horrible earth-shaking might*—played in his mind's eye. *I should have moved my hand away instead of leaning closer.* The strobe effect which had made him feel as though he moved in slow motion came back clear. *Wait. No, I did move away.*

The alarm stopped and, besides infrequent drips, so did the rain. A stampeding rush of footsteps clomped down the stairs.

I am in my lab.

Orcs rarely smiled and were almost never surprised which made the collective, astonished gasps that much more disconcerting.

I must be a flippin' mess.

A deep voice—*Toad*—wavered as it whispered in Giant. "Might-Fist?" The orc cleared his throat and switched to English. "Ben?"

Ben lifted his hand to acknowledge hearing his name. He then raised a finger. *Just give me a minute guys.*

He motioned to the constant pain in his stomach. *Just need a bit longer to heal.*

A lone set of footsteps sloshed to him. Something pressed against his torso, cracking the slab of scab like a bug, just above the pain. The stabbing torment returned to his stomach as something long and thick was pulled out of him. A *thunk* sounded off the wall across room and a light splash followed.

Better. It did hurt, but almost like—Ben struggled to equate the feeling of the object leaving his body to anything else and grimaced inwardly at the only comparison that came to mind—*like being constipated passing.* He went to shake his head against the visual. His scabbed eyes denied the move. *How about it's just better.* He gave a thumbs up.

As though pulled by a magnet, Ben's hand went to where the intrusion had been. His fingers dropped into a moist, gooey hole. *Ugh! I just touched my guts!* His lips moved in his scabbed mask and he rocked back hard enough to crack the remaining casing that held his torso still and smack the back of his head against the wall, which didn't compare. *I just touched my guts!* He gave his hand rapid shakes to get the sticky gunk to fly from his hand. *I'm in water.* He splashed his hand down and waved it in the water.

When the frantic disgust finally passed, Ben heard Counselor Eastly's husky whisper from lessons long since passed. "We make mistakes to learn. Each mistake is a gift. It's called experience. If you think one day you may not remember, you should keep a token to keep you true. Make mistakes. Learn. And repeat. And repeat."

This'll be a horribly grisly reminder, but I definitely don't want to make this mistake again. Ben began to scrunch his features and gingerly lift the edge of the thick scab mask. He took extra care around the sticking points at the corners of his mouth. Able to, he drew a deep inhalation of disgusting air. *Tastes like smoke from a funeral pyre.* The corners around his nose—*easy, Ben. Easy*—also proved a bit tricky. Worst of the three, his eyes as he pulled off—*Ow! Ow! Ow!*—the scant few eyelashes on the inner corner of his right eye hadn't been burnt away.

Bright at first, the room darkened rapidly with each fluttering blink Ben took, as his eyes adjusted to the dim, single row of emergency lights down the center of the room. An orc stood over him. *Toad?* Lit from behind, Ben only had the shape of the body to work from. *No, too broad. Jek? How peculiar. I would've bet that Toad would've been the first to help me. Yup, there's that salami smell.* He held his disappointed sigh. *Crap. It is Jek.* Though he didn't harbor an active dislike for the orc, it would be a long time coming before Ben could forgive the orc who had retrieved him from the Samhain festival and then sat on the sidelines as he, and the other Meadow Towing orcs, fought for their lives.

A glint of steel, close to Ben's body, caught his eye.

The large orc, with grim business in his pale green eyes, leaned close. In his massive green hand, his blood-dagger.

It's angled to cut my throat.

Chapter Thirteen

A TROPHY LIKE NO OTHER

I DON'T KNOW how either ogre shot bolts of raw magic without actually casting, but answer wrong Jek, and you're getting my full reserve. Ben amped up his Argosian font, narrowed his eyes at Jek and, in a low, suspicious tone, asked, "What are you doing?"

"Looks like you're trying to keep it whole. "Jek's gaze shifted to Ben's forehead and then bounced around from his temples to his ears. "Which means cutting where the scab meets hair that didn't burn."

"Oh." Keeping a wary eye on the blade, Ben breathed a bit easier. "Thanks. And you're right. I do want this."

"Let me." Jek placed his large hand on top of Ben's head and moved the knife behind Ben's ear.

Be cool. If he really wanted me dead, he would've shot me when I was in his truck. To show his patience, and ready to pull back if he didn't like the feel—*the pain's nearly gone*—Ben folded his hands on his stomach, which was still covered with crusty remnants. *Is it healed?* He couldn't bring himself to let his fingers wander where the hole in his gut had been. *It could just be numb.*

Jek's nearness pressed the salami smell which began to overpower the nasty order.

What, does he use the meat as cologne?

The orc slid the cold metal blade across his cowlick and met little resistance.

Whoa! My hairline's way back there?

Jek's thick fingers landed on his ears and pulled gently. "I don't think there's a way to keep this intact with the ears.

"That's fine." *Can't believe I'm really going to keep this.* "Just as much as possible."

Jek's feet sloshed in the water as the orc moved around him to get the best angles to slide his dagger along the scabbed hairline across his crown. The tip moved expertly behind his ears in a way Ben had only experienced at barber shops. *I wonder.* "Jek, do you cut hair?"

"No." Driving the blade home into the scabbard clipped inside his jeans, Jek shook his head. "This was like demasking, and after a few hundred, you sort of gain a knack for it."

What's demasking? Opening his mouth to ask, Ben drew a quick breath—*not sure I really want to know*—and closed it. *At least, not right now.*

"Work the back, Ben," Jek said, sloshing a few feet away. "If you're careful, you'll have the thing whole."

Ben closed his eyes. Gathering a bit of courage, he did as suggested—*can't believe I'm doing this*—and lifted from the back. Like pulling off a helmet—*a bit snug against the temples*—he removed the fragile trophy from his face.

Raucous cheers and hoots erupted from the stairs. Feet splashed into the water and trudged toward him.

Open your eyes. Ben turned the scabbed shell-face around to face his own. *Open. Your. Eyes.*

He did.

Chapter Fourteen

CONTROLLING INTEREST

PULLING the cotton Meadow's Towing extra-large—*hard to believe this is the smallest size they have*—white t-shirt down over his head, Ben gathered the excess, tucked it into his blue jeans, and cinched his belt tight to keep it in place. As he came down the carpet-blasted-away, bare, blackened stairs, a gust of wind—*can barely smell that I blew everything up*—worked his loose sleeves and neckline to billow the shirt around him. He chuckled at himself. *Except for the purple star logo on my chest, I look like the Stay Puff Marshmallow Man.* With a *galoosh*, each of his backup pair of black books splashed down into the debris-strewn, mid-shin deep, sooty water.

He eyed the extension cords, some yellow, some red, duct taped to scrubbed clean spots on the blackened ceiling. Like bizarre Christmas lights, a series of car headlights ran the length of the room, creating make-shift rows of ceiling lights. *Wow, those goblins can jury-rig anything.*

His mind's eye went back to the bubbly-swoll of the scab mask made from his burnt flesh fused with whatever chemical reaction the liquid forge and obdurium made. His fingers recalled, all too clearly, the hard bumpy texture of the light-weight reminder to be ultra-careful. Ben shook them to try and lose the feeling.

The ashen water rippled from the force of an industrial, five-foot diameter fans in each of the three other corners. *While they push the air out, they also force the lighter junk toward the stairs.* Mindful of wreckage, floating buckets, and dark green Rubbermaid garbage cans, Ben trudged against the wind, Anvilsmith swinging against his leg, to the lone, four-foot tall, dark brown metal barrel set in the middle of the long wall opposite the stairs.

Hoisting himself onto the barrel. Ben worked his Orion spellcard from his jeans pocket and marveled at how black the formerly gray cinder-block walls were. *How much worse would that have been if Tex hadn't shown me that Pepcon video?* He found his head shaking. *Instead of still kicking, I might have kicked the bucket.* "Well." He exhaled hard to push the morbid wonder out of his mind. "Time to help with clean up."

Ben called the emerald energy from his Anvilsmith to go into his spellcard. Instead of just enough power to summon five gorillas snapping across his skin, in a flash, the Anvilsmith's full reserve flushed into him, looped around his chakras—*I have an eighth one?*—and poured into the card. The excess energy, a majority of what had flowed into him, dumped back into the tablet.

The Argosian energy in his chest crackled. The

Krotostian energy in his gut howled. The Nilosian font in his head sizzled.

Bastion stirred. Ben found his lips moving to voice Bastion's question. "What are you up to, Host?"

Holy! Ben slap-covered his mouth. *He's using my mouth to talk.*

Muffled by his own hands, Bastion answered Ben's thought with his mouth. "Yes and you should use it to answer me."

Ben tried to steel his thoughts so they couldn't be read.

"*I am* your mind." Bastion's sinister, rumbling laugh filled his head. "You can't possibly shut me out. "Nor —" Bastion began to scour Ben's recent memories. "— can you keep secrets from me."

A cold numbing sense of betrayal filled Ben as Bastion rooted through his mind. The cold gave way to a building heat.

"Oh, you don't like this?" Not finding anything for the night, Bastion began to sift through Ben's last day at school before the Yuletide break. "You should be honored to by my host."

Anger formed a knot between his eyes. Ben thought his reply, *I'm not.*

"Well." Bastion stopped Its rooting around Ben's private thoughts. "In that case, if you really want me out, just tell me to get out."

Get out.

"No." Bastion's deriding laughter salted Ben's rubbed raw betrayal. "Tell me with your own words. I want the world to hear you tell me to leave."

Ben went to open his mouth. *What the Hell?* All feeling in his mouth—his sense of taste, his awareness of saliva—fled. Suddenly, he could move his lips, but had zero use of this throat. *He's toying with me.* Then, Bastion released use of his throat, but held all air locked in his lungs. *Asshole.*

Bastion took full control of Ben's body to punch himself in the eye. Hard. "You're my meat-puppet and only have freedom so long as I choose to give it to you." As though pulling covers over itself, Bastion rolled over in the Nilosian font.

"Once I'm done, I'll leave you to your pitiful life," the Beast said. Ben's fist plowed into his other eye. "Don't try to undo my plans." Ben's hands untucked his shirt, worked under the white cotton for a moment before ripping the coffee cup-wide, three-inch thick scab away. Bastion dropped it in the water.

Control and feeling came back to his body. His eyes hurt, but his gut lit with pain from the deeply seated scab being yanked out. Ben had to work to keep from falling off of the barrel.

Inside his head, Bastion's savage voice stung Ben's brain as it continued inside his head. *Or you'll be sorrier than you could ever imagine.*

His five conjured green gorillas, which had remained idle while Bastion seized control, rubbed each other's head as they usually did. After hundreds of cycles devoted to cleaning up during detention—mostly given by Senior Adept Collins—they got to work on the task at hand.

Ben's ability to regenerate made short work of the pulsing aches radiating from his eyes. He pulled his shirt up so the bloodied cotton would get fused to his stomach as the wound started the scabbing process, again.

However, the insult—*Bastion has dominion over my body. How'd that happen?*—continued to fester.

Chapter Fifteen

THE ART OF NOT BLOWING UP

BEN STOOD at the corner of the basement where the blackened metal and glass had been piled. Without working the soot away from the surface, he had to use shapes to tell what was what. *Springs from the goblins hammock... The steel toe parts of my Tore Vex steel-toed boots... Is that the saucer?*

He scooped up the pitch black, tiny plate that had held the Liquid Forge and turned the grungy dish over in his hands. *Curious. I don't know how this survived whatever kind of energy created by that explosion, but I would've thought it would have at least broken when it hit the ground.*

His gazed shifted to a thin, cylindrical piece of metal that used to be the screwdriver pinched on the end to work tiny screws lying on the ground beyond the saucer. *Ah, there is it.* He set the black coated glass down and picked up the handleless, tiny metal shaft. *So, this is what's left?* He sniffed it. *Hmph, smells like, uh...* He searched for a comparison and came up short of a single option. *Sort of smells like a mix of coal and ozone.*

A quick grin spread his lips. *Man, Adept Floyd would flip his lid if I brought this into the Electronics Lab.*

Ben's smile widened at the thought of the Adept's pinched-up face turning a furious red over a double violation of his Lab Commandments. The Adept called them rules, but everyone made a grandiose mockery over the trivialities that would make Floyd go red – which was great fun, until he handed out detention. Without a handle, the shaft of Ben's screwdriver would break Grand Commandment #25 - *Thy tools must have thine name on it* and Grand Commandment #1 - *Thine tools shall be in perfect working order.*

Recalling the bright white flash before the explosion, Ben's amusement drained away.

Now I know why he's such a stickler. Ben nodded, a plan forming in his head. *I'm going to copy his rules, word for word, and post them down here as a reminder.* Ben eyed a section of wall just inside the basement where they would be most visible. *Well, not number twenty-five. That one's a bit much.*

He returned to scanning the pile.

Looks like only glass and metal survived the blast. Scanning for any exceptions, Ben nodded in understanding at a nearly forgotten question as to why everything in the circuitry portion of the Academy's Electronics Lab—*including the very uncomfortable chairs that make your butt fall asleep halfway through class*—had been composed of metal parts. *So, I need to get a metal chair, and a cushion.*

Not needing anything else from the charred pile,

Ben wiped his hands on his jeans. *Well, if at first you don't succeed...*

He quickly went about the building gathering another saucer, another drop of Liquid Forge, and two more spellcards that he had won at the Samhain festival. When he returned to the basement, he stood at the metal drum that he'd been sitting on earlier. *It's as good a workstation as I have right now; and, if I have to suddenly get clear of the flashpoint again, I won't have a chair in the way.*

Stifling a yawn, Ben worked the thin flathead into the grooves of one spellcard and then the next. Each opened with a snap. Tweezers! Ben went back to the jumbled mass of blackened objects, and searched the for tiny tool. *I must be getting tired. I didn't even check to see if I broke them.*

He returned to the drum and gave each half of spellcard a cursory check. *No broken slats. Good.*

Returning to the pile of debris, he searched through the smaller items for a bit before—*ah ha!*—pulling the tweezers from the blackened junk, then shuffled back to the drum and tweezed the obdurium strip from both cards.

He shook his head at the standard circuit board in each and stuffed the four halves of the powerless SD spellcard into his pocket. *Alright.* About to scoop into Liquid Forge, he paused, and rubbed his jaw. *Now to use just enough to wet one strip.*

He cautiously dabbed the flathead screwdriver shaft in the clear liquid and gave one of the strips a dainty coat.

Okay.

His mouth dried out.

"Okay."

As he reached his tweezers to the dry, thin rectangle of obdurium, a nervous flutter filled his gut and his heart started to thump like an orcish war drum. Worse, his hand shook a little.

Get it together. Focused on steadying himself, Ben drew a deep breath in through his nose, concentrated on fully expanding his lungs, and let it out slow. *Fear is an excuse not to try.* His thumping heart eased. He took in another deep inhalation. *You know what will happen. It might hurt like a son of a bear, but you'll survive.* His hand became sure. A conceited quote from Senior Adept Collins that everyone else at the school seemed incapable of not repeating—a viral earworm—pinged in his head. *Fear is for lesser folk.*

Ben shook his head to clear the arrogant infection and spoke his original thought. "Fear is an excuse not to try."

Hand perfectly steady, he reached out and picked the dry strip of metal up with his tweezers. Focusing on the reaction of the wet strip, Ben started with his hand extended his full arm's length behind him. It was as far from the other as he could make it. Taking his time, he eased the dry strip in little by little.

His hand just past his ear, a white flash popped in his peripheral vision.

A jolt of energy shot clamped down on his fingers, pinching them on the tweezers before reporting down his arm.

Oh shi—

The room flashed white. His wrist twisted. Hard.

Ah!

As though he were arm wrestling with a force much greater than he could begin to resist, his forearm spasmed and his bicep cramped. His shoulder tightened bitterly.

I'm not going to cry out in pain. Not going to call others to be blown—Ben screwed his face up as the energy ran painfully along his collar bone to his other shoulder and up his neck—*here we go again. Agonytown. Population me.*

The vision of the double Pepcon blast rang back.

And then...

...then...

...nothing?

Then his neck relaxed and the tightness in his shoulders eased. As did his bicep and his forearm. *Not out of trouble yet.* He rubbed his wrist and tried to get his fingers to release the black tweezers. *Can't let go. Almost feels like I dipped them in Colossal Glue.*

Wait, get back!

Scanning for the Liquid Forge-wetted strip that had been there—*it's gone*—Ben scooted away from the barrel.

No flashing lights. Almost afraid to think it, the thought—*I just might be in the clear*—went through his head when he backed into the opposite wall and began to breathe again. *At least there wasn't an earth shattering boom.*

Trying to let go again, Ben tried to get his fingers to part and—*ow, ow, ow!*—ripped scab away from his index finger. Blood welled in the gash and dried into another scab.

The tweezers remained embedded in the meat of his thumb.

Then, like watching a lit, slow-motion, carbon-snake firework turns from a small chunk of black material into a long stem of spent ash, a morbid fascination kept his gaze locked on tweezers as—encased in a thick, growing scab—they pushed themselves out of this thumb. He held his other hand open beneath to catch them, as the scab fell away with the tweezers. His fingerprints grew out from of the bald, flat flesh.

"Wow." *That was sort of cool.*

Instead of the lone obdurium steel strip being held by the tweezers tips, he found the second strip hugging the first around one of the tweezer's open prongs. *Oh, that's where it went.*

He began to ease the strips off. *They almost feel like strong magnets pulling on each other.*

The strips came off the end with a snap of white light and gust of electrified wind.

Ben shuddered and froze.

Black smoke rose as the two steel strips ground on each other. They became flush, still, and stopped smoking.

Ben remained still, waiting for anything else to happen. He asked, "Are you guys done?" Feeling as though he was tempting fate, he quickly added, "If not, don't blow up. Just take your time. I'm not in a hurry."

Stuffing the tweezers into his pocket, Ben took one of the dozen abandoned Rubbermaid bins to a corner of the room, sat it open end down, and placed the bonded —*or bonding*—obdurium on it.

Meticulously picking the process apart in his head,

he went up to his room, retrieved two more cards and came back down. "Okay, so the flash happened when I had them about three feet apart."

Ben grabbed two more of the bins and sat them, open end down, six feet away from each other. Then he cracked opened two more cars, checked the slots—all good—and removed the obdurium from each to place one strip on each bin. After applying a light dusting of Liquid Forge, he pushed one bin toward the other.

Four feet apart, the two small pieces of metal flew together, snapping light, wind, and smoke as they fell to the cement floor. Like before, black smoke rose from for a few seconds, then stopped.

He picked them up, put them on a bin and—*no need to see what the flash is like if two pairs come together*—minded the other pair in the opposite corner.

Thinking about getting another couple pairs going, the goblins gave out heart wrenching screams.

Oh no, another attack! Ben sprinted across the room and, taking two at a time, bounded up the stairs.

Chapter Sixteen

RUNNING ON FUMES

MEATY SMACKS—*COMBAT!*—CAME from upstairs. *Someone beating the goblins with their fists.*

Adrenaline flooded his body. Ben lunged harder up the stairs.

From playback of the battle that took place on this very ground last month, Ben had learned the video game clanks of weapons striking bodies paled when compared to the true flesh-cleaving *thumps*, bone splitting *thunks*, and true cries of pain.

Pine scent growing. No fire. Reflexively raising his arm to guard against an incoming attack, Ben leapt up the last three steps, then stopped, staring in amazement. The goblins were smacking *their own bodies* while screeching at the screen.

Nuk ended an angry-sounding string of syllables with *wemic*. Uk'so spun to present his rhinestone-clad posterior to the television and smacked his butt at the man/lion graciously explaining the "unique and astounding power of angel feathers" to them.

Just as animated, Uk'so opted for the more common obscene gestures, alternating between one middle finger, then the other middle finger, and finally both middle fingers at once.

Laughter rolled in Ben's chest. He covered his mouth—*hold it together!*—rounded the banister to rush up to the second floor, and leapt the trapped stair just one down from the landing. Having made it up to the hallway outside his room, Ben couldn't hold back anymore and soft chuckles began to escape him.

Don't want them to think I got a bit of perverse joy in them experiencing the same frustration I felt after the bonus stage. Ben snapped his fingers at the lost opportunity. *Man, that would have made an epic Dragon Sage 3, Wemic Reaction video.*

Chuckling freely, Ben stepped into his room. *Hmm, it's a bit chilly.*

Like a Roman emperor perched on a mountain of pillows on top of the brown fur blanket covering the California king beg, Tex looked up from a tablet with an expectant look.

Ben waved a hand to discount his mirth. "Can't put it into words, buddy. But, if you want a good chuckle, watch the goblins react to the Great Sphinx bonus level in a couple of hours." A full belly laugh rolled through him at the thought. "In fact, please do take the time to watch it." He shook with excitement. "Oh! And record it. I'm not going to show it to anyone, but I'd like to see it, too."

"Will do." Tex nodded, then pointed to the sun through the Plexiglas ceiling. "Not including the explosion, you've been at it for more than twenty-four hours." The robot patted the bed. "You probably should lie down before you fall down.

Ben gave a discounting wave, pulled the eight spellcard halves from his pocket, and plopped down into his cushy high-backed desk chair to work at the backup—*now, only*—soldering station that he had set up on the large oak desk. "Bring the tablet, please."

Tex thumped onto the floor.

"And I will. I will." Ben plucked two board-halves from the pile in his hand and let the remaining six halves clatter unheeded onto the desk. *Alright, I'll set my soon-to-be scrap board here, and...* He leaned his elbows on the desktop, and pinched the medium binding clip to place the edge of the card under the clamp. "I just want to get one of these done so I'm just a strip insertion away from having a completed card when I wake."

Tex tapped his leg.

Ben reached down and, instead of just taking the tablet, lifted his companion holding the tablet up to sit on the edge of the desk. He took the Anvilsmith. "Thanks, Tex." *Though I built the schematic and ran it through the om-testers, I want to save the first build of my improved spellcard board.* "Hey, do me a favor. Record this process."

"Okay." Tex stood. His optics wound a little. "Alright. I have a good angle. Say 'go' when you're ready to record, and when making some of the tight printing, remember that I'm on your right."

"Understood." Tapping, *School Work*, *Electronics*, and *Circuitry* on his tablet, Ben scrolled to the middle of the thirty icons and tapped the folder entitled *Circuitry III:*

Final Project. He refamiliarized himself with his blueprint, picked up his tools and said, "Go."

Adjusting his pendant-mount desk lamp for better lighting, he swiveled the magnifying glass over and carefully removed circuits from his scrap board to meticulously solder them onto what would become his masterboard. Fighting against the adrenaline dump and surmounting the weariness of the day, Ben kept his hand steady as he relocated diodes, one by one, onto the new master card. He yawned. *Just a few more.*

His hand dipped and he yanked his arm back to keep from burning the board. *Nope. I'm zonked.*

Running on a sort of last-ditch autopilot, Ben rolled the chair from the desk to his bed, crawled on, and put on his sleeping mask to block out the sun.

Tex asked, "Hey, Ben. Do you mind if I…

Chapter Seventeen

A SENSE OF OWNERSHIP

BEN DREW A DEEP, waking breath. *Bacon. How do the goblins know when I'm going to wake?* On the dense furs, he stretched and twisted. His back sent a series of crisp, relieving pops into the complete silence. *No TVs droning on. No siblings arguing. Just me, and my thoughts. Now, this is how to wake up.*

A soft, rhythmic tapping came from up in his closet.

What's that? Exhaling, Ben removed his sleep mask. In the closet, up on the shelf above his clothes, the glow of his Anvilsmith lit Tex lounging on a couple of hand towels. His companion had set up a cushy little throne for himself next to Kermit—Ben's first companion. The small robot had the tablet propped against the wall with Dragon, Deities, and Divinity on the screen. *Junkie.*

Ben rolled onto his back to gaze out beyond the Plexiglas ceiling into a sky darkening from a deep plum to a midnight blue. As usual, only a few stars shone through. Several clouds ranged high and full of the deep oranges and reds, holding onto the last bit of distant sunlight like delicate candle-boats on a dark lake.

The tapping had stopped then started back up again.

Ben rolled onto his side, to study the green orbital sockets in the Tex's metal face. He said, "I figure you would've gotten enough of the game already."

"Nope." Tex kept his focus on the screen. "I have two more unlocks before dusting this one."

Unlocks. Dusting. More nonsensical game chatter. Ben stretched again and let one leg dangle over the edge of the bed—*whoa, cold*—and snapped his foot back from the cold wood floor. "Where are my boots?"

"You kicked them off the foot of the bed." Without looking from the screen, Tex pointed to where Ben could doubtlessly find his shoes if he could see in the dark. Tex asked, "Want me to raise the lights?"

Expression training to the rescue. "Yes, please."

Tex paused the game and swiped away to a foreign screen with several knobs and sliders. The robot worked them and warm track lights lit and blossomed along the baseboards revealing his boots lying haphazardly on the clean floor. The bathroom lit and the showered started.

Ben pulled the cover up to his neck and whispered, "Is there someone in there?"

"No," Tex shook his head and pointed to the Anvilsmith. "This place is wired up tighter than a smart-house. Everything can be run from the tablet." The robot hadn't move much, but still shifted as though he was settling back into a comfortable spot. "Mind the water, Ben. And let me know when you have it at the temperature you like so I can program it into the system."

This is the life! Ben stretched one more time, hitched his breath, and jogged across the cold hardwood to the cold, beige bathroom tiles. *The cinnamon air freshener is a nice touch in here.* He disrobed, stood on his jeans, tested the water cascading in the center from the three double-showerheads, and hopped in. "Water's perfect!"

A soft ding came from the showerheads, and a yellow flight flashed at the top of the cold and hot knobs.

Given how large Ur-Krurk was, Ben looked around the knobs, and then the showerheads. *There must be some kind of level to expand the area. This stall is wide enough for four, but he was too tall to fit in here.*

Soon lost in the fleeting deep thoughts that only come during showers, Ben washed up, cut the water off, and dried his feet thoroughly. *It's going to be another sprint across icy tile and cold wood flooring to the closet for socks.*

To get a taste of what he was in for, Ben touched a foot out then raised it up in surprise. *The floor's warm?* He set his foot down again and relished the warmth coming up through the tiles. *Very nice.* He stepped out and walked a circle in front of the toilet, each step found toasty new ground. "Hey, the floor is heated!"

"I was going to tell you it could do that, but you shot from the bed like a demon." Tex's synthesized voice came from a group of tiny holes near the commode that Ben thought were a fan to suck smell away. "Normally, you take longer to rouse."

Finding heating vents at the base of the sink, Ben

stopped before the wide mirror, wiggled his toes, and grinned indulgently as the warm air rolled in.

As the smell of bacon frying began to permeate the room. Ben drew a deep, appreciative breath. "Tex, my friend, I gotta admit…" admitting it aloud, Ben nodded in full agreement with his summation of the Meadow's Towing master bedroom. "…this place is five notches above nice."

"I know," Tex replied. "We should move here."

Dumbfounded by the thought, Ben's command of language fled with his ability to keep his mouth shut. Shocked numb by the prospect, he watched his jaw unhinge in the mirror. *At sixteen, can I do that?*

Chapter Eighteen
WORLD AWARE

MOUTH AGAPE, Ben leaned out from the bathroom to read Tex's body language. *Surely, he must be joking.*

Having added a couple of towels from the top shelf, Tex lazed like a Bronze Age emperor on a pillowed dais consulting a large glowing Tablet of the Gods which read: *You have our favor. Now, and forever*.

Ben's jaw quivered. His mouth popped closed as words nearly came, then left him speechless.

"What? You said *this is nice...*" Tex pointed to the ceiling. "The view is great." He waved his small arm in a wide graceful arc. "The room is fantastic." He gave the Anvilsmith a couple of taps, and nodded when the slow opening baseline of *Me and the Moon* by The Dryads thumped. Tex stood and reenacted the late night walker's steps from the video.

Ben's mind went to the last line. *Ain't nothin' gonna stop me this time, because the moon is high, and the night is mine.* The bacon smell made him think of breakfast which brought thoughts of his mother to mind. He founds words. "But I can't. My parents—"

"Can't stop you," Tex cut in. "You're sixteen. It's called being 'World Aware'. And if you want to move with your life, on your own terms, they cannot stop you."

Grateful to have regained conscious control over his jaw, Ben kept his mouth shut as he cast his eyes down to his toes at the threshold between the warm bathroom tile and the hardwood floor. Uncertainty had him frozen as he recalled asking his parents if he could return to the Samhain Festival to observe the closing ceremony. He had posed the question during dinner, and his parent had exchanged expressions back and forth without speaking. His father had seemed for it.

With the idea of being World Aware fresh in his mind, Ben realized that what he had taken as a shrug of *'why not?'* from his mom was a signal of powerlessness. Though he knew her doubting look all-too-well, Ben read the shrug as a new level of 'bad idea'—until something beyond doubt tugged at the corner of her mouth and she said, "We cannot stop you."

We cannot stop you. He rolled the four words around. He hadn't thought about the true meaning of the sentence.

Trying to unravel and name his mother's emotion behind the words, Ben kept his gaze on his toes as he crossed onto the room-temperature hardwood flooring in his room. This new understanding cast a liberating light on his parents and how they'd granted permission for everything he'd gathered the courage to ask for since turning sixteen a couple months ago.

Besides the closing ceremonies, he hadn't asked for much, but it was his desire to visit Crystal the seer, to know if his Samhain Festival winnings were cursed that had sent him to his mom. She had groaned, but granted the request. He'd asked to go to Bauman's Bazaar; she'd grimaced, but allowed it. He wanted to stay the night at Meadows Towing and mustered the courage to ask if he could spend the night a friend's house. She had rolled her eyes hard when he said *friend's house*, but granted him permission.

Understanding turned his lips into a wide smile. *So, that's why I didn't get punished for being away on the night of my sixteenth birthday, and the night I was...* Almost thinking Bastion's name, Ben left a blank and found another way to word the situation he had found himself in. Instead of *abducted* or *captured*, he went with *indisposed*.

The smile turned into a toothy grin full of greed at the endless possibilities and freedom that lay before him. Nodding slightly, he turned his eyes skywards to find the North Star to get Its opinion. But the vibrant clouds had grown dark, blocking the view to *his* star. *Feels like a bad omen.* Mid-nod, Ben began to shake his head.

"You could do it," Tex had been waiting. The robot motioned around the room, again. "We have a roof. The business is bringing in steady funds." His shoulders dropped for a moment before rising for a final point. "If you think about it, it's not like there's any real upkeep here."

Going to the closet, Ben took careful steps as he navigated his counter-thoughts. *Yes, we have a fine roof, but any money this place makes belongs to the orcs and goblins who work it.* About to address the question of upkeep, his stomach growled and he stopped at the work desk. More important to him—right then—Ben's eyes scanned the six spellcard halves he'd saved for the two remaining circuit boards. *They're gone.*

"Good point." As though Ben's gasp had agreed with him, Tex kept on, "You have a staff to cook for you. We have guards."

The clip where he had pinned the half-completed card was empty. He found the board—*this is not the prize-winning design I had been working toward*—finished, and a large, empty sauce pot clamped to the rim. His soldering iron had been strapped to a wooden cooking spoon and suspended from his swivel lamp by six thick, cut-open rubber bands. To the left of the pot were two spent boards with their diodes removed. To the right, another completed board. He eyed the cursory reconfigured extra bits of soldering. *This is one of my designs though...*

Tex said, "The moon is made of cheese."

What the heck is all this extra crap? Ben bumped the desk, making the iron rock. *It's jury-rigged, goblin-style.* He sat and slid a card under the magnifying glass. *This* — analyzing the cross-pointed circuits to boost the cards arcane capacity, Ben rubbed his chin. *This is my Circuitry V final project!*

Tex said, "I swam to China."

I hadn't made a working prototype of this design.

Tex added, "And back."

"I hear you, Tex." Feeling somewhat cheated out of being the first to build his own design, Ben rounded to see Tex imitating a breaststroke in a sea of towels. "Did the goblins do this?"

Tex stopped, stood, and pointed. "The set-up, yes. The boards, no."

Ben scooped up the other completed board to inspect it; the new circuit setup was there, too. "I've thought the design out thoroughly and passed the theoretical ohm tester in the school lab, but I hadn't got around to building it or doing real diagnostics on the design." Having a new respect for this type of work quite literally *blown* into him, Ben's slight jealously at not building the board first turned into concern about destroying Meadows Towing and all inside. He scanned for any burn marks. Ben brought his ramble to a point. "Tex, this configuration hadn't been tested."

Tex replied, "Energy flows. It didn't pop."

"It's great that it works—" Hearing a hanger shift and then the familiar sound of his companion sliding down his coat, Ben turned. Tex had paused his game and left the Anvilsmith behind. "But I haven't done any form of true diagnostics or testing."

The robot pushed over the step-stool the goblins used to access and clean higher parts of the room.

Ben shuddered at the memory of the scraping sound it made. That sound conjured the memory of when he had been helplessly restrained to the bed and the two goblins had checked on him repeatedly. The stool *thunked* against the desk breaking the daze.

"Adept Floyd didn't give your design his *good in theory* ninety-nine percent score, Ben. He gave it a hundred." Tex climbed the step-stool to stand on the desk and looked over the clipped card. "It passed his rigors and—I wouldn't be surprised if you cracked his cards to find your design—your new design works. I tested it."

Tested it? So glad I didn't wake up to an explosion. Ben crossed his arms. "What were the readouts?"

Tex turned to face him, and pointed to the tablet in the closet. His voice modulation took on a confrontational tone. "If it *really* matters, your device has the data."

"Of course it matters." Ben strode across the room, snatched the Anvilsmith down, and swiped away from Tex's game to activate his monitoring program. "There are certain points during the cycles where I need to see the spikes and dips."

Tex's volume raised slightly and his tone modulated to annoyance, "It's all there."

Rotating the tablet to landscape, Ben tapped to the tests and scrolled through the ramp up and steady emerald flow of arcane wattage from the tablet, though the card, and back into the tablet. *Less need. More efficient.* The cyan waste line stayed flat at zero. *Wow!* Well-earned pride pillowed in his chest. *The other cards have loss.* He scanned the readings again. *But not mine.*

"Ben," Tex dropped onto the step-stool. "You know they work. You're always working on the next upgrade." The robot had stopped at the last step from the floor. "I don't understand. Why are you holding back?"

"Well—" Ben drew a sharp breath. He tossed the tablet onto the bed and pressed his fists into his hips. "I don't understand why you're pushing me."

Tex took the final step onto the hardwood floor. "It's called *growing up*."

What? Ben's brow tightened and his eyes narrowed.

"Sorry," Tex's metal eyebrows rose. "I didn't mean to offend, but you have what many casters your age want. More than they could hope for." The robot motioned with both arms around the room and then brought them back in a wider arc. "This place is yours —and, unlike most who deem themselves World Aware, you will not need your parent's support."

Something about the way Tex moved reminded Ben of himself when he had tried to present the idea of independence to Rembrandt, his first robotic companion.

Ben had tried widening the limits, but Remy's processors couldn't handle the parameters of *do as you will*. Even after hacking the robot's programming to not consider repercussions of decisions, Remy would still freeze up with presented with a choice as simple as whether to plug in for power or run until he was at fifty percent.

Tex isn't the opposite of Remy. His brow loosened. *No, this Golemcast is on an entirely different level. Wait.* His jaw shifted to the right. *Perhaps this is why the school gives certain companions at specific ages...*

At ten, like the rest of the Initiates, Ben had been given the traditional Tech-Toad. Kermit, a simple robotic frog, had been good fun. It hopped where directed and was easy to control. At twelve, they received their first robot. Rembrandt proved to be a plodding machination capable of doing many simple tasks, but was quite basic and—ultimately—very limited.

Ben's frown returned as he began to continue down the line of his companions. He didn't want to go further. *But it might lead to a breakthrough.*

One of the few moments, which made him unique amongst his classmates, was when he had earned the fourteenths gifts a year early as a reward for his rapid progression in Spell Programming. What had been a moment of pure pride turned to ultimate shame when his newest robotic companion, Jimmy, went missing overnight and—having lost one gift—he had to return his untouched Aurora tablet and Ranger bicycle.

Ben's jaw tightened. He coached himself. *Get past the sting, Ben. Keep going.*

"Breakfast is ready!" Nuk U'es yelled from downstairs. "Are you wanting Uk'so Tuk to be bringing it to you?"

Ben opened his mouth and drew a breath to yell back.

Tex made a sound akin to what the robot might sound like if he'd had a throat to clear, and pointed his small hand at a tiny, easily overlooked group of speaker holes above the light switch. "We have intercoms. Just push the switch up."

When Ben did, there was a little play for the upturned switch to move a bit higher. *Probably a second setting to be activated.* Ben said, "I'll be down."

As soon as he lifted his hand, Toad's gruff voice came through the speaker. "Ben, a human calling himself Malcolm has been waiting here at the gates for three hours to speak with you."

"Malcolm?" Ben rocked his head back. *What's he doing here and—more importantly—why would he come here looking for me?* He glanced to Tex. "Has he really been out there that long?"

"Unable to verify." His companion shrugged. "This is the first time they've called. Should I stay behind and record?"

"Yes. Please do." Ben cued the intercom. "What does he want?"

Chapter Nineteen

RETRIBUTIVE PARAMOUNTCY

WITH HIS MOTHER insisting that he wear traditional robes when around the house, and having to dress in his Archon Private Academy uniform when going to school or school-related events. Ben had started to look forward to the night that he'd planned at Meadows Towing as being a nothing but a jeans and t-shirt stay. The short sleeves gave all kinds of freedom and the blue jeans just *felt* comfortable. You could do things in jeans that would rip and ruin slacks. *I'll bet Malcolm's going to ruin this day.*

Nuk's high grumbly voice cut in. "Your plate is ready."

The smell of sausage had begun to battle with bacon for scent superiority. Both made Ben's stomach send out a new round of hunger pangs. About to reply, the intercom cued Toad continued, "He's demanding—"

Malcolm's voice, faint in the background corrected: "*Requesting*, you filthy green skin. *Requesting*."

Green skin? Ben considered the words. Though he

hadn't heard them in combination before, he could easy see them being derogatory. Much in the same way that Orcs often referred to humans as *softies* or used the Servant Giant word for human to slander a fellow orc—whether in jest or in earnest.

"Uh, requesting," Toad paused, "a rematch."

When will he quit? Ben drew a breath and shook his head. "Tell him, 'request denied.' And tell him, 'go home. We'll meet in eleven months.'" Giving up his plan to dress comfortably, Ben began to put on his school uniform in the silence that followed. *Malcom's not going to be turned away so easily. And—if so—that's not Malcolm out there.* He grabbed the rusty nail that he had taken from the Dunn-Blatt last month. *Maybe this'll get him to go away.*

Toad's voice came through eh intercom again, "He says that is unacceptable and now demands a, uh…"

Ben nodded. *Yup, that's Malcolm.*

Malcolm's voice came through loud and clear. "Retributive Paramountcy."

The intercom cut out.

Ben's arm hairs rose as he picked up his Anvilsmith. Ambient emerald, cobalt blue, and amber energies danced between his hairs and floated in ghostly wisps around him. *What's the amber energy?* Putting the question aside for another time, he shrugged on his coat and typed 'Retributive Paramountcy' into his tablet.

Rushing his words, worry colored Toad's stammer, "He demands a Retributive Paramountcy and if you deny…"

Malcolm finished the threat he tried to relay through

Toad, "—I'll call a Magistrate Triumvirate to come force the issues."

The definition scrolled on Ben's screen as he rushed back to the intercom and cued it. "No!" *The last thing I want is a Primary at the property, no less three.* "No need for Judges, Malcolm. I accept. Let him in, Toad. I'll be down."

One by one, the three faint wisps of energy dancing on his arm became a visible tether. Each strand, green, blue, and yellow, braided themselves into each other and their tiny hooks coalesced into a single, prismatic hook.

What the heck!

The braided tether drove into Ben's chest. As though punched, the force drove him back a step. Unlike the expanded awareness granted by tethers of what battles of will were going on in the nearby area, a specific knowing of all things Malcolm came to him.

Beside his own, Malcolm possessed ownership over several of his fellow Dunn-Blatt's cars. He owned Clark County Country Kitchens, a small chain of all-hour diners catering to customers with low budgets and late-night cravings. Malcolm also owned a large ranch on the opposite side of town where world-class championship hellhounds—*there are competitions for hellhounds?*—were bred and sold at top dollar. The Dunn-Blatt also had another caster—*can't tell who*—enthralled in a subservient Paramountcy bond.

On a primitive level, Ben understood that similar things about himself—*my secrets are still mine*—were laid bare to Malcolm. The knowledge of each other extend to the physical, too. Each knew, and would know, each other's location.

As though the braided tether wasn't enough. The weight of the challenge began to weigh on Ben conscience. *What in the word did I just agree to?* Reading the definition on his device, he took slow, steady steps across the room.

Paramountcy: Definition (strict) - A three part mystic duel for dominion.

He looked away to put on his tablet holster and spellcard holder.

Retributive Paramountcy: Definition (use) -When a combatant has lost a duel and believes luck played a large part in the defeat, they may call this duel to prove superiority through two more clashes.

Paying more attention to his Anvilsmith than where he was walking, Ben bumped into the doorjamb. He rubbed his shoulder and continued to advance semi-blindly toward the stairs as he read.

The enactor chooses the second duel type and typically plays to their opponent's weakness, though paramountors have been known to play to their own strengths. The paramountee chooses the final combat form. The same strategic thought as above is applied here.

The savory scent of bacon overpowered the sausage as he descended the stairs to the sounds of the goblins' video game characters taking hits. Feeling Malcolm speeding through the scrapyard, Ben scrolled past famous and historic Paramountcies to the note with an asterisk before it at the bottom of the article.

Note[1]: both parties need to exercise sound judgment

in calling for or accepting this retributive duel, as the loser is mystically subjected to an irrevocable subservient bond to the victor.

Ben tried to take an extra step down when he came to the living room. He glanced to the gargantuan TV to see abandoned controllers. *They left the game without pausing again. I have to show them how to short cut the wemic stage.* He grabbed two strips of bacon from the plate on the dining room table and chomped on one as he returned his eyes to his table to read the double asterisks.

Note[2]: it is common for the loser to choose death versus defeat at the outcome of the final duel.

Ben spoke to himself as he felt Malcolm speeding through the gates and up the main thoroughfare. "Good job, Ben. Win this duel or become the jerk's personal, life-long servant." Though Tex had stayed upstairs, Ben could almost hear his companion add, sarcastically. *Well, don't rule out death. It is an option.*

He adopted Tex's deadpan tone. "Fantastic."

Chapter Twenty

MALCOLM'S MOXIE

STUFFING the other strip of bacon into his mouth, Ben slipped his tablet into its holster and chewed rapidly to finish the bacon before Malcolm made it to the front of the building.

Moving through the kitchen to the garage, he spied three frying pans left out and dirty. *That's unlike Nuk and Uk'so. Wonder what they have going on?* Still looking over his shoulder at the dirty dishes, Ben stopped short of moving out into the garage and a feeling—*something's going on*—stole over him. The sensation intensified as Malcolm drew closer. *But what?*

Wiping the grease from his lips with the back of his hand, Ben moved out into the garage. *Empty as usual, but why are all five bays open?* He wiped at his mouth again and pivoted around the corner into a face full of exhaust. *What made that smell? The only cars present are the wrecks.* Not expecting to see anyone, he stopped short. *Whoa.*

A majority of the Meadow Towing orcs—*only*

missing Jek and the gate guards—were present in the hundred-foot span between the garage and the first row of crushed cars. All had longswords and guns strapped to their person. Further out, the orcs who had come on board from Ur-Krurk's Son's traveling vanguard were working in trios as two helped a third into the black studded leather armor they had worn during the battle that ended in them belonging to the property. *Did they feel Malcolm's challenge to me?*

Everyone stopped what they were doing and cheered him as he stepped out into the night. "Ben! Ben! Ben!"

Quiet, motionless, and hunkered down in the shadows, Ben spied the tuzvul. She also belonged to Meadows Towing, but was almost never around. *What brought you out, missy? What are you up to?*

Ben nodded to a couple of the orcs—*Jek's buddies*—as their shouts felt louder *and...* Ben struggled to nail down the growing suspicion. *And...* He eliminated them from the potential problem. Like Jek, the orcs were fairly straightforward. *And, whatever it is, it's not them. Well, not from them, but...* At a complete loss, he bit his lip. *But something else.*

The headlights of Malcolm's Transcend grew closer.

And behind the Dunn-Blatt's, the dark silhouette of a tow truck.

Come on, Ben. Think.

Dirt clouds plumed behind the Transcend in the light desert breeze as the car turned, then skidded sideways on the hardpan, coming to a stop sixty feet away.

The orcs, many with swords in hand, rushed to close

in on Malcolm's car as Malcolm got out, but the swarm didn't ding the Dunn-Blatt's smug smile.

"Hmph." Ben stifled a longer acknowledgment of Malcolm's moxie. *He's awfully blasé about driving onto hostile ground and being at the center of small army of fully armed, armored, and anxious monsters.*

Obscured by the tall broad-shouldered orc, Ben heard Malcolm call, "Baby Ben. You were lucky in catching me in the middle of a very prosperous Samhain Shenanigans." The orcs parted slightly as Malcolm, in his school's violet jumpsuit, moved around the front of his car.

"Look, I didn't know how important this was to you." Hoping this would placate the jerk, Ben dipped his hand into his pocket and fished out the rusty nail Malcolm had said was a family heirloom. "How about you take your tether back and we call this whole Paramountcy thing off?"

In the middle of sneering brutes, on foreign ground far away from civilization, Malcolm wrapped his arms around his abdomen and threw his head back in laughter.

"So sorry, Benny, but that will no longer be enough." The Dunn-Blatt extended his arms and spun a circle to encompass the scrapyard with a snazzy gesture. "I didn't know you owned all of this! Makes me wonder what favor you were playing to years ago by pretending to be the poorest kid at the APA."

Malcolm shook his head in disbelief and continued, "You're the Might-Fist and you have control over a Node Key?" The Dunn-Blatt's smug smile widened as his voice rose in amazement, joy, and greed. "Oh, this is too good!" He clapped and rubbed his hands together. "I'm glad you're not wearing your Might-Fist belt. When it's mine…" Malcolm pantomimed putting it on. "*When* it's mine, I'm *never* going to take it off."

He knew these things and still chose to continue on instead of backing out. "Malcolm, I didn't come across all these things by luck. Do us both a favor, take your tether and go."

"Shit on that! I want the whole burrito, baby." Malcolm bounced in place and, pointing at Ben, settled into a stance like Bruce Lee. "I choose combat in single conjuration personifications!"

Conjuration. Really? Ben wanted to laugh like Malcolm had moments ago. *I've learned from Gary, the world's best conjurer. I know more about conjuring than probably any student in the Las Vegas Valley.* Fighting a secret smile, which worked hard to turn his lips, Ben dropped the nail into his pocket and motioned for Malcolm to go first. "Let's see your conjuration."

Dark purple magic poured from Malcolm's skin. The radiant Krotosian energy formed an amorphous blob too large for a dusk bison. It rolled and folded upon itself before it solidified in a brief howl into a massive stone bull whose shoulders were level with the nearby orc's brows.

Okay. Ben rubbed his mouth. *He's made a super bull. Programming-wise, it couldn't be more than a four-stone creature, but there's no way my two-stone Orion is going to be able to rip one of those thick horns away and put the bull down like it did with the boars months ago.*

The bull stamped, striking sparks form the dessert hardpan. "Look at your face!" Continuing to point,

Malcolm burst out in laughter again. "You thought it was going to be a dusk bison. Admit it, Ben. Admit it."

Okay... Ben felt his breath catch as he modified his initial estimated power level. *Maybe it'd be five stones and, maybe, Gary didn't teach me everything.*

"When you're my servant, I'm to have you lick-shine my shoes before school. Everyday." Malcolm beamed a thrilled smile. "Every single day." As though they were on stage at a talent show, Malcolm extended an opened palm toward Ben. "Okay, baby. Let's see what you got."

Chapter Twenty-One

BEN'S FOLLY

THE SLIGHT BREEZE that had been wafting away Malcolm's dirty clouds died. Without direction, the trailing dirt between the column of wrecked cars began to settle back where it had been disturbed. Without the breeze, the smell of exhaust hung as aimless as the dirt. Ben cut his eyes over to the tuzvul. *Still lurking.* He licked at the bacon flavor on his lips as though he could taste what bothered him about her being out and about.

A loud clack and sparks brought his attention back to the stone bull. *I should—* Ben killed the thought of turning Bastion loose before the beast had a chance to fully form. Since the beast's show of force in the basement, it had become a sleeping dragon. *And there's no way I'm going to go to it for help. This is duel two of three.*

Malcolm prompted, "Any time now."

My parents not allowing me to take the Dueling is coming back to haunt me big time. If I claim World Awareness, I'll be able to take any classes I want at the Academy. Ben nodded. He would take Tex's advice.

For now, though, I should bend to this one and just beat him in another duel. Ben made a face as though someone had served him a heaping serving of sewage soup. *What am I thinking? Give this one a solid go with energy from your tablet. Then, if you do lose this challenge, you'll be at full personal power to stomp him in the third.*

"Alright, Malcolm." Ben laid his hand against his holder, and a finger on his Orion spellcard. "Here we go." Tapping energy from his Anvilsmith, Ben found the energy riding up his arm instead of passing through to the spellcard. Emerald light spouted from his sternum forming an amorphous blob. The energy folded and crackled before shaping into a large, four-armed, green Bastion.

Oh my Gods. Ben's blood went cold. *He's out.*

Malcolm's head reeled back. "A girallon? Perhaps I may have misjudged you…"

Wait. Ben tried to feel for a conjurors bond to the creature and felt a link between the two forms much deeper than anything he'd previously felt. *It feels like they're both my bodies.* Ben shifted his consciousness into —*what Malcolm called*—the girallon. *The tang of fear all over the air. Just under it, anxiety and…* He smacked his lips. *…anticipation.* He balled his four massive green fists and relaxed his hands. *The raw strength… it feels awesome!*

Ben transferred back to his human form. "You have no idea." He extended the nail and offered again. "We can still be civilized and walk away from this."

Malcolm's eyes glassed and closed. Needlessly stamping in place to make sparks fly, the stone bull became more animated.

Ben put the tether away and shifted his sense into the girallon.

The might at my disposal. A grin worked onto his massive mouth. *It's absolutely intoxicating.* He flexed again. His orcs broke out in riotous bellows and cheers.

Malcolm's bull turned toward the orcs.

They scattered.

The bull galloped at breakneck speed away toward the scrapyard entrance.

An instinct to give chase stole over him. Ben fought it back. *Why is he running away all of a sudden? He called this challenge.*

"Get him." Toad urged from his tow-truck, parked behind Malcolm's car. "Make him pay!"

There. That's the trick. Ben leapt, landing before Toad and flexing over the pale green orc.

The shaman bowed deep.

The reek of fear and anxiety oozed from the orc's skin. *What are you up to?* Ben tried asking the words, but all that came from his throat were grunts.

Malcolm's bull continued to move away.

He'll came back eventually. He'll have to if he wants to battle it out. Yet..., Toad's not entirely wrong. Having won Malcolm's rusty nail tether, Ben had considered Malcolm's bully-debt mostly paid off. *Yet...* A small part of him still wanted to hurt the Dunn-Blatt for the physical pain the jerk had inflicted upon him and others not ready to be tethered for the first time. *And in these forms, I can. I can truly fight my former nemesis without doing damage to either of our real bodies.*

Casting one last glance as his and Malcolm's human

bodies standing, eyes closed and vacation by the garage, Ben gave into his want.

He pounded his girallon chest and, tromping hard, Ben tore off after Malcolm.

The smell of exhaust faded. Gaining slowly, his nose locked onto the bull's unique earthy scent well before it turned down a row and out of sight.

Expecting a charge when he would turn the corner, Ben leapt. He grabbed a car eight up, and swung high across the free space to the wall of cars on the other side. Under his powerful grip, metal crumpled, cried, and bit at his hands, but failed to pierce his thick green skin.

The bull stood at the far end, facing him. Sparks flew up from the ground as it stamped twice.

It's almost too far to tell, but even his bull has a smug upward turn to its lips.

On thundering hooves, it charged.

With confidence bordering on conceit, Ben dropped to the ground ready to do to the bull what Orion had done to the boar. *Come on, Malcolm. I'll take you head on.*

He hit the ground and crumpled as the bridge to his human form shattered. *What the!* Stuck in the girallon form, Ben hopped back to his feet, and swung back onto the main aisle.

Orcs were piling into white cargo vans.

Glancing his way, the tuzvul loaded Ben's human body into a separate van.

What's that? A scintillating rainbow circlet had been pushed tight down on his forehead and a cloud of pitch black shadows hung over his head.

The galloping clamor behind him ceased.

Ben spun to see the purple stone bull dissipating into smoke. A revving engine—*a Transcend*—snapped his attention back up the aisle.

Middle finger high in the air, Malcolm hopped into his car.

The plain white cargo van's door closed.

My body's in that one!

They all tore away.

No!

Chapter Twenty-Two

CHASING CARS

MOVING parallel with the distant vehicles, Ben's powerful girallon limbs rocketed him down the row. He leapt, gripped metal, his arms pulling him to the top of the crushed cars in three strong heaves. From up here the dust the vans kicked were well behind him, but they were quickly making up the difference.

Not losing any speed, Ben lunged from his current row to the one across the dirt aisle between.

Two white vans flashed by at the end of the column.

There they are. He crunched down on the top of the wrecked cars on the adjacent row. Moving as fast as this body could take him, his feet and fists pounded on collapsed trunks, roofs, and hoods. The crumpled metal beneath his hands and feet *clunked* and *thunked* as he powered on through the stagnant night air.

The dust clouds had pulled past him.

They're way ahead of me now. From habit, his upper left hand swung back to touch his hairy torso where the *Usian* and *Leap* spellcards would've been if he were in his human form. *If I had my magic, I might be able to rival their speed.*

Ben launched across another opening and poured all his strength into getting as close as possible. *I can't catch them, but woe to them if I'm able to capitalize on any miscalculated turn or any other mistake.*

No! The upper bar at the top of the east gates started to roll up the Koffman security shutters he had installed.

Ben leapt across another aisle and continued on.

In the distance, a series of square taillights drove into the darkness, with the thin slits of Malcolm's Transcend punctuating the long procession.

Incapable of words, Ben roared his frustration as his hands gripped a folded fender of the car beneath him. He flipped it from the top. It crashed into the row below with an ear pleasing crunch. *I'd like to crunch those betrayers just. Like. This.* He hopped to where the other car and been, scooped the front of the wreck he had been on and sent it crashing down, too. *And this.* One by one, he dismantled the wrecked wall below his feet. On the ground, he leapt off the last one and slammed all four fists into it. The compacted hinges cried, the sides buckled, and it slid the few inches into the toppled mess he had made.

He stood breathing steady. *This body isn't even winded.* Considering making the gap in the wall wider, he balled and unballed his fists. About to climb to the top, he stopped. *Tearing this place apart won't lead to a solution to my problem. Get productive. Think.*

"Ben?" Tex synthesized voice asked. "Is that you?"

Ben turned. Ready to run, Tex peered at him from

the distant corner. A growl, equal parts frustration and disappointment vibrated in his throat as he plopped on a compressed hood with a final *thunk*. *They set a trap for me, and I charged right into it.*

He put a hand on his forehead, ran it down his protruding brow, and down the ramp of his nose and mouth. He held his jaw and dropped his elbow on his leg to support his chin on his knuckles.

Tex had drawn closer. The robot motioned to his bulk. "I can see you're thinking."

Lost in thought, Ben became aware of his body again.

Tex continued, "Except for the extra set of arms, that pose is called *The Thinker*."

He shot Tex a short, angry snort.

"It's true and famous," the robot raised his hands as though he had touched something hot. "I wasn't trying to make a joke."

Quite alright, Tex. I could use a joke right now. Ben tried to smile. The corners of his mouth twitched upwards. *What, I can't even smile?* He tried again and the corners of his mouth quivered up. *Next time.* He set himself to try again.

Abruptly, as though hooked and snatched by a high-strength tension wire, his girallon body—with all its mass—flew sideways from the hood.

What the—

Faster than he could get his feet beneath him, or correct to gallop, the invisible force continued to yank on every fiber of his existence, dragging him across the scrapyard grounds toward the east entrance.

The Meadows Towing building shrank into the

distance as his body, scraped deep enough into the dirt, being turned to burger —*I thought it was all desert hardpan*—as it struck long-hidden blacktop, leaving a long streak of blood.

Aware of the damage being done to his body—*it feels like being punched in an arm that's already asleep*—he couldn't help the stray thought. *Wonder if this body will heal as quickly as my real body.*

Then he slammed into the closed Koffman security gate.

At the same time, out in the desert, he felt his human body in the van slam into the van's back doors.

My body, empty, lies out there on a deserted road. He tried to stand. While most of his right side suffered, Ben found several spots of his girallon body had been ground bone deep from the asphalt under the dirt. *What are they doing?*

Distantly, he could feel strong arms wrap around his human torso. They gripped tight, and pulled hard.

"You're at max range!" Tiny in the distance, Tex ran toward him yelling at full volume. "Climb, Ben! Climb right now!"

Ben rolled onto his left flank to get up.

The force pulling on his empty body in the desert thumped him against the buttress. Having experienced it inside his human body, Ben recognized the feel of long tuzvul fingers wrapping around his torso and yank.

The pull translated into his girallon body being slammed against the unyielding Koffman gate. Ben strained up on his good left side and set two hands to climb.

Out in the desert, long, powerful arms—tuzvul arms —gripped his body and yanked, and yanked and yanked, repeatedly slamming his massive body into the gate, causing him to keep losing his grip.

Wait, what's going on with my body now?

The slight awareness he had of his physical body faded as the distant energy source keeping the girallon body together exceeded its maximum range.

His companion continued to close in.

Ben had eye contact with Tex as—*aw, shit*—his girallon body burst into emerald smoke.

Tex covered his face, and yelled, "Nooo—

Chapter Twenty-Three

SMOKE

—ooo!"

WHILE BEN often made observations of the stars and the night sky, he never felt so much a part of them as he did right now. *This is amazing! I can feel myself expanding into... into... The exact name-word escapes me, but this feels great! It's almost like I'm a part of the night and...*

A wide spread of raindrops hung in the air and formed red, green, purple, and black-colored condensation on—*something like a floor*—beneath him.

The view beyond the floor turned into a desolate mix of deep grays except for Tex. His companion had his hands near his bright—*so very lovely and bright*—green orbital sockets, and shook his head repeatedly.

He's upset that my physical being has been taken away. Outside, above, and inside himself, Ben looked at the clear outline of his being. He only had one set of human sized arms. *That's weird, I thought I had two massive sets.*

Well, it's sort of comforting because that feels right, too. The momentary certainty that everything was alright slipped when he felt a—*it's some sort of glass*—wall between him and the downward direction he wanted to go.

The green condensation on the window-floor burst into smaller bits before floating out into the great expanse all around him. He smiled at the change as the green—*the same color as those round sockets*—moved away and evaporated.

The colorful raindrops on the glass floor began to burst into smaller drops as they, too, moved further away. Movement beyond the drops on the glass got his attention.

The sad little robot had a name once, but that had long since vanished, just like his own.

Am I a he? Do spirits have a gender?

The small drops moved further away.

The unhappy metallic being was entirely wrong.

The sense of ease that filled the two-armed vessel that made the outline start to fade.

A dark light emanated from the center of the metallic being.

Want. Want into it.

The tempting light called. Perhaps by joining the energy in the metallic lifeform, it could help the metallic being not be sad.

The floor's in the way. The metal thing's crying.

It reached out to comfort the machine, but the clear barrier still lay between them, and now, his formerly faded form had come back coated with... *Droplets?*

Black, red, and purple bled through the outline and

floated to the center of his arm, almost as though it were his bone marrow.

Bones. He thought whimsically. *I had bones at one time.* His breath began to fog the window. He wiped at it, making the grey turn into a swirl of muck. The three colors didn't mix to form sludge. Each remained its own in the tightly smeared mess, and began to unsmear into thick drops.

August. Benjamin. Brutus. Jacob. Moil. Baxter.

One of those is my name. No. Two. Three?

He put his hand toward the glass obstruction and the black condensation pooled together to form a letter 'B' before he touched it. *Yes. May name was Ben. Is Ben. Indeed. Benjamin Baxter.*

Ben extended his limbs toward a black raindrop coming toward him. As though rushing home, it flew to him and into his shell. He pointed to a red one. It, too, came rushing back. Each drop that came to him made him feel as though he should have the rest of them, too.

Focusing on bringing back all of the dispersed energy at once, his casing filled and was thrown downward. The glass barrier beneath him shattered into innumerable diamonds of starlight.

Chapter Twenty-Four

SELF-MADE

WHY AM I FALLING? Ben dropped on his knees and got his four arms down to catch himself before he fell face-first to the ground. He wanted to curse, but a weak groaning growl vibrated his throat as it rolled from his mouth. *Why do I feel so weak?*

"Ben?" Tex's voice had a note of worry to it.

I remember, I was slammed against the wall. He looked up to Tex and nodded to his companion as he got back to his feet. He sniffed. *Why is the air so stale?*

Tex took a tentative step away. "What number comes after my current version?"

What's with the quiz? Ben waved a hand to dismiss the question. *Not now, buddy. Things are too hazy.*

Tex took another step away. "The answer?"

Ben gazed up to the stars and a fleeting thought—*I could have joined them*—flickered across his mind. *The sky still full of clouds.* His head tilted to a subtle observation. *Wait. Those are the same cloud formations as when I first woke. They've barely moved.* He sniffed at the stale air again and found faint exhaust. *Yeah, without wind, things would get a bit stale.*

He glanced to Tex. **Okay, there was the original, the robot, and the hybrid. So, the answer is four.**

"I need an answer soon." Tex took another step away. "I'm about done waiting."

Of course he can't hear my telepathy. In retrospect, Ben felt sill for even presuming the robot would be able to. He tried to speak. Only a hoot game out.

Ben sighed and extend his upper arm to present four fingers. His thumb proved slow in following directions. *I can barely bend it.*

Tex turned and ran. "Wrong answer, Bastion!"

Bastion? I should call you a robot name that offends you. Ben went to count version on his digits, but stopped. *My fur's black? What happened to the green?* Ben took a few quick steps before leaping to hoist his body to the top of the row. *Why doesn't my body feel so clumsy?* The more he romped along the wreckage, the better his body began to react. The better his body reacted, the more this style of running with all six appendages began to feel natural.

Ahead of Tex, Ben leapt to the end of the next long row at an angle, purposely falling short so he could grab a rear quarter panel and swing out in front of Tex.

He landed and, trying to signal for his companion to wait when he came around the corner, extend his four arms, palms out.

Then Tex came barreling around the corner and lost his footing, but quickly scrambled back to the edge and looked at him.

Now to figure out a way to explain why my answer was

right. Ben went to cross his two sets of arms and found his shoulder's range of motion was worse than when he would put on a school trench coat that he wore two years prior. *Crossing my arms isn't important right now.* Ben eased into a stance just beyond clasping his hands.

Ah, got it! Ben tried snapping his finger at his epiphany, and failed. *Why is my manual dexterity so bad?* He thought back to the well-controlled hand motions Bastion had made to him when they were fighting Ur-Krurk. *How had the Beast been able to sign so well?* Then the memory of It speaking the hiss-gargle language and fluent Ruler-Giant, reminded Ben that he and It were two separate beings. *If that premise is true, then when did Bastion find time to practice?*

Having thought the Beast's name, and It not rising up in his mind, Ben focused inward and sifted through his entire four-armed being for the Nilosian energy the Beast consisted of—instead of just being confined to his head. An elation bloomed in his chest. *Bastion's not here!*

The black nimbus hovering over the rainbow circlet that had been crammed on his head before being loaded into the van… *Was that black cloud the Beast?*

I had thought this entire thing had been perpetuated by Malcolm, but the Dunn-Blatt was just a pawn. Somehow, Bastion—Bastion—had orchestrated all of this to gain control of his body. An angry roar started up Ben's throat, but he stifled it. *Bellowing in primal rage won't return me to my human body.*

Tex turned and ran.

Ben let him go. *I have no way to communicate with him anyway.*

There has to be a way out of this. Trying to improve his

range of motion while he tried to think his way out of his situation, Ben stretched his arms, shoulders, and legs as he shuffled, spider-walked, duck-walked, and crab-walked back to the building.

As much as I would like to go to Master Reynolds or any of the other high ranking APA teachers, all of them probably look on black magic the same way Kograkken and the rest of the Starwise Society did. He stopped his motion exercise to wonder. *Why do they fear Nilosian casters so much?* He continued back to the building. *Heck, I could probably only trust Papa Mojo right now and he'll probably just lie to me to get me to do some kind of errand for him.*

Ben smelled the four dead orcs before he saw them, and stopped his weird walks. The tangy odor of anxiety mixed with the musk of fear as both weighed heavy in the air. *The scents make sense. The only ones who probably weren't in on the revolt lay slain at my feet.* Ben looked each of them over and felt a sinking pain. *These were Jek's buddies. The guys who came to Meadows Towing on their own, without having to be subjugated or blood-oathed.*

Wait. Following his nose, Ben sniffed around the area to find a solid pocket of a clean, soapy, rose-water laced with the perfume of joy in the garage, masked well by the smell of old sweat, and hard mechanic work.

Well, hello. And who are you? Trying to further dissect the scent, he noted, *not nervous at all, no sense of worry, in fact, this jerk actually felt pride in doing this.* Ben's fingers curled into fists as he committed the smell to memory. *This is the one who orchestrated the betrayal.* He looked out toward the eastern entrance. *And they're in one of those vans.*

A distant motor droned toward the property. A set of headlights sped up the main aisle.

Please be Malcolm. Please be Malcolm. Still in the garage, Ben peeked out to see who approached. The shape of the vehicle was unmistakable and much too tall and bulky to be the sleek, low-profile of a Transcend. *That's one of our tow trucks.*

Ben stepped out.

The truck slammed on the brakes when the headlights lit his massive form.

Ben charged.

The trucked stopped, kicked into reverse, and gunned it.

Why are you running? With the power of all six of his limbs, Ben leapt through the air at the truck. *Oh, I got you now!*

Chapter Twenty-Five

NOT ALONE

THE DRIVER CRANKED the wheel to dodge.

Too late, buddy! Ben thumped down on the hood. His two upper arms latched onto the cab as his lower right shattered the driver's side window, and hoisted the driver—*orc*—from the seat. The trucked exuded a strong, familiar, salami smell. His other lower arm grabbed the orc's wrist and held it as firmly has Ben would his little brothers. He leapt away with the orc before the tow truck crashed into a row of wrecked cars. He held the orc before him.

Jek spat in his face. "I won't blood oath."

Ben wiped the dribble away. *He's not leaking fear. In fact, there's a whiff of pride clinging to the orc's heady defiance.* Still holding Jek, Ben set him on his feet and projected his thoughts, *I'm not Bastion.*

Jek's stern scowl stayed strong, but some of the hardness in his eyes eased. "Then who are you?"

You can hear me! You can understand me! Ben released Jek and bounded a quick circled to grab the orc by the shoulders. He wanted to hug his elation. Only his understanding of physical contact in orcish culture kept him from doing so. He gave Jek's shoulders a firm, we meet again, shake. *It's me, Ben.*

The familiar greeting made Jek's scowl ease. "If you're really Ben, who was at the carnival when I picked you up to come face Ur-Krurk's son?"

Not realizing he looked like Bastion, Ben didn't get why Tex had questioned him at first. But with what the monster did, it only made sense. About to answer Jek, Ben stopped and inhaled in three punctuated draws. *Jek's scent, shift from defiance to… To…* Ben tried to name the unsullied fragrance. He sniffed near the orc.

Jek leaned away before offering his hand.

Ben sniffed. Beneath the robust smell of salami, relief. He nodded and projected, *There was a Vibrosian Magistrate and Collins.*

"Collins." Jek tapped his right earlobe with both syllables. The orc nodded along with whatever his thoughts were. "What do we do now?"

Ben motioned Jek to come with him as he went to the truck to check the damage to the rear. *They took my body out the east entrance, and drove far out into the desert.*

"So, we need to go out further into the Might-Lands then." Jek shrugged his signature *no big deal* shrug. "Hop on back."

Ben grabbed onto the tow bar, and made sure to step up onto the truck and not on the wench controls.

Jek opened his truck door. "I'll get some real weapons—" He wiped glass from his seat onto the ground. "—summon the men, and we'll head out to get those guys."

Jek. Even though Ben used telepathy to project his thoughts, his throat constricted and his lips tightened to try and keep the bad news locked away. On a deeper level, the painful realization struck at his heart. He had started to think of many of the orcs as friends. It hurt more knowing Toad was out there with whomever was behind this.

When Ben had first seen the four dead orcs, he was —secretly—glad Toad had escaped the sudden betrayal. Now, he wished the orc had been there. He started again. *Jek, everyone who was here either turned or me or was murdered.*

Jek ground gears. The truck lurched forward and the orc had it to top speed before jamming on the brakes to power skid a short distance from the bodies. The orcs salami scent began to ooze a building dread.

He didn't put it in neutral. The truck inched forward. Ben jumped off the back, opened the driver door and tried to get his foot into to hit the clutch, but his massively muscled leg couldn't fit between the steering wheel and seat. *It's going to run up on them in short other.* Worse yet, the length of his leg didn't bend at the right place. Instead of doing what he set out to do, he found his leg stuck.

Nuk climbed through the passenger window, still wearing his red rhinestone jeans. The goblin squeezed past Ben's mass and hair to press the brake and clutch. Another small body came through the window. Uk'so worked the stick shift into neutral and turned the ignition to kill the engine.

The truck stopped a few feet from a seemingly oblivious Jek and the bodies.

"Benja Min'Fist." Nuk pulled on the driver seat lever. "Push seat back."

Ben did and got his leg free, and Nuk and Uk'so both scrambled from the truck to scamper back into the building.

Leaning close to one of the dead, Jek muttered in his native tongue as he took the sheathed knife from the dead orc's belt.

Jek moved to the next body. The orc stroked his left thumb over his heart four time while muttering something that rhymed at every ninth syllable. Solemn, Jek pulled the scabbard, pressed it against the deceased's hands, and brought to his own chest with a *thump*. He replaced the scabbard, continued speaking as he took the knife from the sheath. Jek moved on to kneel over the next body and start the thumb strikes.

Just from the combats since I've been here, there's—easily —one dead orc for each week that I've been the Might-Fist of Meadows Towing. He cast his gaze up to the purple neon star spinning on its six-story tall pillar. *Since my birth, if a death on the property were a coin, how soon will that stack dwarf the sign?* A trailing thought—*how many years until my own coin tower will rival this one*—turned his guts to ice.

Behind him, Jek said, "Might-Fist."

Ben turned from his depressing, imaginary visualization to the heart-twisting reality of Jek with four extra scabbarded blades on his belt. The sorrow emanating from Jek hit Ben's nose. He wanted to say something to help, but his mouth only gave a grunt.

Jek, seeming to understand, nodded. "Once this is done, I would like to bury them."

Of course. Ben nodded as he shifted his gaze to take in their faces again. *Who were they?*

"They were Cracked Skull like me," Jek tensed his body as though he wanted to turn and look, but some rigid code wouldn't allow for it. "Further, they were my first-blood."

Ben tightened his brow and nodded again. *Cracked Skull is probably his clan, but first-blood...* Not certain if it translated directly, Ben connected the term to a similar concept in the Giant's tongue, which meant each one of the four had direct, strong, sentimental and battle-based connections to Jek.

Jek swallowed a visible lump in this throat. "You should rally your allies to aide us in getting your body and extracting vengeance from the oath-breakers."

Allies. Ben pressed his lips together. *I barely have friends.* He shifted his gazed to the empty work bay where Toad and the others orcs had been when he knowingly came into hostile territory to try and save them. Ben laced his fingers together and squeezed down on his growing anger which came out as a deep rumble gurgled in his throat. *I put my neck out for them and this is how they repay me?*

With no small effort, he tossed aside the sense of betrayal to keep his thoughts from going to a much darker place. For a moment he wondered at Jek's phrasing. *How does one 'extract' vengeance? Better yet, what happens to those who break their oath? Is it like lying or are there further repercussions?*

"If you have no worthy allies," Jek prompted, "then call upon your blood."

Ben shook his head. *My mom is barely an Herbalist, and my dad is a mundane.*

"Mundane?"

Uh... He had thought the term was universal. *A human without magic.*

Just when Ben thought he had the meaning in all of Jek's shrugs down, the orc raised a single shoulder. "Have him bring his guns."

A reflexive, mirth-filled hoot escaped Ben's lips at the thought of his father fighting with his always-manicured, Blackjack-dealing hands. Another hoot popped from him.

Jek frowned. "What about other humans?"

Like this? Ben raised his four arms and pulled at his fur. *I could probably explain my being out here, and might be able to get away with being a girallon... However,* Ben found his head shaking rapidly against the idea. *There are not enough words in the world to explain why my body is composed, entirely, of Nilosian energy.*

Jek gave a quick so? shrug and offered. "Because you're able to tap into Nilos."

Yeah, about that... Ben clasped his hands in the same patient manner Adept Matton would when explaining a seemingly easily overlooked, but blatantly obvious, modicum of decorum. *While using black magic is acceptable amongst goblinoids, there's a saying amongst the starwise 'Those who used the darkest magic deserve the worst deaths.'* It was a common axiom. He had heard it a few times before Kograkken, the giant in Pepperjacks, had grumbled it at him. However, the Giant speaking it while holding a sword under his chin had left an indelible mark on his memory. Ben rubbed his neck. *They would rather kill me than help me.*

Jek sneered. "That's dumb. Why don't they like Nilosians?"

Ben tried to shrug. *I don't know* And almost pulled it off. To be certain he got his point across, he added, *You got me. And I only know two Nilosians—* About to turn his thoughts inward to recall Collins' inky eye incident, Ben found his thoughts centered on Papa Mojo. In his passing thought, the serpent-eyed psychic stood in the shadows cast by a column of wrecked cars.

Where—Wait, I know that arrangement of cars. It's the same one I had ducked behind with Abe and Oscar before we attacked the building. Recalling what Gary had once told him about his third eye, Ben focused on the formation of cars where Papa Mojo stood in his mind's eye. He turned his conscious gaze to the shadows beyond the first row where Papa Mojo probably stood right now. *There.* Remembering the diviner tricking him, Ben found his fist balled tight. *He's right there.*

Why is he here? Ben's brow tightened to a dangerous knot. His fists cranked tighter, making his knuckles pop. *If he had anything to do with this… I want to speak to him, but know—ultimately—that I can't really trust anything he says. But this time… This time he's come to me!* Ben elbowed Jek and projected his thoughts, *Aim your gun one row out where the yellow car is tacked on the black.*

Without asking why, Jek did.

Now, move your barrel toward where the teal front fender drops down over the yellow.

Jek did. "Done."

Mojo, I know you're there. Just come out.

Nothing, not even the wind, moved.

Mojo and Alice have the same kind of eyes. Could I have misread the vision? I hope so. I mean, presuming she recalls what I did for her and her Sister-Mother as a favor, I could sure use Alice's skill set tonight.

Ben nodded at the lack of action. *Have it your way, Mojo. On three, I'm going to have him pull the trigger. How this plays out is entirely in your freakishly-long fingered hands.*

Still, nothing, and no one, moved.

Okay. Ben shrugged. *You want to play chicken with a bullet, that's your choice. *One... Two...**

Chapter Twenty-Six

A SNAKE IN THE SHADOWS

IN THE SHADOWS, just in front of the battered teal fender bent down over a smashed yelled car, a set of bright golden eyes opened.

High notes of pride exuded from Jek's skin as he kept his arm steady. "Just say three."

No. Ben extended his hand over Jek's to push the orc's arms down to point his gun elsewhere and stopped before touching it. *This body's not meant for subtleties. Doing that could break his arm.* Ben tried to cross his arms. Still a bit short of folding position, his four elbows came closer to his sides.

Ben projected, *I can't be your bag boy like this. So, what do you want from me now, charlatan?*

Papa Mojo's deep, gravelly intonations rolled through the scrapyard so clearly that his southern drawl could've been either audible or telepathic. "I can tell, since you are like this, you did not receive my warning."

Ben glanced to the clouds still suspended in the air

and heaved a tired breath. *Do me a favor, okay? Don't try to play me. I'm not in the mood. Tonight's already been a bit of a bear—if you know what I mean. Just tell me what you want.*

Papa Mojo fidgeted a little and moonlight lit his thin fingers as they came up before the shadowed form and folded. "Bluntly, Meadows Towing Might-Fist, I want what you want. I want to live."

Ben rolled his head to the side and blinked rapidly like an enthralled child. *This is where I'm supposed to wonder and ask—with bated breath—'why, whatever could you possible mean, Mr. Papa Mojo, sir?'* He straightened his neck. *However, I'm still waiting for you to cut the crap.*

A soft hiss slithered through the yard and the distant golden eyes narrowed. "The person who is trying to dispose of your body will come for me next."

Ben nodded and unfolded his arms to applaud the most direct sentence the dark diviner had probably said this century. *See? Was that so hard?* As though ready to have a ball thrown to him, Ben extended his arms wide. *You could have answered my next question, too, Mojo, but being forthright is probably hard for you. So I'll give you an easy one. Why does he want us gone? What do we have in common?*

Papa Mojo pulled his steepled fingers back into the shadows. "What's the only possible bond or likeness we can have, brother?"

Ben heaved a sigh. *In case you hadn't noticed, you just went cryptic.*

Another hiss slipped through the area.

Okay, fine. I'll ask then…" Though he didn't have a

physical voice, Ben tried to inflect a falsely innocent, mostly naïve tone. *"Well, Mr. Mojo, sir. How do I save my life?"* He kept the rest of his thought—w*hich will somehow protect yours*—to himself.

Papa Mojo stepped forward. He stopped when a slant of light fell across the top of his bald head. Ben couldn't tell the diviner's exact skin tone, but the mystic shone ghostly pale in the moonlight. "Marshal your remaining forces—"

Forces marshaled. Ben motioned to Jek with his two right hands. *There he is. The only one who hadn't betrayed me and has a reason to help.*

Papa Mojo pointed a long accusatory finger. "Don't be dense, boy."

Don't call me boy, trickster.

Jek asked, "Can I shoot him now?"

After the next insult, yes.

A long, barbed hiss slid across the scrapyard and echoed from rows further away. The mystic's voice had a—*Fear? Rage?*—quiver.

Papa Mojo said, "This is why I had to come. You are not using the greatest resource you have at your disposal. You have goblins, Ben. You have first-blood, Might-Fist."

First-blood? Ben arms folded. *Yes!* He kept his elation from showing. *That's a goblinoid concept.*

"More than that." Papa Mojo stepped back into the shadows. His eyes finally return to their relaxed, oblong shape. "As I am sure you know, Dwarves have a series of words to pinpoint each aspect of such relationships."

While I know the language, I've never met a single one Ben slid his fist past his arms to tighten his closed expression. *Makes it kind of impossible to make a deal with them, don't you think?*

Somehow, a slat of light shone in a narrow strip over Mojo's mouth to light his short, sharp teeth. *Is he smiling?* The diviner's slow drawl felt excruciatingly long as he dragged out his next sentence. "The races of Giants draw the same lines."

Bouncing, flippant hoots burst from Ben's throat. *Even if I could bypass Pepperjack's formidable protective spells, there's no flippin' way Kograkken is going to come and help me.* He projected, *Right. The only giant I know would rather slice me in half!*

"They are often like that," Papa Mojo agreed. He pointed a skeletal finger to the top of the building.

Finally! Ben focused on the seer's digits. *They're as black as before, but pale white skin starts at his wrists. Weird.*

Mojo continued, "You've taken communion of a giant's son." Papa Mojo stepped back and withdrew his arm. The thin fingers retreated as well and folded again before moving back into the darkness.

Bet as soon as I turn my back, he's going to slink away. Still... Expecting to see the goblins on the roof, Ben turned to see what Papa Mojo had pointed at. He scanned the lip of the building and didn't find anyone standing there, just the 'o' in Meadows Towing, where he'd stashed the Imprisoning Orb with Ur-Krurk in it. *I put him up there so he could see what was going on here while locked away.* Ben shuddered at the thought of having to watch your own child be devoured. *Bastion.* Ben found a new level of disdain and disgust for the monster that had inhabited his body. *That ritual must've been soul-wrenching for him to watch.*

"He closed his eyes," Jek reported. Then asked, "Should I start shooting?"

No. Save your bullets. Ben hustled to where Papa Mojo had been. The diviner was indeed gone, leaving behind a heavy smell of baby oil. Ben sniffed to go deeper. In the oil, he found the mystic's underlying, untrustworthy musk. *There's his scent. Even his skin oozes lies.*

For moment, he imagined Papa Mojo at home with a fictional Mama Mojo. In his fantasy scenario, each was famished and trying to trick the other into picking the restaurant where they wanted to dine.

He felt his cheeks lift. *Wonder if I look happy or mad?*

Having enough of the diviner's scent, Ben blew air out his nose. *I could track you, Mojo. Track you and give you an ultimatum to help me or else.* Ben clenched and unclenched his fists. *However, if I did that, I have a feeling that we'd end up no better off than the turtle and the snake in that fable about the two trying to cross a rising river together.*

Ben bounded back to the building and looked up at the 'o' again. *Jek, tell me about communion.*

"Not much to tell, Might-Fist." Jek heaved his *it is what it is* shrug. "Eat the heart and mind of a fallen foe and gain their first-blood. We orcs don't practice it, but ubbos—who, on the whole, always try to consider themselves giants instead of goblinoids—follow the giants' odious tradition."

Ben put his hands against the side of the dark cinderblock building. His fingertips began to dig into the ledges and crannies to grip. He pulled up. His feet left the ground and started to assist in his ascent. He paused to look down at Jek. *And blam, it's that easy.*

Jek gave a doubtful shrug. "You have to kill one first. Then…" Jek's lips crinkled and turned.

Wow, may wonders never cease. An orc is showing distaste.

"Then, carve out the heart and mind, enact some ancient Nilosian ritual, and eat them." Jek's hands moved over each other in a washing motion before opening to show empty palms. "Then yes—twenty-four hours later, *if* you happen to keep the meal down—you *blam* with the first-blood of the devoured."

Ben continued his climb. *When you put it that way…* Having woken up last month with ogre in his stomach, he knew how hard a gut would work to expel the noxious meal. He had asked Nuk about why they had fed him the onion-based broth and they had only said it was to settle the stomach. When Ben had gotten free, he had unknowingly fought the last of the procedure with antacids. *I should've just puked.*

But by keeping it down, did that mean he now had first-blood? It sure sounded that way.

He reached the two-foot tall purple letters and reached into the hole. His fingers wrapped around orb. *It hardly feels right releasing Ur-Krurk to help me after Bastion ate his son.* About to put the orb back, Ben considered Papa Mojo's words again. *He's right. I'm going to need every single ally I can muster.*

Ben tucked the orb under an armpit and climbed down to the ground. Then, holding it with all four hands, he focused Nilosian energy into the orb to activate it.

Chapter Twenty-Seven

DYNAMICS

THIS IS WRONG. Ben found his gaze fixed upon the orb as tendrils of his black magic sizzled around and through the artifact Elder Komir had giving him to capture the very creature locked away. *This monster beat Penelope and made the orcs battle each other to the death only to have the winner eat the dead one's feet.* The underpinnings of what he knew to be a shame-feast rekindled in his head. Ben shuttered. He was still glad to have swiped the definition on his screen away before it got any worse. *And here I am, releasing him.*

A black-laced howling purple streak of magic arced from the orb and slammed into the ground before him.

Ur-Krurk, the super barrel chested, teal-skinned ogre-magi stood free.

With Ben in his girallon form, they were on the same eye-level. For a moment, the ogre stared hard with his red iris into Ben's.

In primal reaction, Ben's body hair bristled.

Ur-Krurk lowered his eyes and turned his head to

spit to the side. He wiped his lips and asked in the strong Ruler-Giant dialect, "What do you want with me, Blood-Son?"

The ogre's breath reeked of jerky. *I left him several cases in case I hadn't been able to return and feed him, but it seems that the ogre prefers it... Unless I miscalculated how much he regularly eats and that's what he's down to eating now.*

Ben didn't answer. He could only look at the monster that had attempted to kill him on his sixteenth birthday, the monster that had threatened the lives of his family, the creature who had lost a son to the unfeeling parasitic blight on his own soul. And now the creature he often had nightmares of was looking around the space between them and around them. *He fears me and can't meet my eye. Too. Weird.* Ben tried to imagine how the ogre might view the situation. *Our moral codes are so far apart; I don't think I could understand his point of view if he wrote a thousand-page dissertation on it.*

To find the limits, Ben asked, **What can I ask of you?**

The Imprisoning Orb in his hands began to vibrate and spit out the various foods Ben had loaded into it. First out, in rapid succession, were eighteen butcher-paper-wrapped cuts of meat. Then, six white Styrofoam family meals from Caliente Chicken shot out, breaking open when they hit the ground – broiled chicken, wedge potatoes, and half-ears of corn lay where they landed. Ben had gotten those over a month ago, but the food smelled fresh. Two bags of beef jerky flew out.

Ur-Krurk walked over to scoop one up.

Movement at the edge of Ben's vision made him take his eyes off the ogre and the food-spewing

Imprisoning Orb for a moment. Jek had opened the door to his truck, and Nuk and Uk'so—each with a small backpack—scurried into the cab.

Crashing splashing retuned Ben's attention to the orb. Gallon jugs of water were lobbed a few short feet from the orb. Some burst open, though most kept their integrity. Last out, cans of tuna, a can opener, and a mounting pile of discarded plastic bags, cardboard boxes, and Styrofoam.

"My Blood-Son, you have treated me well in my defeat and exile. You have taken my title to carry it forward in time so your son or blood-son may honor this ground after your life has been shed, and his son after him." The ogre scratched his crotch as his eyes raise to the sky, searching for a moment before continuing. "You may ask that of me which any blood-son would ask of a blood-father." Ur-Krurk ripped the bag of jerky open and up-ended it into his mouth. Stray pieces fell to the dirt as he chewed and continued to scratch.

While that might help if I understood the blood-family *thing, it doesn't tell* me *anything, really.*

A slight wind stirred and stopped as though the tight grip that kept the air from moving slipped momentarily.

Whoa. Ben thought the ogre would smell foul, but a soapy scent—*pride*—clung to Ur-Krurk's natural musk. *How can he feel pride right now? It has to be a trick. He probably has magic that allows him to control his scent.*

Attempting to get down to the brass tacks, Ben asked, **How long until you turn on me?**

Still chewing, Ur-Krurk tossed the empty bag and

scooped the other unopened one. "Here's something your former race may never understand." The ogre swallowed and ran a thumb over his heart. "You can never betray blood." He then drew the same thumb across his throat. "Never."

Ur-Krurk's conviction struck a chord that rung true in Ben. He found himself nodding.

"Load up" Jek pounded on his truck door twice. The engine rumbled to life. "We're burning moonlight."

Guess I'll take the left side and Ur-Krurk can balance out the right. Ben clambered on. The truck groaned and rocked under his mass.

Ur-Krurk's morphed his ten-foot ogre magi body down to a skinny, almost emaciated, five-foot tall orangeish-brown skinned orc. His nose stretched goblinishly long and hooked down and his chin did the same.

Jek called out, "You've got the sniffer, Ben. Rap on the hood when you got something. I'll stop." The engine revved, the truck lurched, and they were off.

Thinking over what Ur-Krurk had said, two of the ogre magi's words echoed an accusation leveled by Alice last month. Alice had asked, *What are you, Ben, really?* And now, the ogre said. *Former race.*

Ben scanned the dark horizon. His brain burned with a horrible wonder. *What have I become?* Then, as they exited through the eastern gate and zoomed into the night, his curiosity soured to dread.

What am I becoming?

Chapter Twenty-Eight

BEYOND THE EASTERN GATE

LIKE A DOG GOING for a car ride, Ben kept his head either off to the side or above the cab. Though the still desert night air had the same stale, uncirculated smell, the effect of feeling wind through his body hair felt good and proved to be rather relaxing. Even better, when he closed his eyes, had discovered a secondary benefit—it helped him focus on scents.

Ben kept his nostrils flared and his mouth open to allow the air to flow in through his nasal cavity. He initially focused on the convoy's heavy exhaust smell until, one by one, the vehicles started to peel away from the main road to the multitude of dirt trails out here.

His group, on the hunt for his body and Jek's vengeance, had left the scrapyard less than half an hour ago and had long since passed the area where his human body had crashed through the back of the van doors and lain in the dark. At that point, smelling the unfamiliar rose-water scent he'd noticed back at the garage, Toad, Malcolm, several orcs, and a bitter reek that could've been the tuzvul, Ben had locked onto Malcolm's trail. If anything, he could count on Malcolm seeing this through long enough to get his family heirloom back.

The Dunn-Blatt's scent had been robust with pride when the train of vehicles had been closer to the scrapyard. Now, as they moved further into the desert, Malcolm's smell started to change. Doubt ate at his pride and worry chased doubt until the three emotions were measured in equal parts before vanishing in an overpowering sting of fear.

Ben pounded on the roof. *Exhaust from the last van and Malcolm's Transcend continue on, but Malcolm's actual scent has gone cold.*

Jek hit the brakes and started to skid.

When they slowed enough, Ben leapt from the tow truck and galloped back down the road to find Malcolm's scent. He closed his mouth as he started to take air in rapid, short sniffs. *Getting close.* A watered-down Malcolm-smell, the vehicles' tailwind disturbed the air and thinned the scent some, filled his nose. *Whoa!* Ben winced and lifted his head away from the ground. The tart, acrid stink of Malcolm's fear burned.

Ben opened his eyes to see he stood over a puddle of piss that smeared out into the desert—*he pissed his pants and they drug him away.* *Here.*

Footprints flanked the piss-mud and a hint of sour, mischievous deception became high notes in both Toad's, and the rose-water scent. The tuzvul's distrustful scent hadn't changed a lick.

In his girallon form, far from the lights of Meadows Towing, Ben found his vision to be in a high contrast greyscale. As though, by giving up trying to distinguish color, he could see even clearer than if he had cast *Elfsight*. Upon hearing Jek's heavy footsteps closing in behind him, Ben used both his eyes and nose to follow the footprints away from the road.

A light, airy voice called, "Stop, Blood-Son."

That's what Ur-Krurk called me, but who's voice is that? Ben turned.

Jek, Nuk, and Uk'so closed in behind him. A little further away, coming from the direction of the truck, a thin human—about as undersized for a man as the orangeish-brown orc had been—spoke, in Ruler-Giant, with the edgy pattern unique to Ur-Krurk. "You're about to breech Blood-Berry Fairy territory."

Why would Ur-Krurk take on a human form? Ben glanced down at his feet and four knuckles on the ground for any indication that he might be crossing a boarder of some sort. Occasional cacti peppered the distance, a few overly-large rocks lay about the dirt. *Just regular desert.*

Holding his ground and not advancing, Ben stood erect. **The scents go further that way.**

"Yes," Ur-Krurk's light-voiced human form pronounced the sharp consonants of his native tongue. "But there are rituals to respect so the fae see us as visitors instead of trespassers." He whispered, "Also, telepathy isn't secret around fae."

Ben nodded.

As the man—*Ur-Krurk*—drew closer, avoiding the footprints, and piss-mud, his ears stretched up to form points level with the top of his forehead. The body that had seemed narrow grew a few inches taller changing the underfed starved look into a slender grace. Ur-Krurk, now in elf form, flipped opened a lighter and struck it against his leg. Color poured back into the nearby world.

Ur-Krurk pointed to one of the round stone and said, in a lilted voice, "Tuk."

Also avoiding the tracks, Uk'so scampered forward. The goblin went to the large, rounded stone and extend his green arm over it. A patchwork of moonlit scars lit the back of thin, sinewy forearm. Uk'so pulled a knife from his inside his jeans waistline and winced slightly as he slid the edge against—and into—his skin. Uk'so then placed the rune-covered blade level on the boulder and pressed his wound on the flat of the steel. He rocked his arm toward the handle to make the blade point rise.

Blood welled, then ran against gravity to pool at the tip of the blade. Little by little, much more slowly than a typical wound would bleed, the droplet swelled until the crimson threatened to break loose and fly up into the sky.

"Elder, Elven Trader Laely is here!"

Who said that? Tracking the light, tinny voice squeaking in the local Elven tongue, Ben scanned the area. He found a diminutive creature—*it can't be more than a foot tall*—with willowy wings and a skinny body that was as non-committed to gender as a small child's doll.

It flittered and landed on Uk'so's shoulder to exclaim, "Two elves in one evening! Amazing! This may prove to be the best night of the season!"

"Or the worst." Part of the rock Uk'so had his arm

on shifted. Another skinny body, under a foot tall, moved to stand on the goblin's green arm. When it did, the being's rough stone coloring faded, becoming a translucent crystalline form with gossamer wings and a glass walking stick, before taking on the deep green color of Uk'so's skin. "You say *amazing*, I say inauspicious." Voice as light as the first, this one had a grizzled sound to it. "No offense to our most frequent customer, good Elven Trader Laely, but another elf just came through with a deal which was too good to not regret upon seeing a second elf." It pointed the walking stick, which also had Uk'so's skin color at Ur-Krurk. "You are wise. You know of what I speak."

"Indeed, Deep Root Yilst." Ur-Krurk bowed with enough skill to pass Courtmanship III. *And his Elven would earn top form marks from Adept Y'Favo.* "Your instincts lead you to fact. The last elf did not own, or earn, the contents of his side of the last deal."

"You have an odd-acting abomination." Yilst was pointed the walking stick at Ben. "The upward stance, the slack jaw, the amazed twinkle to its eyes…" The fairy pressed his pole to Uk'so's wound. The green flesh pulled together, puckered, and sealed, adding another moonlit line to the patchwork of scars. "It is also comprised of pure magic!"

That sounds like an accusation.

Yilst's wings fluttered and it turned crystalline during its short flight to Uk'so's head where, upon landing, it turned the same deep green as the goblin's bald head. "What's your game, wily Elven Trader?"

Chapter Twenty-Nine

PLAYING DUMB

I GUESS I'm not supposed to be intelligent. As though chasing a scent, Ben took three short sniffs, closed his mouth, and dropped down to rest his feet and all four sets of knuckles on the desert hardpan. A coyote howled in the distance. Trying to seem uninterested, Ben ranged his gaze along the dark mountains in the distance, set against the last deep purple that remained of an astronomical dusky sky. A good ways out, closer to the horizon, clouds moved in that ever-slow way they have.

Don't look up. Ben fought the urge to see if the local clouds were moving or were still stuck like gum under a desk. *Very few animals look up into the sky, and they always have a reason.* Instead he used his peripheral vision to note what transpired with the Ur-Krurk and Yilst.

Ur-Krurk bowed again. "I would feel more comfortable discussing details of the deal I hope to broker if the Wise and Good Deep Root would first accept out blood-tribute. It would surely be my folly if we were not greeted as guests."

The fairy tapped its staff against Uk'so's head. The goblin blinked at each of the twenty taps. "The foolishness of turning away a true friend would stain my name."

Angling its wings for balance, the young-seeming fairy on Uk'so's shoulder ran up his green arm. A satchel appeared around its body, and it produced a miniscule crystal orb from somewhere previously hidden. It held the orb above the blood. Blue energy— *Uk'so can cast spells?*—flowed into the sphere. "Servant magic, Deep Root."

Thinking back to how charged he had felt while cleaning the basement—*as long as Uk'so sang, I was quite happy scrubbing and didn't feel tired*—Ben nodded with new understanding.

The young fairy considered the power as it filled. "Well bred. Good stock." Once full, the orb was stashed back into the bag as both it, and the fairy, disappeared.

Yilst moved on Uk'so's forehead. "I do so only because of the well-tended and richly soiled garden of our entwined history, good Elven Trader.

"In humility, I appreciate your acceptance." Ur-Krurk bowed again. The thin elven fingers articulated a high-court flair Ben had rarely seen and didn't know.

Wow. He's really good! Ben felt his mouth start to gape again at the ogre's masterful grasp of Elven and etiquette. He closed his mouth.

Yilst became clear again as it flitted from Uk'so and fluttered inches from Ben's face. "Too odd, I say." It pointed the clear staff at him. "I'm getting a feeling, deep down in my vines. This embodiment belongs in the husk brought to us. Does it not?"

"Again, Wise and Good Deep Root, your instincts lead to fact." Ur-Krurk extended his hand towards Ben's face and he stepped forward.

If you think I'm sniffing, or licking, your fingers after that extensive crotch scratch, you are grossly mistaken.

Ur-Krurk stopped so his hand remained under the fluttering fairy. "The mystic girallon before you is the new Meadows Towing Might-Fist."

"A human Might-Fist." Yilst's wings gave out and it dropped, taking on the elven flesh tone of Ur-Krurk's hand. "But what of the ogre magi?"

"Please know, Wise and good Deep Root, I speak vaguely because the truth is too deep for a top-soil conversation, but know these facts—the ogre lives, his son is vanquished, and the husk below is now the ogre's Blood-Son."

Sitting for a moment, as though reeling, Yilst lay on its back, eyes cast to the sky.

Ur-Krurk added his other hand to support the fairy's full body across his palms.

Stars which did not shine in the sky above—*and probably never have in this world*—reflected in the glint of the tiny, flesh-colored orbs. Yilst started to stroke the top edge of its wings. The meticulous method of preening made it look as though it would rather be biting its nails, if it had any. *Why is it nervous?* Yilst shifted its eyes to Ur-Krurk. "Human Might-Fist... Human Blood-Son..."

Ur-Krurk nodded. "Dual title. Dual color."

Now they're really talking about me. I feel like a creep

sneaking journals away to gain insight into how others perceive him. Ben looked away completely and spied the distant purple dot which was the Meadows Towing neon star on its tower.

"The dragons were black over red this year." Both excitement and worry flicked into Yilst's voice as it whispered, "They say The Black had purple and green."

"Very ominous," in agreement, Ur-Krurk had lowered his voice, as well. "My information is embarrassingly dated. Tri-color then."

Ben looked to Uk'so who kept his arm against the stone. *How long does he have to hold that position?*

Yilst scooted into Ur-Krurk's right palm as though getting closer would elicit more information. It perked its pointed ears. "Laely, between you, me, and the ether, do tell, what were the two colors you knew."

Ur-Krurk brought the fairy closer—*is he going to eat him?*—and whispered. "Nilos over Argos."

"Yes. Makes sense," Yilst began to stroke its wing in that nervous way again. "While gaining Blood-Son, the human gained Krotos; but how would it gain access to the emerald, which belongs to dimension alone?"

Ur-Krurk nodded. "As though tri-color was not bad enough."

Yilst stopped preening. "Do you know the human's third title?"

How do titles play into this?

"Too deep for top soil," Ur-Krurk answered. "But I would guess it would have to do with his school."

"Yes," Yilst stood. "The husk is still quite young." The fairy cleared its throat as it flittered from Ur-Krurk's hand to the stone, and took on its color. Yilst spoke in Servant-Giant to the others, ignoring Ben. "Your eleven guide has set us to trade." The fairy tapped the head of his staff against the stone.

The rock gave out a groan and then the center lifted to arc high into the sky. As it did, a translucent rainbow film rose form the ground to follow the tip as it hit a summit and began to drop to form an archway. Yilst launched from the ground, turning crystalline for a moment before it shimmered with the lights playing behind it. "Now, come. Let us barter for your master's body."

Chapter Thirty

ARCHWAY OF LIGHT

ONE BY ONE, Yilst first, followed by Ur-Krurk, Jek, and then the goblins, everyone entered the lights as the stone archway finished its descent with a *clack* on another round stone. Complete, the film solidified and flashed bright.

Whoa! Recalling—with utter clarity—the prismatic tentacles that had radiated from Alice toward nearby mundanes, Ben hopped back. *That's the Mystique!* Curious enough to forget his dumb act, Ben leaned closed to get a good look at where the sheet of scintillating rainbow light came from the stone. *Too cool.*

Scents radiated form the pane of lights. Yilst's earnestness, Malcolm's fear, the rose-water's joy, the goblins focus, Jek's—Ben sniffed at the lights again to be certain that the self-loathing and guilt coupled with Jek's scent and not anyone else's. *Why?*—his curiosity as to why Jek would possibly feel anything close to those feelings summoned the image of the four dead orcs back at Meadows Towing. Ben's heart went sore panged as guilt mounted his shoulders, too.

Jek called them into service at Meadows Towing and they died because I was too blinded by the opportunity to thrash an old bully to not acknowledge my suspicions.

Ur-Krurk waving his hand brought Ben back to the present. The elf's hand motions indicated that he should come through.

Ben started to walk into the wall of light. His lips pressed against his teeth and his nose smooshed against his face. In that moment, he felt his Nilosian font being to drain away. *Hey.*

He shifted his weight away. *Hey.*

The wall pulled at him.

Hey! He yanked away and leapt back.

The random rolling swirls and flickers froze and formed solid vertical bands of—*white, orange, red, green, blue, purple, black, and a very thin yellow*—light. *I knew of the other seven fonts, but what's yellow?* He sat on his haunches. *Wonder what it's called. Heck, for that matter, what are the green, and blue called?*

Yilst came back. Its crystal form filled with black energy. "Pure Nilosian!" It sounded drunk. "It's magnificent!" A flapping shade against the arc of light, Yilst turned to face Ur-Krurk. "Beckon your beast. Have it use brute force to pass through the Mystique."

So, it is the Mystique. It's supposed to blanket the entire city. What is it about the stone portal that makes the magic visible?

Still just on the other side of the bands of light, Ur-Krurk's mouth moved, but no sound came through. The elf planted his feet and leaned forward as though to push with his shoulder.

Shoulder through, huh? Ben drew a breath and caught the smell of the stale desert air settling around. *Well, if I stay here, nothing changes.* Ben lowered his shoulder and —*time to Kool-Aid Man my way in*—charged at the light.

As though slamming into an inertia-sucking gel pack, the force of Ben's charge was sucked away. A myriad of smells came to him—*too many to count or sort. Hey! It's still sucking at my Nilosian chakra!* His Krotosian font swelled to bolster the black. A surge of might rippled within his muscles and—*progress!*—his shoulder pushed into the light which bent with his force like Jell-O.

A reality-ripping tear blasted around him as the light-turned-Jell-O turned to fabric and his shoulder caused a tear.

Getting it! Laying into the fabric, Ben pressed with arms, and legs. His face started to go through.

AHHhhhh!

The tearing slapped in his ears, ripping through his eardrums like a diesel truck through tissue paper.

Ahhh! He tried to pull back.

Ahhh! Stuck! Ahhh!

The web of light had him.

Chapter Thirty-One

BLOOD BERRIES

His Argosian power flared and flooded his system. The world flashed red as he channeled his rage against the blood-pounding, reverberating pain in his skull into raw strength and yoked the efforts of his other two energies into moving forward.

Ben's other shoulder and arm pushed through. In his flailing, his hands found the edges of the archway. Getting through, he pulled and pushed, scrabbled and struggled, prayed and cursed.

Finally, as though squeezed through a meat grinder, he fell from the web of light and flopped on his side.

Hopping back to his feet—grasping at his ear—warm fluid flowed through his fingers. No sooner had he stood than his legs and lower arms gave out, and his thousand-pound bulk collapsed onto the sharp stone ground.

Eyes clamped shut against the pain, the world spun as he rolled down hewn-stone stairs, banging his elbows, shoulders, knees, and head on the way.

Clasping his ears, he topped uncontrolled. Though the fall was short, the world kept spinning as he lay sprawled on his side at the foot of the stairs—wishing the pain away.

Something cold tapped his left temple. A soothing wave of energy doused the fire in his left ear. He could hear his hectic bellows as he flopped, but couldn't stop them. Struggling, he managed to get a foot and lower leg against the ground at the same time. Trying to stand, he rocked to the right and, galloping sideway to try and catch his balance, plowed into a rough unworked stone wall.

A humming began near him.

Ben swatted at the annoyance while keeping his right ear cupped. On his second swing, he hit something light in the air. The sound stopped.

Without balance, he pressed against the wall to brace himself, but without equilibrium, the room tilted under his feet before he could recruit his limbs to keep up. He flopped on the floor and rolled along the abrasive ground.

Another cold tap spread relief into the right side of his head.

Agony doused, reason made a rapid return.

An illuminating black, purple, and red glass fairy buzzed away from him to grip a ruddy stalactite. Its wings continued to flutter, making light and shadows dance along the other stalactites that papered the long corridor. One end twisted away and the other ended in stairs—*the stairs that I fell down*—that led up.

Scents, mostly of wild berries filled the air.

The thick uncultivated bouquet would've smelled

lovely if not for the blood, pain, and anguish also hanging in the air. Ben sniffed and found the berry aromas were layered with emotions. The delicious scent of blueberry bonded with a loamy sorrow, both entirely inseparable from the other. *Strawberry and pain. Raspberry and anguish. Blackberry and fear.* Traces of pure huckleberry and boysenberry lay untainted beneath.

The light fairy released the stalactite and fluttered in front of him. "Tri-color indeed!" *Yilst.* Ben recognized the voice and the walking stick it held. Yilst continued, "Your master is strong and worthy of his titles."

Ben found additional fragrances in the air as the fairy's flapping wings stirred scents from higher in the cavern. First the tuzvul's fearless musk, then, Malcolm's unbridled, piss-soaked fear. *They're close.* He scanned the area again. The stairs led up to the antechamber at the entrance, then further up and out of sight. Looking to the other end of the corridor—*I'm pretty sure there's an offshoot to the right there, and there*—he spied more corridors curving out from the natural stone pathways than he had seen at first glance.

Ur-Krurk had already navigated halfway down the sharp stone stairs with his hand out.

Yilst fluttered up to him and landed. "It would surely be my folly to possibly impede the forthcoming Black Dragon and the Century of Shadows, but Good and Wise Elven Trader, there is still a matter of entry fees."

Ben rose to his feet and knuckles. With the tuzvul's scent fresh in his mind, he recognized the pain in the laced strawberry as hers—*uh, disgusting*—and it smelled absolutely delicious. His mouth watered at the thought

of a sundae made from blackberries, then his throat
constricted when the berry's emotion—fear—came
combined with a trace of Malcolm's urine.

Both of them come from further down the hall.

"Good and Wise Deep Root, it would be foolish of
me not to offer additional in exchange for not
presenting sooner. Please understand, concern for the
beast delayed my donation. Tuk." Ur-Krurk extended
his hand with Yilst up toward the entrance. "I imagine
you do not get much *true* servant magic down here."

Uk'so already had the back of his arm cut and three
crystalline fairies similar to Yilst, crowded around the
wound with glass spheres.

Ben started to venture away.

Yilst turned to eye him.

Act simian. Ben scratched his chest, walked a little
further, and plopped down.

Ur-Krurk flourished his hand near his chest, fished
out the Imprisoning Orb and, with a pleased smile,
brandished it at Ben.

Chapter Thirty-Two

INTO THE HIVE

BEN'S EYES WENT WIDE. His guts quivered. He wanted to bolt. *Now he captures me and leaves me here with these twisted fae. And I never saw it coming.*

"Do not mind the beast, Wise Deep Root." The elf tossed the sphere past Ben. "It just needs a distraction."

Whew! Ben bounded after the sphere and—batting it with his lower arms—knocked it further down the corridor. *That would've been it.*

"He was excited to see it, too," Yilst said. "Simple things for simple minds, right, good Elven Trader?" The fairy continued speaking, but distance and the widening passageway effectively muted the light voice.

Minding his way, so he could find his way back, Ben continuing to act like a simple simian as he batted the sphere further and further down the corridor. After glancing a few times to see if he had been followed, Ben kept this ears keyed for the buzzing hum of fae wings as he scooped the Imprisoning Orb and—*mind the stalactites*—went bipedal to get at the scents at the top of the cavern.

Not able to fully stand up straight, his head pressed against the rough ceiling where the smells of Malcolm and the tuzvul had begun to overpower the smell of berries and the emotions connected to them. *Getting closer.* Ben dodged stalactites, alternating between standing nearly erect and using his lower set of knuckles on the unworked stone floor.

More passageways branched from the twisting main hallway at irregular distances. Occasional small offshoot tunnels rose upward or dropped away. *Malcolm and the tuzvul are too large for those.* The owners of the two scents he followed were too large to fit into those passages; still, if enough fairies got together, they might be able to lift Malcolm. When he thought about fairies grouping up to lift Malcolm, he imagined their small faces contorted with strain.

When the same thought turned to the tuzvul, the image was comical. The thought of them trying to lift the tuzvul conjured a cartoon in his mind of dozens of fairies squealing to get out from beneath her as she sat on the ground thinking, *I'm a dainty princess.*

Keeping the rolling hoots locked away, he grinned at the idea. He amused himself so much that he almost missed when the scents separated.

Whoa… Malcolm's fear drifted from a downward slanted corridor while the tuzvul's undaunted defiance came from up ahead. While the perfume of her scent weighed heavier—*she's probably closer*—he continued forward after Malcolm's waning scent —*have they killed him?*

Two downward winding turns later, the hewn stone passageway leveled out to a hundred-foot circular cavern with a fifty-foot wide pillar in the center. Constant, keening screams and full on flapping sounds —punctuated by an occasional grunt or a groan— rained from the ceiling.

With nothing at eye level, Ben eased forward and cast his gaze upward.

Oh my… The purple top of Malcom's school uniform removed to show a plain black t-shirt, near the top, he clung—*no, he's climbing*—to the wide pillar which rose a good hundred feet into the air and petered out long before the ceilingless, midnight blue night sky high above. Dozens of bats—*wait, are those fairies, too?*—flapped around him. Unlike the thin, delicate pixies at the entrance, these flyers had bulbous bodies, sunken eyes, and screaming mouthfuls of jagged teeth. Most cried a chorus of, "Climb faster!" While a few filled in the lulls in the screams with. "We're going to have to skewer you!"

Rotating as it grew slightly taller, the pillar ground against its stone sleeve in the earth. The handholds and crevices Malcolm used to climb lit bright Krotosian purple, as though a distant, dark light shone to light his path of psychedelic sweat. Other bat-winged fairies pressed glass bubbles—*they're the same items the other fairies use*—against the energy to absorb it away. Entire sections of the stone column, in ten foot rings, rotated widdershins while others remained still or went deosil. New handholds and edges protruded while others—*that's just wicked*—clicked flat.

Malcolm nearly summited.

A higher pitched shrill up near the Dunn-Blatt warned, "Watch out!"

Malcolm pulled his body tight against the column.

The bat-winged fairies released a volley of spears, and cried out, "Down! Down! Down!"

"We gotta go down, human." Ben spied a moonlight crystal fairy bound by the ankle to a length of chain anchored in Malcolm's right ear. Flittering to not yank the cord that bound them, it also dodged spears. "They'll let us rest on the ground."

Most of the spears missed Malcolm, but some sunk into his sides while there were others already in his legs.

They're herding him to extract magic and emotions from him... But they're supposed to be friendly guides to—Ben's jaw started to tighten at the vile act being so against what he had learned about the diminutive protectors in Mythic Monsters—*wait, the crystalline one is trying to help. It's just those bat-winged creatures that are bastards.*

His jaw tightened further. *I'm sure this is more than what Malcolm bargained for.* Cursing his desire to help the very person the still unidentified owner of the rose-water scent had used as bait, Ben slipped back out of sight to work rescue scenarios over in his mind. Anyway he ran it—*they control the column*—each attempt ended poorly. *Only if they didn't control the column.*

Ben turned away. He struggled with a last-ditch thought. *Blitzkrieg in, balls-to-the-wall up to Malcolm first, and figure the rest out on the fly.* He shook his head against it. Perhaps once I have my body, and spells, back.

Heading back the way he came—*where'd these paths come from*—Ben found other paths he had not seen on the way in. *It's like being in a beehive.* He shook his head and corrected. *More like being in a hornets' nest.*

To not get lost, Ben sniffed his way back along Malcolm's weakening trail.

Buzzing sounded ahead.

Ben dropped the orb, batted it, and chased it down the hall toward the tuzvul's growing scent.

Four flyers—two crystalline fairies and two of the bulbous bat creatures—seemed to speak to each other in a language of whistles, clicks, and hums. *The bat creatures and crystal fairies are in this together?* Twinkling laughter came from them as they sipped from each other's bubbles. They all fell silent, and watched him.

Keep drinking. Keep laughing. Ben maintained his charade as he moved through the pungent cloud of blackberry-fear beneath them.

Shortly after he passed, they returned to laughing between their whistles, clicks, and hums.

He bounded on after the orb, and maintained the charade until all trace of their sound was gone. To be sure, he plopped down next to the orb, playing with it between his hands and feet for a few minutes as he scanned up and down the stalactite ceiling and hewn hallway. *Alright.*

Ben stood and pressed his head up against the stalactites and latched onto the tuzvul's heady defiance. *Crap.* Malcolm's scent was also stronger. *Too far.* He kept his eyes peeled for the incline where her smell came from and listened for the four flyer.

If only I had my Silence *spell…*

Inching back, he spied the spot where he'd gone down after Malcolm's scent instead of up. Just short of where the four flyers were, he spied the incline. *I got by them once, but if they see me again... Well, nothing for it. Have to try.*

Instead of chasing the orb, he held it tight in his lower hands, and moved out into the corridor sniffing. *It's only natural for a creature to follow its nose.* Thinking about how dogs looked when on a trail, Ben did his best to look natural following a scent.

He closed in on the where they chirped.

They fell silent.

Act natural... Ben raised his head slightly and began up the incline.

They began to whistle to one another.

He continued up. *Just following a scent, boys. Go back to drinking.*

A buzzing closed in behind him.

Pay it no mind, just keep going.

A series of chirps alternated behind him.

Just keep going. Up ahead, the corridor splayed away like it had to Malcolm's. *This one is closed in.* The fairies didn't tell him to stop—*or at least I don't understand if they did*—and so he kept on.

Their chirps stopped. Their buzzing drew closer —*one on each side*—and continued.

The corridor leveled out to a ledge. Straight ahead, across a forty-foot span, on top of another wide pillar like the one Malcolm had been set to ascend and descend, the tuzvul stood astride his human body.

There I am! And I still have my uniform on. He tried to tell if he had his holster and tablet on. *Can't see inside the coat.* The angle of his body didn't allow for confirmation. Ben found his eyes narrowing at the rainbow circlet which remained squashed down on his forehead and, at one-tenth of its former mass, the black cloud—*Bastion*—hovering over his head.

The buzzing at his flanks went back down the corridor.

Working in unison, both the crystalline fairies and the bulbous ones formed squadrons to swoop at the tuzvul and toss spears at her.

If they got her down here, they have to have a way to take her out in a quick fashion. They seem to be playing—

A squadron of flyers threw spears down on her as another flew up the pillar to release tiny spears to pepper her back.

They're using her as practice.

With her long gangly arms, she swiped like mad, but typically ended up short of contact. On the rare instance she smacked one, it fell buffeting to a group of lower flying fairies whose entire job seemed to be the safety net. They'd catch the falling fae and press it against the wall, where it would stick to recover.

Overall the area was a writhing maelstrom of buzzing, flapping wings, whistles, clicks, and hums. He spied a few fairies who seemed to be the leaders calling shots as the others peppered her body. Her hide—like a pin cushion—had hundreds of tiny spears in it. Her regeneration pushed them from her skin and the weapons fell to join the uncountable others at her feet.

Crap! How do I say 'remove the circlet' in Giant? Trying to find the words, he opted for a different phrase and projected, **Take off the barrier.**

The tuzvul glanced at her hands which were hooked into claws and stood tall, sparing a moment to look down at his body before surveying the area.

Ben waved his arms when her gazed scanned over him.

She nodded, "By your command, Master."

Six squadrons of fairies, their leaders included, swooped to take advance of her new posture.

She ducked them, grabbed the rainbow ring on his forehead, and yanked it from his body.

Yes!

The bridge between his mystic self and physical form reappeared in an instant. *Yes! Yes!*

Just as Ben was about to slide across the connection, the black energy cloud above his human head rained upon his brow and his eyes fluttered.

Trying to curse Bastion, a hearty roar blew though his lips and rocked the cave. Ben belted, *Nooooo!*

Once alive with movement, every being in the cavern froze.

Chapter Thirty-Three

TWO SOULS ONE BODY

BEN FOUND himself on his feet, his fist pounding on his chest as the deafening roar, magnified by the enclosed circular cavern, poured out of him in a long furious breath.

Above the steady buzz and flap of wings, a series of whistles rang out as the hovering swarms searched for the source.

Taking advantage of her distracted attackers, the tuzvul grabbed a bulbous fairy nearby who had been motioning orders. She closed both hands around it and —if it made a noise, it didn't rise above the din of whistles—much like an angry child would do to a doll, twisted its head away with a muted snap. Unlike a toy, dark glimmering blood poured from her first.

She grabbed another leader, a crystalline one.

It gave a single, pleading chirp.

The whistling stopped. The sounds of wings grew silent. All the flyers turned to face the tuzvul, focused upon the fairy she held in her massive, gnarled hands.

She thinks I'm Bastion. If he gains control of my body… Ben jogged back down the hall a ways, planted his feet and used all six of his limbs to get him to top speed and —*gotta make it*—leap from the ledge with every ounce of strength within him.

Shit! The arc of his leap topped out. *I'm not going to make it!*

Elation ripped through doubt—*oomph*—when his upper body flopped against the edge of the pillar. His lower hands and feet dug into the crevices as his upper arms landed flat on the top. To get a grip, he had to release Imprisoning Orb.

It rolled forward as he scrambled to get his body over the shelf.

Ben pointed at the rolling sphere halfway across the plateau. **Get the ball!**

A crisp *snap* played on the air when the tuzvul twisted the crystal fairy's head and tossed it away to catch the artifact before the far edge.

The chamber echoed with an ominous thrum of hundreds of furious hums.

As though she were squeezing a juice bag, bright orange sparkling blood gushed from the top of her hand in long squirts. She plopped the crystal fairy's corpse—which had taken on a pale orange flesh tone—into her mouth and chewed as she went to Ben, hooked her hand under his upper armpit, and helped him up.

Atop the column, Ben scrambled to his human body. He grabbed it by the neck with his lower hands and extended an upper hand back. *Come on, give it to me without prompting.*

The tuzvul didn't.

His husk's eyes fluttered. Darkness on black, similar to Collins' cracked contact lenses played beneath the lids.

Please don't let her have seen that. Ben turned his shell's head away from the tuzvul and blocked her view of his human body with his girallon bulk. *How do I gain her trust?* He shook his hand as he raised his husk to standing and remembered a bit from the video of the horrible Ur-Krurkson feast on his tablet.

Ben projected, *You said your honor is mine.*

"And it always will be." She gave him the orb.

The fairy's hum continued to rise in volume.

Bastion, you've earned this. Leaking Nilosian energy into the sphere to activate it, Ben focused the Imprisoning Orb on the black cloud above his head. The orb began to suck it in. *Yes!*

To his chagrin, the sphere also pulled at the Nilosian magic from within him. His girallon body shimmered to red as his Argosian font took over powering his girallon form and artifact.

More of the black cloud from above his head was sucked into the orb.

His husk's eyes stopped fluttering.

The blackness that was in his human body flew from the top of his head to join the thinning cloud. Thicker, it pushed upward to slowly start floating away from the sphere.

No. Bastion's getting away.

"Liar!" The tuzvul wrapped her powerful arms around his wide girallon torso and squeezed.

The bear hug pushed air from Ben's lungs. He released the sphere and caught it with his foot.

She slid her hold up his body and locked his upper shoulders in a full Nelson.

Too—Ben struggled against her might—*strong*. Ben released his human body.

"Liar!" She yanked his bulk back, and back, and back toward the ledge.

She's going to heave us both from the top.

The last of Bastion left his husk. Amazingly, it also continued to pull think wisps of itself *from* the orb.

No matter, the link between his two forms was perfect and unimpeded. Ben tossed the Imprisoning Orb to his human body, released control of his girallon form, and slid across the link.

Back in his skin—*whoa, this room is dark*—he spied the orb come at him. He caught-trapped it against his body. *Got it!*

Ben slapped a hand to where his spellcards should have been. *Just holder, nothing else.* His girallon form poofed away into swirling motes of black, purple, and red smoke.

On the edge of the pillar, the tuzvul struggled for balance.

Cradling the orb like a football, Ben ran over and kicked out at her torso.

She bent her stomach away from the attack and latched onto his trench coat.

Moving the orb from one hand to the other, Ben spun and slipped out of his jacket.

Clutching his school coat and cursing him in Giant, she fell backward over the ledge.

The throngs of angry fairies went down after her.

As at Meadows Towing, he became keenly aware of

Malcom's location and weakening condition. *Sorry, Malcolm, but this is much more important.* Ignoring the knowledge, Ben tossed the sphere into Bastion's escaping—*so hard to see in here*—black cloud. While the mystic prison sucked in what wisps it went through, the majority of the Bastion-cloud—pitch black against a dark background—continued to rise.

Ben caught the orb and sent it up for another smoke-vacuum trip.

A distant *thud* came from below.

Well, that should take care of her. He caught the orb, took a careful step closer to the ledge, and sent it up again. It sucked at more of the cloud. Ben caught it.

The deadly hum of murderous fae started to rise.

Annnd now they're going to 'take care' of me...

Chapter Thirty-Four

DEATH ON TINY WINGS

I HAVE MY BODY BACK, but these senses seem so dull compared to the girallon. Now I only smell berries—in general—and not the emotions entwined with them. My hearing's dulled, but only a person incapable of hearing would miss this deadly buzz.

Bastion-smoke trailed from the Imprisoning Orb to the retreating cloud.

No way am I going to get in that stream. Ben set the Imprisoning Orb down and bent at the waist to be in a perfect folding bow—*sure hope they respect courtmanship*—before they came over the edge.

Uncertain what to do, being bent in the most supplicated courtly position made his mouth move before he really knew what he was saying. "Good fae-folk. I am Benjamin Baxter and I am not your enemy." Avoiding his growing grasp of Giant's tongue, he repeated his introduction in all the core languages he knew: Elven, Gnome, and Dwarven.

The humming continued to build and then closed in from all directions as he started his Dwarven introduction. A tiny prick dug deep into the right side of his neck, making him stutter.

"Ahh!" He stopped Dwarven and retuned to English. "Today's enemy was the tuzvul, and she fell." Ben repeated it in Elven and, when he started to say it in Gnome, another prick dug deep into the left side of his neck.

"Ahh! Her master escapes." A desire to point at where Bastion's cloud had been swelled in him. He stamped it down. *Who know how they'll take the sudden move and, worse, what if Bastion's no longer there?*

Two tiny feet landed on the back of his head, positioned on either side of his spine. A needle's point pierced his skin.

Trying to escape the pain, Ben pulled his chest and head tighter to his knees, but the slow, constant burrowing into his spine continue. *Persevere. Persevere.* Straining to endure it, his teeth ground together and he grunted through his grimace. "Good and Wise Fae, if he escapes, the Century of Shadows is certain."

He remained silent. *If they don't like Elven, that'll be my third strike, and this one will go into my spinal cord, making me a quadriplegic.* Ben struggled for something more to say.

A sharp whistle lit behind him. The digging pinpoint stopped its dig. One tiny voice spoke in English. "Say in Elfish."

Ben did. *It's worth a chance.* He added, "The cloud is known as Bastion. He's wholly Nilosian. Granted, he is more my problem than yours, but soon, he'll be an enemy to all."

A volley of heated whistles and clicks preceded the fine tip being ripped out of his neck at a cruel angle.

"Uhh!" The pain made his knees almost buckle.

A light, musical voice spoke in elegant Elven. "Gather your capturing device, young Baxter, and lock away The Foe of All."

'Foe of All,' have to look that one up. Note for future research in place, Ben put Adept Matton's final lesson before failing him in Courtmanship V into practice. *Respect is in the bow. Grace is in the unfolding.* Controlling his breath to keep from greedily sucking air, his lungs quietly expanded as he stood. "Thank you, Good and Wise Fae." He scooped up the Imprisoning Orb, glanced to find Bastion's dark cloud moving sideways, and began to toss the prison up to gather the smoke.

Inching closer and closer to the ledge until his toes over the edge, Ben kept sending the orb up and catching it. One last time, Ben extended his arm over and tossed the sphere up into the retreating smoke and caught it. He gathered most of Bastion, but he'd need three or four more throws to collect the rest and he could go no further.

Worse, thin wisps of Bastion constantly leaked from the orb to rejoin the mass. If he didn't get all of the Nilosian energy, this who struggle would be for naught.

A whirl of hums surrounded him, and a miniature tornado lifted him from the column. Dozens, if not scores of fairies, both crystalline and bulbous, swarmed around him, waving their fingers in unison, directing him through the air like a balloon on a string.

Unabashed, Ben grinned when he imagined the flight of joy-scented bubbles floating from his skin as he captured the remaining bits of Bastion.

As soon as he completed the task Ben's thoughts turned to somehow saving Malcolm. *But how?*

Chapter Thirty-Five

ON A DARKER ROAD

BEN HAD no idea how hard of a bargain the fairies would drive. Still, leaving from the fae caves with a live Malcom rambling non-stop about how great it was to be rescued was better than leaving him behind. Well, almost.

Jek wasn't pleased in the least, but the orc kept his silence.

In the cab of Jek's truck, the engine droned as they motored away from the fairies' hive with the headlights off. Ben looked past Malcolm between them to Jek's sloped profile against the night sky beyond. Partly feeling the same way, Ben kept his mouth shut, too.

Perhaps, for Malcom's part in the murder of Jek's first-blood, Ben should have left Malcom with the fairies. He had been so against what the fairies were doing that he had forgotten that this night wouldn't have gone the way it had without the Dunn-Blatt assisting the rose-scented person.

Jek's eyes went wider with greater annoyance as

Malcolm started in again. "I swear, Baxter, I don't know what I would have done if you hadn't come when you did."

Arm on the window, Ben enjoyed the air running up his coat and shirt sleeve. *Feels great to be above ground, even if I have to put up with the smell of Jek's truck.* He glanced ahead to see the teeny purple neon dot of Meadows Towing sign against the bright lights of distant Las Vegas.

"They were going to kill me." As with the last couple cycles, Malcolm looked up. "I cannot possibly thank you enough."

Ben nodded. "You're not out of the clear yet." Not entirely please with the arrangement—*I feel like that fairy anchored to you, except, instead of giving you a reason to go on, I'm preaching false dread*—he reminded Malcolm of is duty. "You still need to return, monthly, to prove you are worthy of keeping your life."

"I will. You can bet I will." Malcolm went back to looking at his hands. "Twily's life depends on it too."

Ben shook his head as more evidence stacked up against the fairy Malcolm believed was on his side. *Twily, that's almost a perfect anagram of Yilst.* His mind went back to the berry smell of magic and dark emotions. "You know it's probably going to suck."

Malcolm nodded at this hands. "It's better than death."

Cursing in Giant, "Son of a bitch!" Jek punched the roof and pointed forward.

Malcolm slid away from Jek. "What'd he say?"

I don't see anything. Ben scanned out into the dark

distance where Jek pointed. He switched to the Giant's tongue. "What is it?"

Malcolm tensed as his eyes shifted to look over Ben's shoulders.

Ur-Krurk's gruff voice came from Ben's right. "Gotta admire the balls on those bastards."

A set of tiny taillights lit far off in the night.

Jek started to slow. "How do you want to play it, Might-Fist?"

"What do you see?" Ben switched back to English. "The only things I see out there is a set of brake lights."

Jek glanced at Malcolm between then and continued speaking in Giant. "A white van is being let into Meadows Towing." The orc reached under his seat and pulled out a large handgun. "If I drop the hammer, we'll make it before the gates close."

"No." *I get that you want revenge, Jek, but us rushing in will benefit them more than us.* "We need to move tactically. We have no way of knowing how many of them are in there."

"Speak Giant, Might-Fist," Jek cut his eyes to Malcolm. "You never know how close your true foe might be."

Ben did. "My Giant is not good enough. No can say —" He switched back to English. "I can't say exactly what I mean quite yet."

"Blood-Son," Ur-Krurk's massive teal face filled half the window. His red irises set against black orbs were fixed on Malcolm. "Do not commit an error. The enemy of your enemy is not your ally."

Ben stole a glance at Malcolm sinking into the seat before replying in Giant. "He has no love for them."

"Nor he for you," Ur-Krurk put his black-nailed thumb to the corner of his eye. "Right now, he's loyal." The ogre pulled down on the flesh to peel his lower eyelid down. "Once he forgets the value of his life, he'll betray you."

"True." Jek agreed and did the same eye-thumbing move. He motioned forward and slight disgust worked into his voice. "Well, the gates are closing. So, what now?"

The complexion of this would be changed greatly if I had access to either my tablet or my spellcards; preferably both. Knowing another gate lay deeper into the scrapyard back lot, but not able to see anything, Ben gestured out into darkness to the left of where the taillights had lit. "We take the entrance closest to the north-east compactor and drive halfway to the building. Ur-Krurk drops me on the roof and I get my Anvilsmith while he surveys the enemies."

"Solid strategy—" The ogre shook his head. "But it won't work. From the looks of things, they were Black Sky orcs."

Ben asked, "Which means?"

Jek answered, "*Which means,* they started ransacking the place and dividing up your possessions the moment they got back on property." He dropped the truck into neutral and let it roll. "And, the longer they have stuff they don't need, the more likely it is to be broken."

"I'm sorry, Ben." They all looked down at Malcolm who had slunk low in the seat. "It's all my fault."

You had no way of knowing this would go so far sideways. Still... Ben opened his mouth to soothe

Malcolm's guilt and paused. *Maybe he knows more.* He asked, "How so?"

"I just wanted my hook back." Malcolm gripped his hands, wrung them, and shook them violently before he pulled his hood over his head. At this angle, lavender symbols lit on the inside of the Dunn-Blatt's uniform before darkness filled the hood and obscured his features.

Ur-Krurk's throat rumbled as he spoke English. "Hiding in shame is pure weakness, Boy."

Wow, that almost sounded more like guidance and an insult. Ben turned to see the ogre pull back from the window. A wet snort of snot being summoned rose before Ur-Krurk hawked it into the night.

The pool of shadows around Malcolm's face evaporated as an indignant sneer twisted his lips. Different symbols lit around his sleeve band. Menacing Krotosian energy surrounded the Dunn-Blatt's hand as it sunk into the cuff to form the precursor of a blast around his fist.

Ben had been so focused that he jumped a bit when Ur-Krurk's voice rumbled again in English through the window. "The fairies bled you good, Boy." A hungry smile played on the ogre's black-toothed maw. "Think hard before you start something my Blood-Son wont' be able to pull you from."

Malcolm relaxed his hand, and the power faded.

Hold on a second. Curious, Ben lifted Malcolm's arm to inspect where the symbols had lit mere moments ago.

Malcolm started to withdraw.

Ben grabbed Malcolm's arm. *I just may have spells to*

cast after all. He twisted the cuff and pulled from Malcolm to scrutinize the lines of faint needlecraft.

Malcolm sat upright and went with the sleeve. "What are you doing, Ben?"

Ben's eyes narrowed at Malcom the basics of new a plan started to form. "How do Dunn-Blatts cast?"

Chapter Thirty-Six

BACK IN BUSINESS

MALCOLM SQUIRMED in the seat next to Ben, stirring up the pervasive smell of salami ground into the seats. The Dunn-Blatt twisted to yank free and slid his arm free of the sleeve

The cuff remained in Ben's hands. *Wow, this is really soft. Considering how many of Malcom's fellow schoolmates are jerks, I just figured the material would somehow be—*he rubbed it between his thumb and forefinger—*agitating.* Ben ran his fingers over the outermost threads. *Whoa.* Well-crafted knots called for power. About to let a bit of Argosian energy slip, he licked his lips in anticipation. There, Ben rediscovered the taste of bacon... And his hunger.

He tightened his stomach to quiet the rumbling. *All in due time.* Ben let his red magic flow into the sucking knots. A hiss-gargling sentence—

"Malcolm?"

No answer

—flashed through Ben's mind before crimson

energy flowed out of the threads. It swam around his fist.

Malcolm gasped.

"Cool." Ben admired the flow for a moment as a Blast spell were his to release. He opened his hand. The spell disbursed and his energy flowed back into his reserve.

Malcolm gasped. "How many sources of magic do you have?"

"Might-Fist," Jek said. "Another set of taillights."

Ben glanced to see the red lights and pulled on the sleeve. "Give me your hoodie."

Malcolm jerked away. "No!"

The ogre's big, teal hand reached in, grabbed Malcolm by the arm, and unceremoniously yanked the former bully out of the window. Malcolm's knee whacked the top of the door.

The soft sleeve slipped from Ben's hands.

Ur-Krurk held Malcolm close to his big, bull-dog like face. "You're in no position to deny anything, Boy."

Malcolm gave his zipper an angry downward yank.

Ur-Krurk snatched the Dunn-Blatt school top from Malcolm before he fully removed it from his body. As requested, the top went to Ben.

Sorry, Malcolm. Ben flipped the cuffs backwards again. The right cuff had seven well-spaced rings across the width. Over half of the left was covered with four similar rings. *There's space for three more.* Ben jumped from the truck. He slipped from his coat. No longer protected from the night's winter chill, a sharp cold began to slip into his skin.

Ben tossed his coat to the Dunn-Blatt.

Malcolm chose to shiver instead of putting it on.

Man, I really hope your school provides a similar comfort knack. He slipped on the violet hoodie and, once he zipped it up, felt the fabric flash warmth into his skin —*ah*—and the mystic threading gave a steady *feed me magic* pull. Ben flipped back the cuff and looked from the fine needlecraft to the shivering, silent Dunn-Blatt. "What spells are these?"

Malcolm crossed his arms, clamped his eyes shut, and turned his face away.

Ur-Krurk tightened one of his large hands into a massive fist. The knuckles popped. "Speak or bleed."

Without opening his eyes, Malcolm pointed to the right and tried to ramble too quickly to be understood. "Burning Grasp, Napalm Arrow, Darkness, Scorching Ray, Fireball, Lighting Bolt, and Firestorm."

Ben ran a finger along each spell thread as Malcolm rattled them off. *Burning Grasp and Napalm arrow must be fire-based versions of Shacking Grasp and Acid Arrow.* Ben slid his thumb along the opposite cuff as Malcolm continue to rattle. "Purple Princesses, Writhing Wreath, Cone of Flames, and you already know how to summon a dusk bison."

I do? Ben thought back to the duel they had last month when he had went to summon one of his conjurations at the same time as Malcolm and discovered he could use his energy to counter the Dunn-Blatt's spell. *Well, I'm not going to correct you.*

"Again." Knuckles popped on the ogre's other hand as it balled into a fist. "This time, say them slower."

"I got 'em." *Well, I have no idea what the Princesses and Wreath spells are, but I know enough.* Ben threw a thumb toward the back of the truck. "Ur-Krurk, hop on." He turned to look at the goblins. "Nuk, Uk'so, watch Malcolm and don't let any harm come to him."

The ogre flew to the back. The goblins hopped down. Nuk held a length of chain and Uk'so Gripped a tire iron.

Ben pointed at Malcolm's feet. "Stay put." He jumped into the cab and shot his hand forward. "Jek, get through the gate."

Jek shifted into first and jumped on the accelerator. Grating rocks spat from under the spinning wheels like a machine gun before the tire caught traction and they launched forward.

I don't know. Those lights look pretty far away. Ben began to doubt Jek's judgment. *Well, if the Black Sky orcs see me, they're going to come after only me.* Ben pulled the hood over his head. The lone stitching along the rim gave that slight, magic-hungry pull as the cuffs. *Sweet, I can activate the face obscuring magic that Malcolm usually uses.* Ben let his Krotosian energy flow into the hoodie to conceal his identity.

A veil of darkness blotted his sight—*shit!*—before, granting him clear vision across the desert, similar to his Elfsight spell. *Instead of stars raining light, everything simply looks slick with the Moon's glow.* Now, unlike last time, he could see the white van around the glow of the tail lights as it pulled past the closing gates. "Slow down. We're not going to make it."

As though it granted the truck more speed, Jek leaned into the steering wheel. "We'll make it."

"Stop!" Ben ordered. "We're not even close."

"So, what, we wait for another one?" The orc

jammed on the brakes and punched the dash. "Great, they'll have an army by the time we get in there."

"I doubt it." Noting the lack of movement atop the large brick columns the gates were anchored to, Ben pointed at the scrapyard. "Drive slowly to stay quiet and head in."

They began to inch forward. "The gate is closed."

"I know." Ben rubbed his palms together. "But if these Black Sky orcs scavenge as madly as you two say they do, they wouldn't have set sentries nor would they have taken the time to reconfigure the gate code." He grinned at Jek.

The orc's blank face reminded him that the hood hid his features.

Ben put a small laugh into his voice. "Heck, I'm willing to bet they're even using the remotes from the other tow trucks.

Jek gave a slow *I get it* nod.

Small rocks crunching and dirt shifting were the only signal of their approach. Closing on the scrapyard the ruckus sound of Orcish war-rock—deep drums and chaotic metal striking metal—carried, unimpeded, across the desert.

"Not even Gromsk will be able to help them." Jek flashed Ben a bloodthirsty grin. "You're brilliant. This'll be the perfect ambush."

Chapter Thirty-Seven

FAMILIAR GROUND

AMBUSH... Ben hadn't stopped to consider what they were doing. *Ambush is the right word for it and it's no more insidious than what they did to me...* Still, the word sat wrong on his conscious. *Think about it later.* Ben rubbed the magical stitching, noting the bunches, grooves, and binds in the fine threads. The word began to roll back to the front of Ben's mind before he intercepted it with a different word. *Gromsk.* He asked, "What is Gromsk? Is it a type of weapons?"

"No." Jek's leaned into the steering wheel again and kept this eyes forward, scanning around the ground, up along the buttresses, and the Koffman Security Gate. "He's an Orcish War God."

"Ah." The war-rock had long since swallowed the sounds of the truck rolling forward. *He seems awfully confident for having seen two vans enter the property. I mean, sure, we have Ur-Krurk, but we'll still be greatly outnumbered.*

Ben glanced in the side mirror to glimpse the ogre

magi gripping the crane the back. *Still can't figure out why the monster's supporting me. He had two chances to betray me—once with the Imprisoning Orb and he could have just beaten me senseless once we were outside the fairy hive and sold me, and Malcolm, back.* Trying to figure it out still made his head spin. *Well, I'm not going to think of him as a pure ally, let alone a horrid ritual-granted father figure. He's probably waiting for the perfect moment to betray me.*

A *click* brought Ben from his thoughts.

Jek lowered his hand from the remote clipped to the visor to the steering wheel. "Jackpot." The orc grinned as the Koffman gate began to roll up and the double wrought iron gates parted in the center to yawn open.

If not for the war-rock, a keen-eared sentry probably would've heard that. Concern about Ur-Krurk boomeranged back into his thoughts. *Can ogres call for a Retributive Paramountcy? It's so farfetched—Well, Councilor Eastly might have the answer, but then the old bat would demand to know why his* valuable time *was being squandered on* useless twaddle.

They cruised through rows and rows of wrecked cars.

Ben's mouth dried and his stomach tightened as they had the first time he had come to Meadows Towing. From habit, his fingers went to where his Achilleus spellcard would normally be in his holder. His fingers brushed against his empty holder and slacks.

"Being in the cab makes you an easy target." Ur-Krurk opened the passenger door. "Get on your feet so you can move."

Minding his pace, Ben hopped out and sped-walked

alongside the truck. Drawing a breath of steel-laden air, he found courage as his eyes landed on a crumbled aqua sedan under a faded brown station wagon with wood paneling. *This is no longer unfamiliar ground. In two more rows, we'll be on the main path to the building.* "Jek." Ben leaned into the window so he wouldn't have to yell over the frantic clanging metal-music and pointed across the cab. "Turn down this row."

Ur-Krurk had taken to the air and flew just above him. "Since you can multicast, now would be the time to get any defensive spells in action."

The ogre's hot breath wafting over him sent a chill through Ben's spine. *Hope that didn't show.* "I don't have my necklace or tablet, and Malcolm, apparently, doesn't believe in defense."

"Foolish boy. Even the mightiest of offenses cannot be sustain forever." Ur-Krurk drifted from being directly over Ben to hover above the truck's sun baked hood. The ogre raised his voice to be heard over the clamor. "You are going to have to deal with him, Blood-Son."

"Harshly," Jek added.

Ben sighed at the inevitable reality. *They're right. If only I could get Malcolm to act less Malcolmy.*

Light reflected on something small that moved a ways down the row. *Tex?* Ben's hand dropped to his hip to pull his Anvilsmith so he could call his companion. And grabbed air. *Crap!* He shook his empty fist in frustration as the robot moved further away and disappeared around a corner. *We could really use a scout right now.*

Choosing not to compete with the music, Ben

projected, *"I'm going to see what kind of numbers we're facing."* Not waiting for their feedback, Ben sped up to a light jog to outpace the truck. The hoodie blew soft, cool air against his torso to help control his body heat. *That's a neat knack.* At the corner, he dropped to a knee and peeked.

The bass-drum of the heavy war-rock thumped across the hundred-foot span to the first row of cars. *Wow, I can feel that on my face. They're going to blow out the speakers in the work bays.* Every light in the place was out, and most of the windows were shattered. *If it weren't for the tools and small fixtures strewn across the clearing, I would've bet the beat broke the windows.* About a dozen motorcycles had been hastily parked around six long, white passenger vans, and Malcolm's Transcend. The two-foot tall *Meadows Towing* letters had been re-worked to read *wooT Mead wings*.

An offended sneer flashed across Ben's face before he hustled back to relay the set up to the other two. Ben thought his question to them, *"About how many orcs per van?"*

Jek answered, "There'll be between six and twelve." He knocked his knuckles together to represent tight seating. "When given a chance, we orcs roll thick."

Ur-Krurk landed and took Ben by the shoulders. The beef jerky reek on his breath had faded and only blackberries pillowed his words. "Blood-Son, draw more blood than you give. I'm taking the orc to a vantage point. We'll wait for your mark." The ogre lifted Jek and flew to the top of the wall of wrecked cars.

Noticing the bulky riffle slung over Jek's shoulder,

Ben wondered, *what kind of gun is that long one? It looks one hundred percent pure business.*

Ben ran a finger along the dusk bison stitching in Malcom's hoodie. He opened his Argosian font. The red energy flowed into the hoodie. His pulse quickened, blood heated, and a tremble washed through him as two long and lean Argosian dusk bison appeared. Almost as tall as him, Ben was about to compare their length to his car—*only two?*—when his thoughts got away from him. *Where'd the rest of my power go?* He tried to pull the remaining two casting's worth of energy from the Dunn-Blatt uniform, but it felt dry. *Crap, I gotta use more energy in this.* Ben gave the uniform a dirty look. *Greedy thing.*

In the moment's distraction, one of the dusk bison— the most feared of school mascot conjurations in the Las Vegas Valley—pulled the long, deadly tendrils on its back tight, plopped on its bottom, tucked its head, kicked a hind leg out and started to preen itself like an idle house dog. The other searched for a scent, prowled it to the corner, and waited to get into action.

Preener and Prowler. Ben shook his head against the names. *No need to become familiar with conjurations I'll never summon again.* Still, he made notes of the names as he grabbed Preener's reins. *Mimic Prowler.*

It did.

Wonder if— He glanced.

With Jek in arms, Ur-Krurk hovered just below the top car.

They're waiting on me. Ben drew a slow, steadying breath as he stalked to the end of the aisle near the readied beasts. He peeked out one more time to survey the building for movement.

Orcs partied upstairs, orcs partied in the kitchen, and, beyond them, orcs partied in the livening room.

Well… Why am I hesitating? Reluctance? Ben let the initial thought peter out. *Fireballs. Two of them.* He rubbed the fifth stich on his soft right sleeve. It sucked at his fingers like a starved calf working an udder for milk. Mentally, he aimed upstairs and at the archway dividing the downstairs rooms. *Alright*—he let his Argosian energy flow into the stitch—*let's do this.*

Chapter Thirty-Eight

RETAKING THE SCRAPYARD

As BEFORE, a hiss-gargle sentence echoed through Ben's mind. *Cool, the hoodie converts — whoa!*

Unlike summoning dusk bison, the magic from the fifth stich came back fast and — *hot potatoes!* — ready for release. Two glowering, crimson beads — *four?* — jumbled restlessly above each of his palms. *If I don't release* — sulfur filled his nose — *they're gonna pop!* He stepped sideways, picked locations near his original points — *twenty feet apart* — and let them fly.

The two roiling orbs from his left hand shot to the kitchen and living room. The two from his right entered separate smashed-out windows on the second floor. There, Orcs, who had been rocking to the raucous music, froze in place. The faint light of his magic reflected in their widening eyes. Colored by the magic, their teeth shone red as their mouths started to move to call out a warning.

Thoom!

All four beads exploded and filled each area to the

brim with sudden flame. Framed by the windows, the orcs not instantly incinerated to twitching skeletons, were wreathed in flames, and writhed in pain.

It's like a grotesque shadow puppet show.

One of the burning orcs on the second floor leapt out the window to land flat; unmoving.

Prowler and Preener ached for release.

Go.

They charged across the clearing.

A gunshot barely reported over the noise of the blasting war-rock.

Blood splattered from Prowler's right hindquarters.

The beast turned back.

Go. Ben urged the beast toward the building as he seeped energy in the fifth stitch again. The hiss-gargle sentence—*I can almost make it out*—echoed in his mind as a bead appeared in each of his hands. He sent another to the second floor, and popped around the corner and let the second fly at the shooter.

He barely got a look at the jackal-headed dog-man pointing a gun at his beasts and the two still engrossed in a dice game at their pawed feet—*the orcs weren't the only betrayers*—before the fiery explosion engulfed the gnolls. The three bodies bobbed around as meat burned down to bones in seconds. Their charred skeletons dropped to the ground.

Orcs began to pour out of the building like angry ants.

The lead orc's head kicked back, popping into red mist. The chest of the one behind it burst open form the same round as a *crack*, clearly audible over the music, came from Jek's position.

Purple bolts of magic—*Ur-Krurk*—struck opposition on the roof.

Ben let more red energy flow from his chest chakra into the hoodie and—*something something, Argosana, something*—the hiss-gargle sentence flashed through his head before rewarding him with four more glowing orbs. He strafed them across the front of the cinderblock building.

Most of the orcs that spilled out were swallowed by the flames.

One orc, a massive brute with flames riding his back heaved a greatsword at Preener, chopping it in the gut.

Ben switched to the second stich to blast the orc with Napalm Arrow when something bit into his right flank, lanced pain through his abdomen struck a rib—*I've been shot*—and ricocheted of a rib to exit his back. Another stabbing pain went through his right leg.

He hobbled backward.

Something slammed his ankles together and swept his feet from under him.

"*Ooph!*" He glanced the direction of the shots.

A lone, wiry orc charged down the second row at him. He had a pistol in one hand and a whirled a bola above his head.

Ben released his Argosian energy into the stitch. In rapid successions, four solid-fire compound bows appeared, twanged a sizzling arrow at the rushing target, and faded.

The orc leapt the first arrow. Let his bola fly as he sidestepped the next. The third hit his leg and the fourth—

Rough twine struck Ben's neck and yanked. The

wizz of it wrapping tight warned of dread before the tightening registered on his neck and the weights *clacked* together. Against his spine. The force flopped him onto his back.

It's choking me! His hands slapped against the tight ropes. He groped for purchase on the edge of the twine —*too tight*—and found none. *Prowler to me.*

The bitter taste of fear rose in his throat.

Keep cool.

Ben struggled to control the emotion that threatened to suffocate him faster than the bola.

Calm yourself.

He glanced to the orc who threw the weapon and found a lava covered twitching mass.

Burning hands. Opening his chakra, Ben's finger landed on the first stitch. It sucked the raw magic in, hiss-gargled at him, and sizzled the spell into being.

Fiery gloves coated his hands. He gripped the ropes. The smell of his flesh cooking with the ropes, pooled in his nostrils as his flaming fingers dug at the layers of tightly woven cords strangling him. He grimaced against the burning. The choking rope muted his agonized cries into a pissed-off rumbled in his throat.

A gnoll turned the corner with a knife.

Prowler snatched it up with its tendrils and curled in to gore the whining creature.

Ben's fingers gained a millimeter of ground. *A rope broke!* A wisp of air entered his mouth. He sucked at it, and locked it in his stinging lungs as a second rope gave.

More air.

He thought to exhale the old and bring in new, but

—*running on automatic*—his lungs continue to expand from the tiny slip of air.

He pulled his knees up to his chest and rocked forward into a kneeling position.

Another gnoll came around the corner. Its black-clawed paw-feet scrabbled and found enough ground to shift its weight and, wild eyes laser focused on Ben's neck, cock a moonlight-sheathed sword back.

Oh shit.

Chapter Thirty-Nine

SITTING DUCK

BEN'S EYES WENT WIDE.

A fine froth broke out at the upward corners of the overjoyed gnoll's furry maw.

Shit! Shit!

It swung.

Ben scrunched down.

A red tendril lashed out. It knocked the gnoll's arms up.

Instead of being beheaded, the blade skimmed the top of Ben's skull. The chop chipped away a fragment of skull, sliced his scalp clean away, and took part of the hoodie.

The pain! Still unable to yell, Ben grasped at the last of the burning ropes around his cooking neck—*the stench!*—and the outer layer fell away. He exhaled and sucked in cool, coal-tasting air. *More.*

The gnoll's paw-feet turned away. Its sword flashed out at the dusk bison gnawing on the first gnoll.

Ben lunge-crawled forward on the dirt covered

blacktop. He caught the gnoll's thin ankle and discharged the *Fiery Grasp* spell into it.

The jackal-headed creature yipped and whined as its fur went up in flames and its skin began to boil. It dropped to the ground and began to roll.

Prowler leapt in and clamped its jaws on the gnoll's neck. The dusk bison's fore hooves crashed on the creature's chest as its mouth came away with the majority of a bloody throat.

Engines roared and revved to life and shots rang out over the war-rock.

Ben yanked the last of the rope away with his fiery hand and drank in a true lungful of air. His neck cried against the wide expansion. *So. Much. Pain.*

Vans and motorcycles began to flash past him.

Purple energy—Ur-Krurk—lit from the side of the building.

Surrounded by orcs, Preener crouched defensively in front of the building. Ben touched his fifth stitch. *To me.* Magic flowed in. *Something, blank-cana Argosana, something.*

Enemy orcs cheered and swung at the conjuration as it leapt away, but were soon dumbfounded by the red glowering beads within their midst. Then the spell exploded, engulfing them in fire as they tried to run.

The pain in Ben's gut and leg were all but a memory as he rolled over and eyed a line of motorcycles. Ben touched the sixth-stitch—*chew on a Lightning Bolt, jerks*—switched power reserves to Krotosian magic and let it flow into the hoodie. The purple magic floated around the summoning threads. *I don't want conjurations, darn it.*

Lightning Bolt! He directed the truant magic into the stitch which took it happily.

A howling lavender lightning bolt cracked from his hands and down the line of retreating bikers, electrocuting all but the few furthest away in rapid succession.

Ben called both Preener and Prowler near him for cover as, knees to his chest, he worked away the twine of the bola puzzle from his ankles with his remaining flaming hand.

Three bullets rocked into his back. Two passed clear through, but the last exited his stomach and lodged into his upper leg. He flopped over—*there!*— grinding his teeth to bite back yelling. *If my neck hated moving to draw breath, it'll throttle me for shouting.*

He sent Prowler to finish the crispy, gun-toting biker who had survived the stroke of lighting.

Ben scanned around. Other retreating orcs were in range. One by one, *crack* by *crack*, they fell as bits of their skulls, if not the entire head, were blasted away by Jek and his massive gun.

Save your magic. Ben worked the ropes keeping his legs together. *Mind your surroundings.* He kept glancing around. Each time his eyes scanned over burned bodies, charred bodies, and limp bodies missing heads. About to relax and focus on the ropes—*stay alert*—he kept reminding himself to stay mindful of his surroundings as the pain from his bullet wounds began to lessen. *Being shot sucks.*

The slug in his leg pushed back up the hole it had made as muscles mended, finally falling to the ground as the bullet wound healed over. Likewise, the bolts of pain coming from the top of his head eased.

Ur-Krurk landed next to him and cut the rest of the rope away with his black claws. The ogre hauled Ben to his feet to inspect the growing blisters. Something about the way the monster's face twisted in mild disgust shook worry into Ben's core. How bad does it look? Ur-Krurk asked, "Who got close enough to burn you?"

Don't laugh. Ben tried fighting the simper threatening to turn his lips, but lost and winced from the pain both on, and in, his neck.

Ben projected his answer in Giant, *Me.*

Ur-Krurk slapped him hard on the shoulder.

Ouch! So worth it.

Ben finally got to see what mirth looked like on the big, teal, face. The ogre's lips pulled back to show a sneering grin of jagged black teeth. Instead of laughing out, Ur-Krurk sucked air in desperate intake sound as though he were surprised and couldn't get enough breath on one drag.

He rubbed his shoulder—*so worth it*—and pointed to his neck. *Why's this not healing?*

Ur-Krurk recovered quickly. "Fire is the only thing that does lasting damage to us." He lifted Ben from the ground. "Get some ice on that. I'm going to chase down the runners."

Ben fought the urge to rub the searing burns. *Jek?*

"I'll drop him off on a pillar to snipe any who head out toward the goblins." As though waiting to be dismissed, Ur-Krurk gave him a nod.

Ben gave a thumbs up.

The ogre took to the air and scooped up Jek.

Ben gauged his red conjurations' condition. *Boy, you guys are really beat up.* He wanted to thank them aloud, to say their names, but the growing blisters kept him quiet as he wondered about his earlier Liquid Forge detonation in the basement. *How was I able to regenerate from* that *damage?* With an intimate knowledge of what it felt like to have your flesh cooked away, Ben grimaced. *It felt like fire.*

He dismissed the two Argosian dusk bison and remembering the hoodie needed double energy to summon one—*all I should need*—he let a double-casting's worth of Krotosian energy slip into the conjuration stitch. Louder than when he conjured before, and as clear as the *Fireball* spell, a hiss-gargle sentence sounded in his mind. This time, all the words, besides *Krotosiana* where *Argosana* had been, were beyond his understanding.

Two violet flashes energy ushered in purple-black dusk bison. Similar in size to their red versions, these two conjurations had a more healthy-looking muscle mass to them. As before, one prowled forward to stop at the work bays while the other dropped onto its bottom to preen itself.

Motioning for Preener to him, Ben quickened his stride to get up next to Prowler. *The place may have emptied out, but there still may be more hiding inside.*

Moving closer to the booms and clangs of music —*have to turn that music off*—he stepped over charred remains at the entrance to the work bay. *Uhh!* Ben pulled the neckline up to cover his nose and mouth. Too late. He could taste the foul, burnt bodies and entrails on the air. Bile began to rise.

Not having to hold it back or put a strong front around Ur-Krurk or Jek, Ben rushed into the kitchen, leaned over the sink, and let the rising disgust—*I've killed them. I've killed them all*—heave out of him. Two rounds of bile splattered into the basin before he ran dry and continued to heave. Each pulse of his throat inflamed the burns.

Finally, he got his stomach, disgust, and remorse under control. He rinsed out his mouth, washed his hands, and let the water run to carry his mess down the disposal.

Using the hood to mute the smells, Ben held the neckline to his face as moved against the ruckus and entered the work bays to pull the plug on the pounding drums and rhythmless clangs.

The vibrations immediately ceased feeling like they were rubbing along his neck. *Thank goodness.* Ben stifled a sigh when loud grunts and giggles died seconds after the music.

Ben rushed back through the kitchen to the living room.

Clear.

Prowler preceded him up the stairs.

The door to the left had been blasted form its hinges. He scanned the bodies. None stirred. He turned to his bedroom. Prowler moved by his side as he hustled to the door and threw it open.

The conjuration lunged. Preener followed.

Two shots rang out before a high-pitched scream filled the area under the dusk bison's hissing.

Don't kill. He directed. *I'm probably too late.*

"This is not how you issue a Might-Fist challenge!"

Toad's voice brimmed with righteous indignation. "This is no way to challenge for the belt."

Son of a... Ben pushed the door open. Blocked mostly by Prowler's length, the body of a slim orc lay beyond the hissing conjuration. A gun lay against the far wall near shattered remains of brown beer bottles. Toad stood on the bare mattress of his bed, wincing as he rubbed his hand. *He's wearing my belt and spare coat.* Noting the pale green orc's total lack of other clothing, Ben switched his gaze to the other being in the room. A short—by orcish standards—pitch-black skinned female orc stood wrapped in blankets, the furs from the bed piled around her, and she held a serrated longsword at the ready.

Like flipping a switch, Toad's tone changed from fear to pleading sympathy. "Malcolm, I swear I didn't know they were going to double-cross you." A nervous laugh bubbled from his throat. "I'm glad you are well." The orc sobered and swallowed hard. "Could you, uh, dismiss your creatures, please?"

Disbelief tilted Ben's head. His wounded neck throbbed. *Does he think Malcolm so dim or easily won over?* Moving at a sloth's pace, Ben raised a hand to the center of the hood and touch the sigil to dismiss the magical darkness concealing his face.

A range of emotions danced on Toad's face as he stuttered, "B-B-Ben..."

"Toad." Fists clenched as hard as his teeth, every wrecked syllable made the boils on Ben's neck blaze. "Who, exactly, did you best to become Might-Fist?"

Chapter Forty

AFTERMATH

TOAD DIDN'T HAVE an answer ready.

The bedroom reeked of beer and feces. Ben's gaze went to what had to be a case of broken bottles smashed against the northern wall. *Can't believe...* The sound of Toad's breathing began to steady. *I trusted...* Ben's eyes went to a pile of shit on the nightstand where he had placed a small oil painting of his family that his father created and given to Ben last December 25th. Under the bottom coil of light brown waste, Ben spied the barest hint of the frame's corner. All of his energy sources began to churn and heat within him at the blatant disrespect. *I should...*

Sensing the coming storm, Toad extended his hands out, palms up to bend in a supplicating bow. "Ben, Might-Fist, please let me explain. I—"

"Get—" Ben reined-in the growing contempt and loathing before they collided into hate. Each word felt like a barbed-wire choker. "—Out." A dim light threw soft shadows from the orcs against the wall. Ben glanced to the heat building around his fist. There, his three energies, black, red and purple, swirled feverishly like electrons around a nucleus. The hoodie sleeve swished out to touch the power which remained just beyond the fabric's reach.

Ben eyed Toad and projected, *Unless, of course, you want to challenge me for the title.*

"No, no," Toad unbuckled the belt. It flopped on the mattress. "I'm not challenging you."

Ben managed to relax his hand. The energies flashed into his fingertips. He pointed to the door. *Then go. Get out of here.*

Toad straightened. "Wonder why I turned on you?"

Don't care. To give the orcs a clear path to the door, Ben motioned Prowler to back into the bathroom and Preener to slide to the left near the closet where it melded with the darkness. He moved around the broken pile of wood that had been his desk and over the body of the slim orc to stand near Prowler.

Ben projected, *If you don't start moving, I'll have them attack.*

Both beast reared their tendrils back and growled as they lowered into a ready-to-charge crouch.

Minding the conjurations, the female kept her sword at the ready for a moment longer before dropping the blade on the bed. She fished black leather clothing from the furs and dressed quickly.

Toad stepped off the bed opposite the woman, closer to the pooped-on painting. He grabbed his jeans and hoisted them on. "You were lucky to retake this place by yourself." Toad zipped his pants and tossed the spare trench coat onto the bed. "Then again, you've always been lucky." He spoke Orcish to the woman.

Continuing to dress, she barked back.

Ben's gaze flicked to the coat to determine if it had waste on it, too.

Pointing to the ground by his side, Toad stabbed the air with his finger.

She shook her head.

Ben projected in Giant, *You do not have to be with him, but you do have to go.*

She nodded, strapped a scabbard to her hip, and soundlessly slid the sword home.

Toad grumbled and scooped up a white Meadows Towing t-shirt.

"No." Ben winced and nearly groaned as his neck tightened to stop any more words from passing through. *Leave the tee, too. You've lost all rights to be anywhere near this place. Ever.*

"You're making a huge mistake, Ben," Toad said, clutching the shirt like a child would his most comforting blanket. "You'll never be able to hold, much less run, this place without me."

Sadly, at one time, I really believed that, Ben pointed toward the door. *However, you've made your choice. Now, out.*

The black-clad woman grabbed a quiver of javelins, hooked it over her shoulder and moved around the bed to bow before Ben. She spoke two sentences in Orcish before leaving.

Speaking pleading-sounding words in their language, Toad followed after her.

With Prowler right behind him where the beast

could whap Toad with its tendrils, Ben followed Toad
closely.

The orcs argued down the hall and down the stairs.

She never stopped, but Toad froze halfway down
and covered his nose.

He pushed Toad to start him moving again. *Every
single one of these deaths is due to your betrayal.* As much
as was possible, Ben had grown accustomed to the foul
stench of burnt flesh sticking to each breath.

Toad continued down. "You've become quite the
killer, Ben."

Ben adopted a stoic demeanor. *All on you.*

The orc motioned his head to the sofa. "Some of
these orcs were children and had nothing to do with
what happened earlier."

You involved them, Ben refused to show any
weakness, sympathy, or regret. *It's probably a trick of
some sort anyway.* He gave Toad another push when the
orc slowed. *Now, you have to explain to their loved ones
what happened here.*

Pointing to something beyond the sofa, Toad
continued to the door.

Where Toad motioned, a circle of several small,
charred bodies remained. *Probably goblins.* Ben couldn't
help but notice marbles at the center of the circle. *Oh...*
His throat throbbed as it began to constrict with sorrow.
He pulled the hood and, wishing he could make the
world dark to him instead of his face dark to the world,
used Krotosian energy to activate the darkness. His
gazed went back to the marbles one last time as they
moved from the living room, through the kitchen and
out into the work bays. Remorse stung his eyes.

Worried his telepathy might sound as tear-choked as his voice would, Ben didn't correct their course to the main entrance when they started walking east.

Feeling the world close in on him, Ben welcomed the scrapyard's metallic open-air smell as they moved away from the reek of burnt bodies around the building.

As they walked, Ben let the distance between him and the orcs grow, and discontinued feeding energy into the hoodie to keep his face obscured. The magic persisted and would for some minutes. *Papa Mojo had said the assassin would be going after him next and I've already burned through—*

Ben had never known how much magic lay within him and had often wished for a personal awatt-like counter. The Dunn-Blatt hoodie relayed, roughly, how much power he had left.

—I have a quarter of my energy left and will probably need every ounce of it.

Without warning, a sudden breeze from the east grew rapidly into a strong gust. Ben scanned the orcs who trudged on with heads bowed—*they're not doing this*—and beyond them. *What now?*

Chapter Forty-One

JEK'S VENGEANCE

THE WIND GREW STRONGER and stronger. Carrying stinging desert grit, it soon howled through the rows of wrecked cars and whistled through the tiny fissures in the metal.

Out ahead, Toad kneeled to lower his profile.

The shadows filling Ben's hood protected his face and neck from the sandstorm. Though Ben didn't want to concede to the force, he tucked his hands into his armpits and followed the shaman's example.

Arm raised before her face, the black-clad orc leaned into the mighty draft and battled to gain inches.

Ready to release a volley of *Napalm Arrows*, and not in direct danger if the wind carried the magical shots away, Ben thumbed the second stitch and projected, *Is this of your doing?*

"No!" Toad yelled over the wind and looked back at him. "Someone must've cast a spell to hold the wind still and now..." Toad brought an arm in to protect the side of his face from the cutting sand. "Now, nature is trying to catch up with where it should be."

Papa Mojo must've divined the assassination attempt and stopped the wind so I, in the girallon form, could track my human body. A small, ever-hopeful part of him considered an unlikely possibility. *Perhaps I misjudged the diviner?* Not wanting to put the charlatan in a better light, Ben frowned the thought away. *If he helped me, it's only because he thinks me key in his own continued existence.*

Running his hand along his side to finger a gunshot hole, Ben marveled at the hoodie. *It mended.* He pulled at the side so he could see without turning his neck. *And the bloodstain is shrinking away.* He ran a hand over his head to feel the hole there had been closed over. Ben thought about how he had bought more coats since he turned sixteen than he had during his prior six years at the Academy. *Man, too bad my coats can't do this.*

The near-gale force winds eased to gusts again.

The black orc had advanced several feet against the squall and stumbled forward at the sudden ease.

Toad remained crouched and kept his arm up, protecting his neck and face. "Might-Fist, if you would but give me a second chance."

Ben rose. *One more word to me, and we'll be dueling.*

Silent, the shaman bowed as he stood, then turned on his hells to catch up with the female to rekindle their arguing in Orcish. They went back and forth as they moved through the scrapyard.

Though Toad had the belt on in the room, she seems to be the one in the power position.

"He survives?" Disbelief painted Jek's question.

Ben ranged his eyes up the exit column. Jek had

been rubbing his eyes, but swiveled the tripod holding the massive rifle to have the business end directed at Toad.

Crap. I forgot Jek was out this way. Ben grimaced against the pain as he nodded. He projected, *His shame will follow him home.*

"No!" Jek dropped to a knee and pressed his shoulder to the butt of the weapon. "He dies here!"

Toad yelled at Jek in Orcish.

Jek yelled back and switched to English in the middle of his reply, "—which is why I'm going to coat the desert with the cowardice that fills your guts."

Attempting to lower the tension, Ben extended a hand. *Jek—*

The rifle cracked.

Ben tried to look away, but wasn't fast enough to not see Toad's upper chest disintegrate from the high-caliber shot. The remaining body parts thumped and slopped to the ground.

"Might-Fist," Jek's voice carried over the slight ringing in Ben's years. "I won't let you make that mistake."

The woman had started shouting. When Ben turned back, she had one of her javelins cocked back, ready to release at Jek as she continued yelling.

Jek, for his part, stood from the rifle; he had one of his pistol pulled and aimed at her. With his free hand, he ran his thumb over his heart in the opposite direction he had done when speaking over his dead first-blood. With each slow strike, she reduced her volume until she quieted altogether. He stopped midway through the final stroke and rotated the pistol so his hand was palm down while pointed at her. He grunted two Orcish syllables.

Putting the javelin away, she turned her head and spat air at Toad's remains. She then closed the remaining distance between her and the Koffman security gate barring her from exit.

Jek holstered his pistol and dropped his thumb across his heart. Looking at Ben, he pointed to the remaining orc. "She would rather live."

There had to be more exchanged between them than that. Though curious, Ben had no way of being sure. An inner heat began to slowly rise in his neck. Having had a minor burn before, he knew the burning sensation would echo back and would be a long time leaving.

Ben projected, *We cannot open the gates, but you are free to leave.*

She nodded and moved to the column opposite Jek to begin climbing out.

Ben turned away and started back to the building to follow Ur-Krurk's advice and find some ice.

Chapter Forty-Two

NOT YET DONE

SORT OF GETTING into the cold relief the ice granted, Ben winced against the heat building further in his neck. His upper back pressed against the smashed front corner panel of a pink, pre-2000's luxury sedan, he sat a few feet away from where he had lobbed fireball after fireball, holding ice wrapped in a dishtowel to the front and sides of his neck. A second towel-full of ice perched across the back of his neck, and he kept his head bowed slightly so the makeshift icepacks would stay in place.

A gentle breeze from the east kept fresh air coming in, pressing the smell of death and carnage west. From where he sat, he could only see Bola—the body of the orc who had hit him with bolas—if he looked to his left, which he didn't do too often.

A rumbling engine trundled down the main row from the east gate. *Probably Jek with Malcolm and the goblins.* Ben didn't check to see, but thumbed his fifth stitch, in case he was wrong. Glancing toward Meadows Towing would mean looking over the carnage and he felt stuffed to the proverbial gills with seeing shot, blasted, burnt, clawed, and gnawed dead bodies.

It's just like Master Reynolds always says in his annual welcoming speech to the Academy's Initiates. I've finally hit the day when the wonder fades and reality sets in. If only I could've better followed his closing advise to 'hold onto the wonder as long as possible.'

He glanced right, looking down the long row between towers of wrecked cars extending to the eastern wall; then left, to Bola and the long row stretching out to the western wall, and sighed. *The wonder's gone.* Both directions were longer than the school's longest target fields. *Never thought I'd be in a place like this.*

The rolling tires and rumbling engine came to a stop. Doors creaked open. "Benja Min'Fist?" Nuk's raspy, child-like voice called out anxiously, "Benja Min'Fist?"

He answered, *I'm on the first row, to the right.*

"Are you hurt?" Nuk asked as two sets of feet padded over. He turned the corner with Uk'so on his heels before finishing the question.

Hearing the concern, and seeing the two of them made Ben smile.

"No, Benja Min'Fist." Nuk hustled over and hooked his calico hands atop of Ben's wrists. "Ice be making burns worser. Heat no can get out. You keeping the cooking in." The goblin yanked.

The dishtowel came away with bloody burnt skin fused into the fabric. Ben sucked a long hiss of air at the sudden pain. Mildly stunned, the dishtowel fell from his hands and some of the ice fell onto the ground. Warm fluid ran down his neck into his collar.

Nuk tapped Ben on the side of his head, like Ben would've done to his youngest sibling. "You being putting cooked black skin under running water. Then wind dry. Then water."

Is my skin really blackened? Ben hurried up to his feet to get out of the goblin's reach. **I appreciate your advice, and I'd love to, but the person who set all this into action is still out there, and...** Ben bit his lip against the inescapable truth about his debt to Papa Mojo for, more than likely, being the one to still the wind. **And I need to return a favor.**

"Ben?" Tex's synthesized voice came from his right.

Ben turned.

Tex looked him up and down, then crossed his arms. "Why are you wearing a Dunn-Blatt top?"

Inwardly, Ben laughed. *You jerk.* His chest heaved a bit. He'd gotten good at not moving his neck or contracting the muscles. He slowly unzipped the hoodie to reveal his damaged and damp—probably with blood and puss—APA school button on.

"Ee-yuck," Tex turned his head to look away. "Never mind, Mr. Burn Unit. Zip up. Zip up!"

Thought so. Ben kept his slight smile to the corners of his lips and zipped up.

Tex dipped under a car, by the wheel well, and came back out with an Anvilsmith tablet.

Ben projected, **Thanks.** And took it.

"And no 'thank you?' Ingrate." Tex feigned to look around. "Where's the guy who burned you? I want to call him back to give you another lesson."

Forgot, can't mindspeak with him. Ben opened a chat window and typed in, "Thanks, Buddy. Oh, and I'm the one who burned me. I'll be glad to give out another lesson." He set the tablet down and, when his companion looked down to read, channeled Argosian energy to power into *Burning Hands*.

Tex looked up, and jumped back at seeing the fiery gloves. "No. No more lessons needed."

Ben recalled the spell. The ruby energy flashed back into his fingertips.

Tex ducked back into the little wheel well, this time coming out with a checkered washcloth tied up on a stick like an old fashion hobo bag. "I wasn't able to save everything..." He extended the pack. "...but I kept going back until the probability of being able to get back out dropped below ninety percent."

Ben opened the pack to see a handful of goldfish spellcards—*nice, just what I needed*—and the four sets of bonded obdurium steel strips. He gave his companion a thumbs up, plucked three spellcards and returned the bundle to the robot.

Tex blinked at him. "Why only three?"

Ben picked up his tablet, loaded a spellcard, and started the quick reformat of the card. He typed, "That's all I'll have time to reprogram on my way to the bazaar."

Nuk reminded, "Running water..."

Uk'so nodded in agreement, and stepped forward to hand Ben his tablet and spellcard holder.

After I get back, Ben projected.

Nuk said, "Sooner is better."

Ben strapped the case on, slid the tablet home, and turned the corner to head to Malcom's car. *I—*

Ur-Krurk was there. The ogre had a massive teal hand on each of Malcolm's shoulders and held the Dunn-Blatt as though he were a fish trying to wiggle out of his hands. He shook Malcolm. "Tell him."

Malcolm opened his mouth. His gazed dropped to Ben's neck. "Oh my God!" He tried to cringe away.

Ur-Krurk shook him again. "Tell him."

Malcolm clamped his eyes shut, making faces every time Ur-Krurk corrected the direction of his head to face Ben as though he could see the mess of Ben's burns through his closed lids as he explained. "Purple Princesses is Black Tentacles repackaged Dunn-Blatt style, and Writhing Wreath is a four-stone spell of my build that amplifies any other fire-based magic that you cast."

"And…" Ur-Krurk shook him again.

"And…" Malcom added rapidly, "You can shoot a couple of Blasts and Scorching Rays from the wreath, but the spell's real purpose is to augment other fire spells." Malcolm tried to shrug the orc's mighty hands away. "Okay, I told him. Let go."

"You're at my whim, Boy." Ur-Krurk shoved Malcom to the ground. "You might want to keep that in mind *before* you go trying to tell me what to do."

Half the goblin's height, Tex tapped Uk'so's waist and whispered, "Are you hearing Ben because I don't hear him saying anything."

Ben tapped his temple.

Ur-Krurk answered, "Robot, he's using telepathy."

The ogre kept eyeing Malcolm as the Dunn-Blatt got to his feet and dusted himself off.

"Great, everyone's hearing voices but me." Tex threw his hands up. "Never knew sanity would suck."

Ben extended his hand to Malcolm. *Ignition code please.*

"What?" Malcolm glanced between Ben and his car. He nearly screamed, "No way."

Ur-Krurk took a step toward the Dunn-Blatt.

"Seven, six, six, nine, zero." Malcolm fumed.

Thanks. Ben focused solely on the black bison-painted, purple Transcend, and made his way to the car. *If anyone is looking for me, it'll help keep the scent off my trail.* The few blackened or bloody lumps on the Meadows Towing grounds that he had to navigate to get to the car weren't bodies. Ignoring what they were, Ben hadn't classified them as anything else. They just were *not* dead bodies. He opened the car door and slipped into the fine nylon webbing the Dunn-Blatt had for a car seat.

Ur-Krurk gave an attention-getting grunt. He stood behind Malcolm. The ogre pointed down at Malcom's dark hair, then to his own chest. He smiled as he ran his thumb across his throat with a finalizing nod.

What? No! Ben's eyes went round and his neck burned as he adamantly shook his head to deny permission. He switched to Giant. *Do not kill him.*

Malcolm turned to see what was going on behind him.

Unabashed, Ur-Krurk towered over the Dunn-Blatt. "Is there a problem, Boy?"

Malcolm shook his head and moved away.

Ur-Krurk started after him and answered in Giant. "As you wish, Blood-Son."

Ben looked over the standard Kentmoore dashboard set-up and noticed Malcolm had upgraded from the two rows of five buttons numbered zero through nine to the five button, double-number, quick toggles. He touched the seven, rocked it to six, and rocked it to six again. Tapped nine, and rocked it to zero.

The Transcend started up and revved with a dusk bison, growl-like rev.

We have unfinished business, you and I. Ben turned his gaze to Malcom who stared back defiantly. *You'll stay here tonight, and we'll settle it tomorrow at sundown. Understood?*

Malcolm narrowed his eyes and nodded.

Ben eyed Ur-Krurk and asked in Giant, *Understood? *

The ogre nodded and grabbed Malcolm by the neck, leading him to the building. "Time for you to face the carnage you caused."

"How do I strap myself in?" Tex climbed into the passenger seat and looked around the center console.

Wishing he could take his companion along, Ben sighed and suffered the pain to shake his head sadly.

"I know I'm not allowed in the bazaar itself, but I could help you reprogram the cards, or, be ready with the car in case you have to make a hasty retreat." Tex started to climb out. "Or, you know, just hang out in the car."

Ben's chest warmed at his companion's dedication. He lipped, *Sorry.*

"I know," Tex said as he perched on the doorframe.

"You'd use me if you could." He dropped out of sight. A light *tink* indicated that he had hit the ground. "Be careful."

An inward cringe shook Ben as he thought about checking his neck in the mirror. *Nope.* He hit the gas.

Chapter Forty-Three

HOW BAZAAR

BEN PULLED INTO THE LARGE, over-stuffed dirt lot surrounding Bauman's Bazaar. Just like every night of the Samhain festival, the cars, carts, and wagons of the starwise filled the area to near capacity. As before, most regular spots were taken and most of the overspill had jammed up the parking lane thoroughfares. Far off, the tents and lights of bazaar played on the not-so dark, distant horizon like a spiced cider-scented mirage. About to head back out to try one of the other entrances, Ben noticed an arrow directing him further in to *Vendors' Parking*.

What in the world could Malcolm possibly have for sale?

Ben followed the arrow deeper into the lot. As he approached a fully-blocked lane, a glowing, forest-green ramp appeared, stretching ahead before curving off to the right. *Okay…* He drove onto the ramp.

The Transcend shut off, the ramp lifted the car to a second-tier track parallel with the ground, and, without turning back on, the car sped down the track like a miniature train.

He passed over people laughing, people arguing, and even some folks conducting transactions between cars, some of whom looked up at him as he went over.

The car crossed into the *Vendor Lot* where it passed over several empty spots and then stopped four rows out from the entrance to lower the Transcend into the closest of the remaining available spots.

If someone is waiting for Malcolm or surveying this... Ben touched the center of the hood and pulsed Krotosian magic into it. As before, it seemed to fill with warm water before activating.

Ben undid the spellcard holder and pulled out the reprogrammed spellcards. He stuffed *Shield* into the hoodie's right pocket—*what's this?*—where he discovered the rough length of a rusty nail. He shrugged at the discovery of Malcolm's hook and placed *Achilleus* in his left pocket. Lastly, he put *Blast* and Malcolm's tether together in his front pants pocket.

Keeping his tablet between his leg and the car door, Ben cued up Eleven Soul Sight and slid the duration to his maximum. *Sixteen awatts for eight hours. That's a huge chunk of the hundred available. It'll be better to cast it hour by hour... But casting from the tablet in there, among the shoppers, would call attention.* Ben pressed the *Cast* button formed from clusters of stars on his tablet.

The Anvilsmith drummed on the door as it vibrated between against the handle and his leg. Starlight started to rain down as the energy settled in his eyes. The spell made the colorful tent city take on an otherworldly sheen.

Ben got out and—can't resist—twisted his torso and leaned back to keep from turning his neck to look to the dark sky above. The North Star shone brightly and had a few friends shining with it through the vault of light over the city.

About to stride across the few rows to one of the pay stations, Ben stopped. His eyes narrowed as he took in the distant auras of the mingling crowds. *What about this made me stop?* He folded his arms and took a moment to analyze what worked at the threshold of comprehension. *Oh...* His eyes widened and his hand went to his chin to keep it from dropping in astonishment.

Most of them only have one type of magic, the blue kind, at their disposal. He held his jaw. *I always thought* everyone *had access to one of the five colors that comprised all traditional casters' mystic energy.* He gawked at the auras that ran the full spectrum of blue from a very faint azure to deep cobalt. The center masses were mostly cerulean and only one out of ten had a font of Vibros, Argos, or Krotos rolling around one of their chakras. *Even fewer have two... I would have never thought...*

Moving through the cars, he made a mental note to question Uk'so about the blue magic the goblins possessed. Closing on the entrance, he steeled his thoughts to obscure them from readers.

Ben stopped at the vacant booth and grabbed one of the small glass orbs. It reminded him of the Blood Berry Fairies' bauble. *It's just a little bigger.* No one ever was inside, but the entrance fee had to be paid or the invisible magical barrier would bar entrance. Keeping his neck stiff, Ben twisted his torso to see if anyone watched him.

Other patrons were infrequent and at other nearly vacant booths on this side of the bazaar.

Alright. Ben took one more look then lowered the orb and placed it against the tablet's microUSB power slot where it ebbed out an arcane watt.

"Keep it." The whisper came from within the booth. A floating feminine face appeared. Her eyes dropped to the Anvilsmith, then rose to wink as they searched for eye contact. The face motioned him to go in. "Don't worry. You're good."

Ben's brow rose in surprise and immediately knitted in suspicion. *Glad my face is hidden.* Bending from his lower back, Ben bowed to show appreciation.

Bodiless, the face lowered a similar distance.

Prior to this, only Toad and his fellow APA students had shown him this much cursory respect. For a moment, Ben considered the deep folding bow Jack— the tattooed thief who had stolen his possessions months ago—performed before him, and quickly discounted it. *The thief used my need for respect to establish, and sustain, his deception.*

Ben placed the glowing emerald bauble into his right front pocket and headed into the Bazaar. Expecting to smack against the invisible field as he had seen anxious kids do before their parents paid the admittance, Ben continued forward as though he knew it wouldn't happen.

The sudden sweet scent of spiced cider signaled that he had passed through the threshold and transitioned into the temporary resident tents on the marketplace's outermost circle. As usual, several of the jovial renters milled around, socializing with one another. Any who noticed the tablet hanging from his hip gave him a deliberate smile and a slight nod.

Further in, unless you were an Archon Private Academy student, merchants at standing stalls on the edge of the bazaar always pressed new arrivals trying to make a quick sell. The crush on him, as a Dunn-Blatt was everything Ben had always seen at a distance. However, instead of hawking their wares, they pressed items upon him without stating a price.

First in his hands was an open backpack from an exotic, scantily veil-clad, dusk-skinned woman. "For your books, a new haversack."

Next, a quill from a tall Asian gentleman in pale robes tailored to be above the knee. "For your papers."

"For your threads." A dark hand rattled a package of needles at him, and Ben's gaze followed it into the backpack. It landed upon a growing pile of items that he had not seen placed into the leather backpack.

What's going on?

The crowd parted, and he stopped before a stocky, eight-foot tall, bald, female merchant in sparkling, full-length orange and red robes. She, with great, purposeful disgust, had looked away from him and any other Academy student who came through. She presented three purple—*it's the same shade of violet as the Dunn-Blatt colors*—velvet-bound vellum volumes.

The hawkers around him gasped appreciatively.

She placed them in the backpack. "May your magic blossom, Bravado, and thrive."

The other vendor's stunned reaction signaled how

big a deal this was. Ben bit his lip to prep for the blazing pain before bending his neck in admiration.

Flaring her sparkling robes, she moved to the side and bowed low.

What is going on? Striving to understand, he eased forward. The bazaar proper now lay before him and most of the merchants further in were looking his way to see what was happening. *I wonder if there's a way for them to tell who I'm supposed to be based on the hoodie. If so, what makes Malcolm such a rock star?*

Ben flipped the incredibly light backpack closed, buttoned it, and slid it onto his back. He adjusted the straps to rest on the edge of his shoulders, far away from the burned, sensitive flesh. As he moved deeper into the marketplace, random shoppers patted him gently on the back, and a majority of the merchants took the time to formally bow when he passed.

Trying to scrutinize Malcolm' apparent fame, Ben gritted his teeth. *Alright, he gets preferred parking, free gifts, and general admiration?* He massaged his temples. *Not being able to figure this out is really starting to piss me off. Think, Ben. Think.*

Distracted by his own conundrum, Ben barely managed to stop just in time to keep from bowling into a patron wearing an APA tan trench coat. *Hey a fellow student!* Ben recognized the short, curly-red-haired Dueling Adept instantly. *Adept Love...* Twisting his torso instead of his neck, Ben naturally looked around for others, but, against his own advice, Love shopped alone in the bazaar.

The small man pressed his fist on his hips, narrowed his eyes, and spat anger in his familiar nasal whine,

"Bold, Dunn-Blatt." His green eyes appraised Ben in a ruthless way no instructor, Collins included, looked at students. The Adept's lips barely moved when his eyes went form the Anvilsmith on Ben's hip to peer into the dark hood with a deadly, emerald spark in his eyes. "Very. Bold."

Chapter Forty-Four

LARS

BEN'S BREATH abandoned him when he became cognizant of the circle of nonchalant-acting patrons forming around him and the man who taught everyone at his school how to duel.

Love flipped his coat back from his holstered tablet.

Holy.

Shit.

Ben's guts turned to ice and his lungs went cold. His breath refused to return. His knees began to shake. His bladder and bowels quivered with a very real, imminent threat to release their contents.

About to bow deeply to yield, Ben stepped back and bumped into someone inside the circle. He clenched his cheeks. *Don't crap your pants. Don't crap your pants.*

He pivoted to see the Arch-Primary of Las Vegas, Las Lightningpalm. The Chief Magistrate's robes had the same cut as any of his Lesser Judges, but his were a resplendent golden yellow. With the back of his hand, he pushed Ben to a Primary at the side, but still in the circle. The blond man moved his waist-long mane behind him and stood tall without his baton. He set a resolute fist on his hip as Adept Love had.

The hair on Ben's arms stood when he spied the raised gold lightning bolt set in obsidian signet ring.

Both men stared at the other. Neither spoke.

Adept Love didn't bow, but he did turn away.

Lars lowered his fist.

The Adept's red curls bounced as he burst from the circle. Forcing his way through the crowd, he called back over his shoulder, "I'll get a student, then!"

Ben found a breath. And then another. Little by little, his bodily functions began to resume their standard business as usual functions. He unclenched his cheeks.

Lars moved to stand before him.

He clenched up again.

"Relax, Bravado." Lar's breath smelled of dragon fruit and his smooth tenor voice held an intriguing, old-fashioned-radio-announcer quality to it that begged for attention. "I can have Primaries escort you to your car if you are not ready for a duel."

Wide-eyed in being spoken to by the Chief Magistrate as though he were an equal, Ben recovered, blinked, and shook his head—*ahh!*—and grimaced.

"Good." The Arch-Primary nodded to the milling crowd who all turned their backs to walk away. Unlike before, even the nearby merchants abandoned their booths. Lars gathered his hair, wrapping it around him like a shawl as he removed a pin. Released, his hair dangled near the ground.

Wow.

Lars presented the needle for Ben to see.

What are you going to do with that? Ben found his breath leaving again as the Chief Magistrate moved the point closer to his chest. A hand-shaped metal badge appeared around the needlepoints as the tip kinked into a lightning bolt across the palm.

"I can always use folks of your caliber, drive, and dedication to keep magic pure. For tonight, you shall have my shelter from any non-student caster." Lars pointed to a minuscule amber stone inlaid where the end of the bolt met the palm. "Touch this after you kill another. I'll come collect the body, gift you with a seven-stone spell of your choosing, and will have delivered to you, the Ape's weight in obdurium. I expect big things from you, Bravado. Big things."

Stunned, Ben nodded before remembering to bow. *How deep do I go?* He kept bending, moving his head deeper, and then closer to his knees.

The heels of soft leather boots clicked the moment his forehead tapped his shins. "It is I who should bow to you." The Chief Magistrate didn't. He turned to walk away and paused. "Once you have your fill of seven stones, I will up the bounty to eights." Lars strode away and called to the retreating crowd, "One by one!"

The masses pivoted and, instead of repeating what had been said like the night prior, they answered, "Until there are no more!"

Each of the patrons and vendors had returned. Most moved directly toward him to toss small gems, platinum, and gold coins as his feet. They all murmured various forms of sincere appreciation for "the deed that needs doing" or "the task at hand" or "purifying the traditions." Nothing direct like *thanks for killing an technomancer*.

A second wave of passersby lobbed silver on top of the gold as Ben stood rooted to the spot, anchored, completely, by the hatred of the mystical world as it showered him with riches. Even the preteen, who had stolen the white wand, threw a copper on the pile.

"Hold on, Sir," a child, no taller than his waist, in rich orange mink fur smiled up at him.

"Yeah." Another child, this one bald, with a long gazelle-like neck beamed. "We'll get these for you."

A third squat boy with pigtails laid a sack on the ground. "Courtesy of my father." He pointed to the mustachioed merchant who had wanted to buy the platinum sword focus from Ben. The rotund man rubbed his belly before bending as far as his girth allowed. The boy grinned and gushed, "It's a quad-stitched holding bag."

The three worked at a quick, playful pace, each trying to collect more than the other two. The coins and gems were gathered into the sack before they tied it onto the bottom of his backpack. Waving farewells, the three of them went back to their respective parent's tents.

Ben released the breath he'd only just realized he'd been holding.

Blood had withdrawn to his stomach leaving his arms and legs cold. He struggled to grasp what had just happened. *I've just received more respect and adoration than any technocaster in the history of our craft.* The first step away from the spot proved to be the hardest.

They want us all dead.
He took another step.
Every one of us.
And another.
Dead.

Chapter Forty-Five

ONE OF THEM

WITH THE FINAL clue to the riddle of Malcolm's rock star status, the smell of sage-seasoned meat, spiced cider, and various baked good melded into a blur around Ben, punctuated by the frequent murmured affirmations and the endless pats on his back. Everything, even the nodding, smiling crowd parting before him, became vague background observations

The Adepts at the Archon Private Academy made sure to drive home the point about how technomancy was disliked by those outside of the school. The frequency of their warnings increased as they neared major events, and on the week before Samhain festival, each Adept would stress the fact at least twice per class. For students attending the festival, they advised against leaving the fenced fairground and encouraged students to travel in pairs. Having seen other schools' practitioners employ the same tactics, Ben always figured his teachers were spouting, what should've been common sense.

What they failed to mention is how murdering an Academy student—Ben absentmindedly brushed his hand against his tablet—*or appearing to have done so, makes the killer a hero. Lars Lightningplam, the Chief Magistrate himself, offered me nothing short of a true bounty with a promise to keep the slayings secret.*

Recalling the various Initiates and Apprentices who —*faces regularly seen in the halls one week, gone forever the next*—Ben had always figured either failed out or quit the APA, his slow pace began to pick up as his senses returned.

Merchants who spied the device on his hip continued to bow, the crowd murmuring and patting his back.

Ben's posture changed as, behind the hood's darkness, he frowned at the traders and well-wishers. His back rounded as he increased his pace and leaned forward to stalk through the bazaar. Ready to do damage, he hoped *Man, oh man. Please let me be there when the assassin comes for Papa Mojo. I'd love to unleash my Rage from these pompous traditionalists at someone deserving.*

His energies began to roil.

People stopped patting his back. The murmur of congratulations changed to "man on a mission" and "happy hunting" and "put another one down."

Why haven't my parents told me? Do they know? Do any of the other guys or their parents know?

The weight of a hard stare snapped his attention back. *Please be the assassin.* Ben spun.

The small merchant at Goodspice's Goods, the one who had sold Neil a full collection of four and five-stone spells, stood on the stacked barrels outside his solid green tent. The merchant extended his hand and rolled his wrist to point his thumb at the ground. He then crossed his arms over his paunch, and turned his back.

Ben's fist balled tighter. *How dare you thumb me down, you—* As though the realization were a wall, Ben came to a sudden stop. *He's not thumbing me down, he's thumbing me for the very same reason others gave me gifts, currency and adoration.* Ben marveled at the strength of the merchant's character. *And he's doing it publicly.*

"Roasted walnuts, sir?" a short, skinny baker next to Goodspice, who had noticed the thumbing, called. The man waved a peacock-feathered fan. A magical breeze carried several homey scents to Ben's nose.

Ben's stomach growled.

The man switched to fanning loaves of bread. "No one can best my banana. No? Perhaps pumpernickel is more to your liking? No? How about rye?"

Nearly forgotten, a deep hunger gnawed at him. *Right now, I rather starve than eat anywhere I'd be welcomed.*

Amongst the sea of robes and fur coat, a blue jean jacket caught Ben's eye which took in the brown flattop haircut. *Is that that the same guy…?* He recalled the man from a month ago. *Yeah, that's one of the guys who handed mundane cash through the white Legerity's window at the Pinball Hall of Fame and drove one of the neon cars that shot at, and chased, me.* Thinking about breaking off a piece of his rage for this guy put a small smile on Ben's lips. *Blast him, like he did me.*

Ben considered the man's blue aura and the Krotosian

energy that floated around his crown chakra. No. Ben let his smile fall. *Perhaps I'll challenge him properly after Mojo is safe. I'd hate to squander power now and come up dry when it matters most.*

On brown flattop's right, as though pulling up next to him in a car—*the other jean jacket guy, the one with red hair*—closed on his compatriot with two tall mugs. Between the two mugs, a familiar red-and-yellow amulet—*Komir's amulet*—bounced on his chest as he bopped and whistled.

Seeing the gift given to him, personally, by Elder Komir on his sixteenth birthday, a symbol that didn't exist on this side of the mystical door deep in Pepperjacks, Ben jammed hands into the hoodie's pockets. Gripping his *Shield* and *Achilleus* spellcards, he channeled Argosian energy into both. The refreshing smell of fresh-cut pineapples filled his nose before Shield's mint scent had a chance to register. His blood started to race as the air before him hardened. *If Red isn't the one who took my body, I'll eat my coat and loafers!* Ben fished the rusty nail from his pants pocket and let Krotosian magic slip into it.

The emerald challenge tether shot form the nail. Arcing around and over the crowd of other casters, it dipped down at the last moment to drive the tiny hook squarely into the whistler's chest, just underneath Komir's pendant.

A myriad of roasting meat, fresh fruit, drink aromas, colognes and perfumes from around the flattop poured into the tether and wafted to Ben.

He fingered the second stitch inside both sleeves —*Writhing Wreath* and *Napalm Arrow*—and fed

Argosian energy to both hungry spellstiches. The ground around him lit as two solid-fire compound bows appeared, twanged sizzling arrows at Red, then faded. The arrows left flaming trails as they raced down the line to the target.

The shaft stuck into the air, just short of contact. *Crap, he activated the amulet.*

Azure energy twisted up Red's throat in a waving line.

He's using silence? In a duel? Still, Ben wished he had a way to counter it.

Frantic powder-blue energy caught his attention as it bounced in a star formation in Brown Flattop's chest before a small pyramid shot from his forehead.

What's that spell? Readying for the worst as the spells flew at him, Ben tightened.

Chapter Forty-Six

SPELLBOUND

A STREAM OF AZURE ENERGY, the *Silence* spell anchored on something—the wreath—above Ben's head. The world lost sound as the powder blue pyramid expanded around him, rotated point down, and faded without apparent effect.

Two at once, Ben. Not smart. Keep his left hand on Writhing Wreath, Ben laid a finger across *Napalm Arrow*, *Fireball*, and *Firestorm*. *If only I had the other guy tethered, too.*

A yellow-robed arm reached out from his side. The hand with a gold lightning bolt set in obsidian signet ring—*Lightningpalm*—reached out and—*what? How?*—snatched the tether from Ben's chest to take the challenge on for himself. *Why?*

Streams of golden lighting shot down the line.

The whistler's mouth sprang open, twisting in silent agony as the yellow power beat relentlessly at the barrier before his chest.

Brown Flattop turned away, and ran.

Ben reached out to take the tether back.

Mouth moving, as to give order, Lars knocked Ben's hand away before he could steal the challenge back, and pointed after Brown.

Before Ben could project, *To Hell with that guy. This one has my amulet,* a powder-blue pyramid flashed before his eyes and his telepathic sentences came out horribly jumbled, twisted, and warped. *What the heck?* Ben's neck flared in pain when he shook his head to dismiss the glyph. He made another play for the tether—

Lars frowned.

—Ben stopped.

Lars pointed. Lars made a fist.

Damn it! Not wanting to, Ben tore off after the guy with the brown flattop. *If Lightningpalm had only tried to give me audible orders, I—Silenced—could've ignored the command, but the hand motions left no questions. He wants me to get this guy and beat him down.*

There was enough distance between him and the runner for the crowd to have parted for the sprinter and come back together after he'd passed.

Even with the extra prowess from Achilleus, there were too many people for Ben to try and navigate. A powder blue pyramid glyph flashed before his eyes again as he tried to project, *Move out of the way!*

Ben ran to the side, jumped onto a merchant's table, and ran across it. The backpack of hate-goods swung and bopped on his back. *Slowing me down.* He shrugged it off, leapt to the next table, and the next.

Further ahead vendors scooped their wares table clear and, their voices muted, cheered him on.

The crowd turned his direction. Chanting, they parted for him. The glyph flashed before he eyes when he tried to read their lips. *What are they saying?*

The runner glanced back, zigzagged, and disappeared down a narrow corridor between red tents.

Holy crap, if this guy's an assassin, too, he's probably head right for Mojo now! Committed to get the guy for his own reasons now, Ben forced his way sideways, bounded off a merchant's table and leapt at the second red pavilion. The tight fabric absorbed his moment and he slid down the mouth of corridor's tight opening.

The few merchants along the narrow way between the shops glanced at the tablet on his waist and pointed to the left side of the intersection ahead.

Ben leaned to take a step in when a hook landed in his shoulder. *Crap!* With a challenge tether hooked into him from behind, he could go no further away. Waiting for Lars to snatch this one, too, Ben turned. *Impossible.* The challenge's arched tether curved high and away into a distance reserved for only the longest-range spell. *No tether could cover half that distance.*

Yet, as the challenge began, nearly the exact same mixture of scents he had sampled when he issued his challenge to Red came to him.

Somewhat amazed, by the incredible distance, and unable to continue his pursuit, Ben watched the bazaar patrons part as the high emerald arch dropped to form a straight light.

Recalling that reasons behind challenges could be felt, the same damn Silence glyph appeared before his eyes when he tried to send the urgent need to postpone the challenge in order to save a life. He tried to swat the tiny pyramid, but it faded and he found expressing his feeling through the tether as difficult as trying to project his thoughts to others. *Well, I have no issue feeling their murderous intent.*

Down the cleared path, some five hundred feet away, three casters in APA tan trench coats stood.

I don't have time for this, guys! Ben bowed to send his surrender down the line.

Surrender denied, their outrage boiled back to him.

As though someone pushed the badge the Chief Magistrate had pinned to his chest, Ben spun. At the edge of patrons forming broken circle—to let the challenger through—Lars stood. The Arch-Primary made a series of motions.

Right. Grab the tether, and… shake it? Dance?

From down the line, the challenger closed at speed beyond perception.

Kevin, looking more like Collins now than when he threatened to duel LeRoy last night, stood fifty feet away—the shortest range for a clean duel.

Closer—*come on, let go*—Ben tried to relent again.

Jaw locked and teeth clenched in the way of Collins, Kevin's lips moved as he gave his head a slight shake.

Well—Ben thumbed the spellstiches—*this sucks.*

Chapter Forty-Seven

DUELING

No one in the crowd around them pretended to mill around. No, these patrons' mouths twisted in yells and chants Ben couldn't hear. Like the throngs who packed the stands at the old WDF Circuit matches, they were animated and most, desiring the duel end either his or Kevin's—preferably Kevin's—death, formed an *X* with their forearms. The stink of their excitement crowded in and curled Ben's nose. *Monsters. And you think you're civilized.*

Lars pantomimed grabbing the tether, again.

Sensing Kevin about to attack, Ben focused on his aura to read what would be coming—*where's the magic*—and blinked stupidly.

Kevin's aura was a dull, matte gray. *There's life, but not a lick of magic.* Kevin shook as the edge of his aura where the Anvilsmith laid against him started to flash green, pumping emerald energy into the otherwise mystically empty vessel. The power rolled in Kevin's stomach before shooting up to his shoulder.

It's a Blast. Without the spell handy, Ben planned to release a blast from the Writhing Wreath above his head as he grabbed onto the tether—

BEN'S AWARENESS EXPANDED. *Three other duels are happening in the bazaar. A large battle raged at the base of Sunrise Mountain. A powerful ritual to drive demonic spirits from the last house on Camino Del Norte neared its height.*

THE HALO of light around him vanished as the magic in Kevin died and sound returned to the world.

Everyone, shut up! Their yells, chants, and cheers were incomprehensible. Consonants and vowels had no basis and oft warred to topple into each other. *It's as though everyone knows a private dialect of gobbledy-gook.*

One voice rose above the hubbub. Smooth. Confident. Made sense. *Lars.* The words Ben heard didn't match the motions of his mouth. *His voice is coming from the badge.*

Lar projected, *Challenge him with manabarbs. Apes can't keep up.*

Energy from Kevin's Anvilsmith jackhammered into his empty shell. The emerald energy settled in the gray chest before evaporating.

What spell is that? An ice storm broke out around Ben, plunging the temperatures to below zero. His ear and nose froze, becoming frostbitten. Hail rained down. Some of the crowd were in the spell's radius, but the tether assured Ben was the only one to suffer the effects. Ice pellets the size of tennis balls slammed down on him. Two, in rapid succession, cracked on his chest and broke his collarbone.

Ben bit his lip and forced the bellow rising to his throat, down into his chest. His Argosian font swelled. He thumbed the fourth stitch to summon a dusk bison.

Channel raw energy at him. Lar's voice insisted from the badge. *It'll guarantee you the win.*

Ben squeezed the tether. *I don't want to exploit a weakness, but time is on the assassin's side.*

Hailstones pummeled Ben's back. He opened his Krotosian font and channeled it at Kevin.

Violet energy danced down the tether toward the target, just as the yellow had from Lars. *Pure Krotosian energy.* It howled like a banshee at Kevin who flinched away.

Emerald energy shot from Kevin's Anvilsmith meeting Ben's Krotosian energy a few inches before his schoolmate's chest. The device flashed full of green power and, in a painfully sluggish way, began to deplete downward. *It may be a sure win, but it's so freakin' slow.*

Kevin tapped at his device, but it continued to flow in the line to keep the purple from hitting.

Have to make this faster. As though he were casting a second spell, Ben opened his Krotosian font.

Kevin's tablet looked like it had been mystically punctured when energy from the power slot arced out to spill into the tether.

I should open a third... The ice storm ended and Ben's broken bones began to knit.

Kevin shook his Anvilsmith and yelled at it.

Ben empathized with Kevin's frustration. *Wanting to*

cast spells, but having to watch the awatt meter tick down to nothing is difficult.

It took thirty seconds for Kevin's Anvilsmith to empty. When it did, Kevin bowed.

The crowd's roar rose to a fever pitch as many of them stroked their arms down through the air signaling for Ben to cut off Kevin's head.

Ben ignored them, his thoughts turning back to chasing the, jean jacket-wearing, brown flat-topped, possible assassin. He began to turn and leave when everything, and everyone, in the bazaar froze in place.

Ben projected, *Hello?*

Chapter Forty-Eight

TO THE VICTOR

Everyone's frozen. Ben tried to move again. *Me too.*

Unable to move his eyes, the disgusting bloodthirsty mob around them remained unchanged. Men, women, and children, like a picture, fixated on what they expect to happen.

Kevin stood at the center of his field of vision, his head bowed. Looking at his defeated schoolmate, a vague, revolting understanding—*if I pull on the tether, I'll rip his soul out*—washed over Ben.

No way!

He tried to release the tether—and found his Krotosian energy reluctant to release.

Let go—Wait...

A realization—*Kevin has over fifty arcane abilities, mostly tether-related, and they can all be mine if I pull the tether*—settled on Ben's soul. Gary's lecture during Samhain, about the dangers of dueling and gaining abilities came back to him. Oh man... Over fifty arcane abilities—everything Kevin had worked for—mostly tether-related could be his.

I only have to pull and the Impossible Shot, the Distance, the Near Instant Travel all flow down the tether. All that—plus more—mine.

I only have to pull.

Oh man...

Chapter Forty-Nine

TOP JUNIOR CASTER

No.

As Ben's hand sprang open, movement and sound returned to everyone. Tears forming in his wide eyes, Keven stood upright, looked into the darkness of Ben's hood, and instantly doubled over into a folding bow.

Lightningpalm's face screwed up in confusion as the normally well-composed Arch Primary grabbed his forehead trying to understand why Kevin's soul hadn't been yanked clean.

Kevin's aura remained gray, but his Anvilsmith began to recover energy.

Whoa! Ben's own energy reserves swelled to half full. *Alright!* Ben clacked his heels to acknowledge the deep bow, and took off down the tent corridor. *First left,* he reminded himself, and repeated. *First left.*

A blast slammed into Ben's shoulder as he started to make the turn, turning his world green. He stumbled into the tents and rolled on the ground. *Ah, Kevin, you're just like Malcolm.*

That stupid little pyramid glyph flashed before his eyes, and kept flashing. He glanced back.

Similar to his vision from last night, LeRoy stood at the mouth of the tent corridor, yelling in that same gobbledy-gook that everyone but Ben could understand, motioned for him to get up.

No tether? Ben scanned. *Stupid glyph. No, no tether.* He scrambled to his feet—*Mojo's still at risk*—and took the first left.

LeRoy yelled after him.

"I understand about not publicly executing the ape and forgive you." Lars' voice came to him through the pin, "But you got that one in private. Finish it."

Screw you. Ben stopped at an intersection where, straight ahead, it would lead out into the open bazaar. *Making a left would do the same.* He turned to go right and a second green blast slammed into his nearly-healed shoulder, spinning him like a top into a purple tent.

Crap, which way?

The light blue pyramid glyph continued as he scanned the four directions, spotted LeRoy winding up another spell, and used his schoolmate for bearing.

This way. He got to his feet and ran into a deep dead-end. *Might be some small corridors.*

There weren't.

As he went deeper, he finally spied two dusty black tents at the far end of a row with a rope dangling down. *Just like Diviners' Row at the Samhain festival.*

A third blast slammed into his lower back, sending him flying forward to flop on his face.

Ben spun as he stood.

The colors of the tents, the length of the corridor, the smell of spiced cider, the sound of a pot boiling where and how LeRoy stood...

This was his vision from the other night.

Tablet in hand, LeRoy extended his arms to touching the tents by his side as though to show there was nowhere for Ben to go and no way for him to get out without going through him.

If I turn and run to the rope, he'll blast me and we'll end up dueling. Ben scanned the area as though searching for an alternate escape. *Play worried.*

Play worried? Ben repeated the thought as it occurred to him that he'd just dissed LeRoy.

Before tonight, this exact scenario would've made me break out in cold sweat. I'd hope to be having a nightmare so I could wake up from it. Now... Ben smiled grimly at having complete confidence—*not cocky, not conceit, just confidence*—in his ability to protect himself. *...I'm just playing worried when I'm not. Not in the least.*

The only "worry" he felt was for Mojo.

LeRoy raised his hands with whatever he was saying and returned his arms to their wide open length as swagger poured into his walk. His mouth kept making arrogant turns and twitches as he spoke his tongue waggling as he kept pace with Ben backing further and further into the dead-end and closer to the ropes dangling between the tents behind him.

The glyph flashed and faded in the middle of LeRoy's boasting. "—go ahead." LeRoy crossed his arms and stopped advancing. He flicked a finger at the rope. "Climb on up, you little bitch. I'll still be here to kick your ass when you come back down."

Ben bumped into the rope. *I don't believe you, LeRoy.* Sensing a trick, Ben slowly put his hand into his front pocket.

"Go ahead, Dumb-Blatt. Tether us. I'll kick your ass and then snuff your ass."

Ben grabbed his Blast spellcard. He made sure not to turn his back as he moved around the rope. Slowly, he extended his other hand to grab the rope.

Energy bounced from LeRoy's gut to his shoulders as he fired two emerald blasts.

Ben channeled Argosian, Krotosian, and Nilosian energy into his card as he returned fire with a triple Blast.

The red and purple diffused LeRoy's greens in midair, and Ben made the third, black, bolt dissipate inches from his schoolmate's chest.

Eyes wide and expecting to be knocked back, LeRoy stumbled backwards from the dissipated black energy.

Ben projected, *You may be able to best your schoolmates, but I'm a whole different matter.* Ben grabbed the ropes with both hands. *It's your choice if you want to be here when I come down.* He pulled on the rope.

Chapter Fifty

TOO LATE

THE TENTS and bazaar fell away to the—*optical illusion*—of infinite darkness. *Papa Mojo's sanctum.* Ben sniffed and then forced air out his nose. *Still reeks of mildew and mothballs.* Recalling his first tip into the diviner's wagons, Ben spun. *Where's the light? Where's the crystal ball?*

Crap. Though it would present him as a target—*if the assassin's in here*—Ben channeled Argosian energy into his *Writing Wreath* spellstich to light the area.

Ben spun again. On the whole, the darkness of Mojo's walls prevailed, but— *There!* He moved toward the diviner who sat still with his skeletal fingers gripping the crystal ball.

Mojo. Ben projected. *Let's get out of—*

As he reached Papa Mojo, he abruptly realized that the diviner had been turned to stone.

Ben tried to yell his rage at not being able to save Papa Mojo in return. His throat burned as his wrecked voice warbled. He balled his fists and looked around, but there was nothing more to Mojo's area than the entryway and the room containing the small table.

To be certain, Ben searched again, but the dimensions of Papa Mojo's stinky sanctum hadn't changed. He sat down across from the diviner and looked into his empty stone gaze.

"Sorry." Pain reawakened, Ben's throat seared as he stood and walked away. As he reached the exit, he looked back once more at the diviner who had saved his life, the scene etching itself in his memory.

Ben sighed. *I really hope LeRoy's not there.*

He turned away from Mojo and left the diviner's tent.

Chapter Fifty-One

JUST IN TIME

THE SMELL of spiced cider swirled back to him as the long corridor where he left LeRoy swam back into being.

LeRoy was there, but his schoolmate stood frozen mid-turn as though he were about to leave. Lars Lightningpalm had just finished cutting a deep line on LeRoy's face with a black blade, and raised the tip to LeRoy's throat.

Hearing distant footsteps, Ben projected, *"Their Master's coming!"*

Lars glanced to him, then in the direction of the footsteps and touched his ring.

Ben felt as though Lar's hand were on his chest where the pin was as magic flowed through the badge. He caught a glimpse of Kevin at the end of the corridor before the bazaar spun away and he stood alone next to Malcolm's car in the parking lot.

Not knowing what Lars had cut into LeRoy's face, Ben enjoyed the trilled rushed of having stopped the

Chief Magistrate from jamming the blade into LeRoy's throat. *That was close.* He thought about Kevin at the corner. *Lars could've had them both.*

"Thank you for the heads up." Lars' voice came to him from the pin. "I still expect big things of you, Bravado. Do not disappoint me."

Ben took the pin off and tossed it in the car. *So very sick of you.*

A hook sunk into his back. Ben sighed.

"I don't' want to duel, Malcolm." It was Neil's voice behind him. The tether confirmed the necromancer's intention to get an item from him. "You went to school with us and I considered Ben a friend. Give me his Anvilsmith so we can bury it in place of his body, or—" Neil's voice took on a fierce edge. "Or perish."

If he could speak, Ben would've been at a loss for words. Holding the hoodie to obscure his burned neck, he turned to face Neil and enjoyed the way his normally indifferent schoolmate's pale eyelids rose in surprise when he pulled the hood back disbursing the shadows that covered his face.

Chapter Fifty-Two

(IN) THE END

SITTING on the back of Neil's Transcend, just outside the property line of the red behemoth that was Pepperjacks, and against the sky threatening to break into dawn at any moment, Ben reached over his schoolmate's dormant Golemcast, and pulled a bottle from the Goodspice Spiced Ale four-pack. As he lifted the bottle out, another rose up from the bottom of the cardboard container to fill the empty slot.

How many bottles does it hold? Ben asked,

Neil sat, staring at Pepperjacks. *Forty-eight.*

Well, Ben began and paused. He kept glancing to Neil's companion and expecting it to move. It remained still. *I'm not sure where to start or how much to share.*

Neil twisted the metal cap form his bottle, tossed it next to the robot, and took a swig. He projected, *Start with how you got Malcolm out of his hoodie and conned him out of his car.*

The Golemcast leaned over to collect the top at half the speed Tex normally used.

The slow movement elicited a smile, and Ben twisted open his own bottle. The cinnamon-apple scent filled his nose. *Okay, I need a believable lie.* Ben took a deep, appreciative whiff before raising the drink to his lips.

Ben pulled it away without a sip. *"The bottle's warm."*

Neil spared him a glance. *"Goodspice's magical bottles makes their ambrosia act like it was freshly drawn from the tap."* He held his bottle up to the moon.

Ben smiled to himself. *I'd bet he's appreciating the magic more than the contents.*

Neil took a sip. *"Quite a hefty deposit."*

Ben raised the bottle and took a pull. *Mmm.* The delectably warm mix of apple, cinnamon, and nutmeg matched, exactly, the beverage he'd had in Goodspice's tent. Moreover, the fluid quieted the pain from his neck. An appreciative sigh escaped him as the goodness dropped into his stomach and spread warmth through his chest.

Got it. Ben smacked his lips. *I'll layer in some truth. "Took Malcolm's hook during Samhain, and he really wanted it back. Anyway, he called for a rematch."*

"Sounds like Malcolm." Neil retuned his attention to Pepperjacks. *"What were the stakes?"*

Ben tossed his cap further from the robot. It stood, lumbered over to the metal top, picked it up, and retuned to plop where it had started. *"He wanted to pit a platinum coin against the hook that he could beat me."* Ben turned his own gaze on Pepperjacks. *It looks ready for business. Why are they keeping it closed?* He continued, *"I felt confident and asked that we up the stakes."*

Neil nodded. *Malcolm had always been ambitious, but both car and casting device seems like a really risky wager.* The albino turned his powder pink eyes on Ben. *While I believe he might have gone for it, I really doubt you would have accepted. No matter your level of confidence.*

Looking back into the eyes, Ben steeled his thoughts. *Can't believe I let my guard down.*

Neil looked away. *You do not need to confide in me.* The sides of his face looked as though he were smiling. *I am glad Malcom finally got his proper comeuppance.*

Instead of replying, Ben took a drink.

Neil sipped at his bottle and fell silent, too.

For several minutes, they both sat silently, nodded absently, and enjoyed their drinks.

Neil slid down the side of his car. He placed the empty bottle next to the dormant robot and flipped the seat cushion to pull out a first aid kit. *Changing topics before you lie again.*

Ben smirked.

Neil turned the case over and started to punch in a combination.

Whoa. Ben averted his eyes, staring off at the casinos and the colors their lights—MGM Grand's emerald, Paragon's gold, the Luxor's white—turned the sky above. A bit of Vegas pride swelled in him. *How many other cities paint the night so beautifully?*

An opening click sounded. *Check these out, Ben.* Neil moved away from the kit. Inside were a score of bright green spellcards. *These little guys can hold second tier spells.* Respectful of what he held, Neil presented the case to Ben.

Thanks. Ben grinned. *If only you'd given these to be me before I blew myself up.*

Neil pulled at a Velcro strap and saw, organized in tight elastic slots, twenty unique spellcards.

Ben gawked. *Wow.*

A small smile played on Neil's lips. *Since we're in business together, figured I'd give you all of the four-stones to start working on.* Neil pushed the Velcro back, closed the case, and added, *They bring the quickest return.*

Ben looked up when he heard Neil's car door open.

His albino classmate slid in and started his red school-colored Transcend. Neil angled his rearview mirror instead of turning in his seat. *Once you've filled five with any of the different spells, shoot me a text.*

Ben finished his bottle and set it next to the robot as Neil had. *You can count on it.*

I plan to. Without further ado, Neil drove away.

DAWN HAD MADE good on its threat, but had yet to blossom into its full radiant glory before Ben made it back to the Meadows Towing.

All the bodies, and body parts are gone. Thank goodness.

Anxious to crack open one of the new spellcards to see if he had been right as to why his goldfish spellcards—*with their single obdurium strip*—would not hold a second tier spell, he rushed into the still-charred kitchen.

Licking barbeque from his fingers, Ur-Krurk stopped in mid-motion when he saw Ben. The ogre large, light-blue face had guilt written across its features like a dog who had been caught digging in the trash.

Ben scanned the blackened kitchen for any indicator of what Ur-Krurk had been up to. His eyes landed on a few naked orc daggers, the kind the dead doubtlessly had carried on their hips. Two of them had blood on them and the other looked licked cleaned.

"Blood-Son," the ogre edged toward the archway to the living room. "You normally only visit weekly."

What did you do? Coming closer, Ben stepped through the archway separating the kitchen and living room. Instantly, he cringed at the sight of Malcolm, in purple underwear, bruised and battered, his hands tied together. The unconscious Dunn-Blatt hung by his bonds from a hook in the center of the room, swaying slightly.

"Blood-Son," Ur-Krurk's voice turned timid as he eased closer. "From day one, you must lay the ground rules so they understand what can happen…"

Memory of the rope-burn rings on Penelope's wrists came rushing back. *Malcolm's not as bloody or beaten as she had been…* But the ogre had done serious damage in the few hours he'd had to work. Ben's gaze followed a thin stream of blood trickling weakly down the length of Malcolm's leg. It dripped from his toes into a deep soup pot beneath him.

"If you don't," Ur-Krurk's tone turned placating as the ogre's warm breath pillowed Ben in the smoky barbeque scent. "They'll begin to think they have equal ownership of the property."

Ben watched another drop fall.

"I didn't do his face." As though Ur-Krurk had

made the ultimate concession and Ben knowing would make it better, the ogre added, "He's not dead."

His fingers working *Writhing Wreath* and *Napalm Arrow* spellstitches, Ben rounded on Ur-Krurk who shrank toward the work bays. *Wonder how you'd like to be left hurting with permanent damage?*

Projecting his thoughts, Ben bared his teeth at the ogre, *You will take him down and place him in the guest quarters.* Ben moved backward to the sink to block Malcolm from his view and pointed to where the Dunn-Blatt hung. *Have the goblins tend to his wounds.*

The monster, which had been the cause of many of Ben's nightmares for the past couple of months cowered and bowed to his commands.

Ben added, *You will not torture—anyone—again unless directed by me. Understood?*

"Understood, Blood-Son."

Ben leaned against the sink for a moment. *I should have never left Malcolm alone with that monster.* Ben crossed his arms, summoned the will to watch, and went back to the archway.

The ogre went into the living room and took the limp body down with care.

Heavy footsteps tromped into the work bay. "Might-Fist..." Jek sounded surprised to see him. "We haven't had a chance to get things all cleaned up."

Ben glanced at the orc entering the kitchen. He pointed into the living room. *Did you know he was doing this?*

Jek moved next to him and watched as Ur-Krurk took out a knife to cut ropes. He gave his usual *doesn't concern me shrug.* "He's an ogre, Ben. Why would you expect anything different?"

I didn't know ogres had a thing for torture. Ben opened his mouth to reply. Instead, he shut his mouth and watched as Ur-Krurk lifted the body and went to the far stairs.

Jek opened the blackened refrigerator and pulled out two bottles of beer. He removed the tops with the knife on his hip, and extended one to Ben.

Ben shook his head. The pain silenced by Goodspice's cider roused slightly.

Jek put away his knife, shrugged, and set the bottle on the counter. "Granted, I don't know humans as I know my own kind, but a part of you must realize that you can never trust that human." Jek took a half-bottle draining guzzle. "Whether you agree with it or not, the kind of treatment Ur-Krurk just doled out will color that man's decisions for as long as he remembers this night."

Ben tried to see it through the orc's eyes. Though Malcolm had played a key role in Toad's plot, the Dunn-Blatt had been doubled-crossed and—*counting what the Blood-Berry Fairies did*—now doubly punished. *He called him a man. Sounds like he had plans for Malcolm.* Ben considered putting the cold beer bottle on his neck for a moment.

As much as Ben didn't want to admit it to himself, Jek had a point. Only time would tell if the coloring would be for betterment or ill.

Ben projected, *He's not much older than me. Why do you call him a man?*

"You own this place. You are a man." Jek picked

up the second bottle and moved to the sink to sit on the goblin's work stool. "The Dunn-Blatt came here and challenged for dominance, like a man. And when all this is done, he will reap what he sowed—like a man."

Ben forced his muscles to not shudder when he recalled the way Jek had shot Toad's chest into little more than mist. *Unlike Ur-Krurk, I know you'll disobey any order I give to leave Malcolm alone on a permanent basis.*

Wanting to consider the possibilities for a little longer, Ben prepared for the pain, changed topic, and whispered, "Tell me about the Blood-Son bond."

Jek rubbed his neck, got up to check the living room, and downed the rest of the first bottle. He rubbed his neck a second time and stepped close to Ben. Beer breath haunted his whisper. "I don't know how you came across the knowledge, but the ritual you performed has been the cause for many abrupt changes in allegiances between Giant-kin."

The orc raised the second bottle to his lips, took a long pull, before continuing. "There's a saying amongst the big men which goes, *'Feed your sons the beating heart of your brother, and his strength will be added to your line.'*" Jek took another swig and rocked his free hand from side to side. "Or something like that. The important thing is this." He leaned closer. "Giants believe in the shit and have magic to reinforce it."

Unable to take much more of the beer breath, Ben leaned away.

Still whispering, Jek backed away, "You and the tuzvul ate his son's heart, so, in his eyes—though she's dead—you are both his kin now." As though saying such things left him parched, Jek upended the bottle and guzzled it.

Ben switched back to his Dunn-Blatt problem, and projected, *About Malcom, give me some time to figure it out.*

"Sure thing, Might-Fist," Jek nodded and put both of the bottles in the sink. "I'll make sure he knows—with words alone—the consequences for trying to leave the property."

Ben considered the words. *"Fair enough. Thanks."*

Jek went into the living room.

Planning to go up to his bedroom, Ben followed and froze. Without Malcolm hanging there, his eyes went to where the circle of small charred remains had been. *"Jek?"*

Picking up the pot of blood, the orc turned. "Yeah?"

Ben did his best not to look like he wanted an affirming answer. *"Do goblins like marbles?"*

"More than ogres love to torture," Jek answered without hesitation. He then gave an *I don't get it* shrug. "The little guys can't get enough of 'em."

Conscious eased greatly, Ben went up to his room.

———

PRECISELY AT SUNDOWN, after dinner, Ben, now in his own school uniform, led Malcolm—in his colors—outside for a walk around Meadows Towing.

The neglected metal-and-plastic smell barely hung in the air, and the sky had that nice blue-purple color with several stars shining brightly overhead. They strolled in silence down rows and columns of stacked wrecks until they arrived at the water tower at the center of an almost fairy circle grouping of compactors.

Ben stopped and faced Malcolm. *I brought you out this far because I wanted to assure you clear line of sight to see no one will interrupt our duel.*

Malcolm crossed his arms. His injuries were well hidden by his school uniform. "So?"

Presenting Malcolm's rusty nail, Ben began to back away. He had to focus on Malcolm's wrist to see the rope burn. *When I took your hook, I said you could get it back after a year and a day.*

"You did." Seeing where this was going, Malcolm pulled up his sleeves. The bruises and cuts were quite obvious.

Don't feel sorry for him. Ben told himself. *His situation is all of his own doing.* Ben established eye contact to overlook the wounds, and kept moving backward. *But you didn't wait.*

"No, I didn't." Malcolm's prideful smile kicked up. "I had a shot at getting it back much sooner and when opportunity knocks, I answer."

Which is exactly why the orc who spoke to you last night will blow your head off if I cannot find a way to control you.

"Control me?" Malcolm laughed. "Good luck with that, Benny." He guffawed louder and leaned back to look up at the water tower."

Ben used the rusty nail to hook Malcolm.

"Ah, yes, the Retributive Paramountcy." Malcolm continued to smile and scan the water tower. "Is that orc hiding up there?"

No. Ben had moved fifty feet away to initiate a clean duel. Hoping Malcolm would say something, anything, which could resolve this in another manner, Ben returned to his line of reasoning. *I would let you go, but the orc will kill you, and if the orc fails, the ogre will hunt you down.*

Mention of Ur-Krurk took Malcolm's smile away and turned him feral. "When I beat you! When! I will have you order the orc to murder the filthy goblins, then demand the ogre kill the orc, and command the ogre to sit on a thirty-foot, barbed spike." Sneering Malcom began to roll his shoulders to loosen up. His voice cracked and his eyes moistened. "Then I'll work you like a puppet for the rest of your life." Malcolm's face twisted into a vengeful scowl. "I'll have you working the darkest skin-trade pits catering to those with the worst of desires."

Ben leaned back. *Wow. Where'd all the extra hate come from?* Jek's words about coloring Malcolm's perception rang back. Ben sighed, and projected, *I don't know what I did to you in the past, but I'm sorry it has come to this.*

"I'm not." Malcolm began to dance in place like Bruce Lee. "Come on! Name your duel."

Manabarbs.

Malcolm stiffened. "Come on. We both know you have three magical fonts at your disposal. You'll clobber me. Choose one I have a chance at winning."

Prior to hearing what you have in store for me and mine —by the way, the goblins aren't filthy—I might've. Ben projected. *Have to act now, so he doesn't talk me out of it.* Ben opened his Argosian reserve to send a ruby stream of crackling red energy down the tether. *Now, I know there no question. I have to win.*

Malcolm let out a ruby line of his own.

The energy clashed into a crackling crimson start at the center of the tether.

Malcolm released his howling, violet Krotosian energy.

Ben did the same.

Lavender collided with the violet a few feet from his chest to make a keening purple star.

Sorry, Malcolm. Ben next opened his Nilosian font down the Krotosian line. The vivid purple star darkened and sizzled as it flew down the line, stopping an inch from Malcom's chest. Ben then switched the Nilosian energy to the Argosian line turning the star a deep, sizzle-crackling brown. This star slid down the line, until it also hovered inches from Malcolm.

Ben kept rotating his Nilosian to the Krotosian and Argosian lines to make sure the stars stayed close to Malcolm. Concern wrinkled Ben's brow as his three sources of energy dropped below half. *Malcolm still looks strong.*

Sensing weakness, Malcolm leaned into the tether and grinned like a man possessed.

I have to bring this to an end. Ben opened a third line. Nilosian energy, blacker than the night, sizzled between the others to beat at Malcolm's two.

"You can tri-cast?" Though the struggle was ongoing, Malcolm's determined smirk dropped to a frown. The Dunn-Blatt shook his head. The mad grin returned and he leaned further into the tether trying to dump all of his energy into the line. "To Hell with you, Ben! To Hell with you!"

Shocked, at the stars flying his way, Ben opened up fully and dumped his mana.

Malcolm didn't get a chance to fret as the two stars went out and five lines of scintillating red, purple, and black energy blasted into his chest, throwing the Dunn-Blatt back, unconscious.

The tether between their torsos returned to a wispy emerald line. Ben's end centered in his chest, while Malcom's tether rose up his still body and anchored in his forehead.

A thorough awareness of everything about Malcolm filled him; volumes of information rolling through him.

Malcolm was the youngest of four children, the only one born without the ability to cast in a family of legacy magic-users. Desperate for some form of magic, Malcolm applied for, and was accepted into, the Archon Private Academy which ostracized him from his family. When he turned thirteen, an accident at the school opened him to Mindist energy, enabling him to weave spells like traditional casters.

Mindist! Ben captured the name of the blue energy.

Proving the magic to his parents, they snatched Malcolm away from the APA and enrolled him to the Dunn-Blatt Institute, where he could learn *real* Magic. But he was mocked as an Ape there until he initiated, and won, a Retributive Paramountcy challenge over Allan.

Ben recalled the miserable-looking kid in the back seat of Malcolm's car who had owned a string of twenty-four hour diners and a ranch where hellhounds were bred, which became Malcom's—and were now Ben's.

Malcom groaned and rubbed his temples.

Worked like a puppet, eh? About to command Malcom

to stand, the Dunn-Blatt popped up to his feet before Ben could fully form the thought. *Astonishing!* Ben clapped, and made Malcolm clap, and then felt brief shame before amazement pushed it away. *It's almost like he's a conjuration that I control.*

Ben nodded to his next thought, **I want you to make my trench coat mend itself like your hoodie.**

Malcom's eyes became glassy and his voice took on a monotone quality. "It will be done." The Dunn-Blatt blinked and rubbed his temples again. "If you're going to make me do things, at least have the decency to not make me acknowledge it."

I wonder if this link is truly like a conjurers' bond.

Ben cautiously extended his senses into Malcolm. *Whoa!* Sorting whose senses were who's made his knees wobble. *Almost like being in the girallon.* About to swoon, Ben put his, and Malcolm's, arms out for balance. *Whoa.* It helped, but—w*hoa!*—Ben pulled back his senses and caught himself before he fell.

Okay. Ben extend his vision. Their points of view wove together. *This is going to take serious practice.*

Ben closed his eyes and viewed the world through Malcolm's sight. *So, that's what it like to be just a little taller.* He opened his eyes and had Malcolm close his. **Can you see anything?**

"No." Malcolm replied, "But if you allow me to, I could."

Ben tried to make it happen.

Malcom fixed his posture and lowered his sleeves. "Damn, I look like Hell."

Ben thought about how he had heard that Malcolm used to make people he beat in Dueling give him a piggy back ride. *I should do the same to him.* Ben dismissed the thought. *That'd just be petty.*

Though he hadn't projected the thought, Malcolm said, "You know, Ben." Malcolm smiled. "You should. You've totally earned it." Malcom bent at the knees.

Tempting, but no. Ben waved off the ride. **Come on, let's get back to the building. We've got some stuff to talk about.** Thrilled at the possibilities that lay before him, Ben smiled all the way back to the building.

ABOUT THE AUTHOR

Ezekiel James Boston hales from Las Vegas and currently resides in the Great Northwest. Favoring fantasy, science fiction, and paranormal occult, he's authored over a hundred short stories, a score of short novels, and half a dozen full length novels.

Aside from being an avid writer, Ezekiel enjoys reading and games of all sorts. He chose to give up "active" sports after jamming his fingers and discovering that an author cannot slam their forehead onto the keyboard and have the story appear on the screen.

For exclusive content, please visit:

ezekieljamesboston.com / subscribe-to-ejb /

ALSO BY EZEKIEL JAMES BOSTON

Novels:

Birthday Bedlam: Book One

Samhain Shenanigans: Book Two

Yuletide Yield: Book Three

Novelette:

Nexus Bar & Grill: A World of Benjamin Baxter Starwise
Novelette

Short stories:

Gateway Blood, Buck Tales

Soul Survivor, Buck Tales

Jamal & the Skeleton's Heart, Buck Tales

Collections:

Benjamin Baxter — Darkness Within Trilogy

COMING SOON

Imbolc Insanity, Book Four

Please note: Word of mouth is crucial for any author to succeed. If you enjoyed this book, please consider rating it or leaving a review where you purchased... Even if it's just a line or two.

Thank you for reading.

www.ingramcontent.com/pod-product-compliance
Lightning Source LLC
Chambersburg PA
CBHW020248200626
46816CB00001BA/181